DEATH
DOESN'T
FORGET

ALSO BY ED LIN

The Taipei Night Market Novels
Ghost Month
Incensed
99 Ways to Die

The Robert Chow Novels
This Is a Bust
Snakes Can't Run
One Red Bastard

Other Novels
Waylaid
*David Tung Can't Have a Girlfriend Until He Gets into
an Ivy League College*

DEATH DOESN'T FORGET

ED LIN

Published by Soho Press, Inc.
227 W 17th Street
New York, NY 10011

Library of Congress Cataloging-in-Publication Data

Names: Lin, Ed, author.
Title: Death doesn't forget / Ed Lin.
Other titles: Death does not forget
Description: New York, NY : Soho Crime, [2022] | Series: The
Taipei night market novels ; 4 | Identifiers: LCCN 2021060874

ISBN 978-1-64129-480-5
eISBN 978-1-64129-328-0

Subjects: GSAFD: Mystery fiction.
Classification: LCC PS3562.I4677 D43 2022 | DDC 813/.54—dc23
LC record available at https://lccn.loc.gov/2021060874

Interior design by Janine Agro, Soho Press, Inc.

Printed in the United States of America

10 9 8 7 6 5 4 3 2 1

For the Sunflowers and the Umbrellas

The wide and multifaceted world itself exists as an historical truth. But does that mean that the marginal world is any less true?

—Pa'labang, from "The Mother of History"
in *Indigenous Writers of Taiwan*

CHAPTER 1

On the morning of the last full day of his life, Boxer pulled the corners of the 7-Eleven sales receipt flat onto the desk with his thumbs and index fingers. He was afraid the slip of paper would lift up its edges and fly away. Reluctantly, Boxer lifted his right hand and gingerly picked up his phone.

The display read 8:03 A.M., a few hours before he usually woke up. He pressed the home button and tapped the Ministry of Finance app, the one that automatically reads QR codes. He muted the phone, focused the camera on the receipt, and tried to hold his hands still.

Maybe it had all been a dream. Maybe Boxer was in for yet another rude awakening.

The phone buzzed and a pop-up message indicated that the receipt was indeed a winner in the latest drawing—200,000 New Taiwan dollars in cash! That was as much as he made in half a year.

He thought about his old friends, guys he had known since they shoplifted candy together. Boxer and his friends had learned a lesson early on: leave the tourists alone. One time, when Boxer was eight years old, he asked a white couple by

Longshan Temple for change. He wasn't even trying to pick-pocket them, but a policeman had dragged him into an alley, and beat and kicked him until he passed out.

He touched his right eyebrow at the memory of the thrashing. As a grown man, he understood now what had set off the policeman. What would happen if the visitors went to the local precinct and complained about the beggar boys? The cop would have been demoted or fired because it had happened on his beat. Moreover, if Taiwan's reputation wasn't good, no one would visit and spend like they were handing out play money. Whenever they paid for things, tourists always chuckled to themselves.

The trick to avoiding harassment was to rip off other Taiwanese. Boxer did so for a long time. He and his friends stole scooters and bicycles for years. The gang only broke up as its members moved on to bigger things.

Tiger, who had deep pockmarks like black dots on a big cat's face, started hanging out in clubs and selling drugs for a syndicate. He had died in jail.

Ah Quan had moved into computer fraud early, with fake magnetic strips to withdraw money from ATMs. One day he disappeared. Boxer had heard that Ah Quan changed his name, moved south, and became a legitimate programmer.

Jessy was a rich kid who just wanted to steal. He was sloppy and his dad got him out of trouble so many times. Finally, enough was enough and his father shipped him off to Canada.

I'm the only one of my generation striving in the streets of Taipei, thought Boxer, but my day has finally come. Now that he was sitting pretty, he could call up his co-workers at the bar and show them how much they had underestimated him.

"Boxer is really a generous guy!" he could hear them

say. He would ply them with food, drink, and maybe more, depending on how appreciative they were.

He just had to get the money first.

Most receipts could be redeemed at convenience store chains like 7-Eleven and FamilyMart. But his prize was far above the NT$1,000 limit. He had to go to a bank to collect. If he wanted to get to the closest Chang Hwa Bank branch when it opened at nine, he had to leave soon.

The thought of leaving the apartment gave him a panic attack. Boxer clamped his entire left hand flat over the receipt in case it started yelling.

He had to make sure not to wake up Siu-lien!

Boxer cautiously turned his head, expecting to find her still asleep beneath the threadbare sheets. Instead, Siu-lien was sitting up in bed, her arms hugging her folded knees.

"I heard your phone buzz," she said, her words and eyes tired and angry. "The sound of that receipt checker woke me up."

Boxer cleared his throat.

"Good morning, honey," he said. "I didn't mean to disturb you."

You mean you didn't want to wake me because you wanted to get the money for yourself," she threw back at him. "That's *my* winning receipt you have over there, right?"

"*Our* receipt," Boxer said too loudly and too quickly. "You paid for the cigarettes, but if I didn't ask you to buy them for me, we wouldn't have won."

EVERY PAPER RECEIPT IN Taiwan is a lottery ticket for cash prizes from the government. It's the Ministry of Finance's way of ensuring that people ask for receipts for their purchases. When the QR codes are scanned for lottery winnings, they create electronic trails of taxable income that can be checked against businesses that try to cheat. The tax money that came in far outweighed the monthly prizes, which topped out at NT$10 million—about 340,000 American dollars. If you hit that, you could move to America.

Boxer and Siu-lien hadn't been good about keeping receipts. The agency only held drawings every two months, and the government counted on people like them to discard potential big winners or put them through the wash. The latest drawing had been held a few weeks ago, but Boxer and Siu-lien only managed to retrieve receipts from their pockets and wastebaskets last night to check them. The first seven were all duds. The very last one caused Boxer's phone to exclaim "You've won!" in a chipper cybergirl voice.

They were amused at first. "Free bag of chips," Boxer said. Then they read what the app said.

"WE'RE LUCKY THAT I smoke," Boxer declared, smiling as if to offer his yellow and purple teeth for proof of his habit. "And you've been trying to get me to quit for years."

"We're lucky that I managed to hold on to that receipt!" Siu-lien said.

Boxer picked at the mole on the side of his chin. "We said we'd split the money evenly."

Finally, Siu-lien wavered. "We did," she said.

He stood up triumphantly with as much dignity as a lanky, shirtless functioning alcoholic could muster. "I'm going to the bank now to get our money."

Siu-lien slid across the mattress and put her feet on the floor. "Hold on, Boxer. I'm coming, too!"

Boxer shoved the receipt to the bottom of his left pants pocket and wagged a finger at her with his right hand. "You don't trust me, huh?" He snatched a work shirt from the back of the chair and punched his arms through the short sleeves.

"You never think I'm good enough for you, Siu-lien. Is that it? Are you trying to make me leave you?"

She sat on the side of the bed and put one foot on top of the other. "Of course I trust you, Boxer. I just think we should both be there in person. Don't you think it's something we should do together?"

His shirt was now on, and he was finishing the fifth and last intact button. "Don't get sentimental on me," said Boxer. "It's just money."

He scratched his right ear and tried to stand straight. Siu-lien reminded him of a judge who had considered his fate back when he was a juvenile. She had known, just as Siu-lien surely did now, that Boxer was likely to deviate from The Good, but if called out on his bad intentions, he would deny them, and later do something even worse to make up for being humiliated.

"Okay," said Siu-lien. "I'll see you at work, then, Boxer." She knew well enough not to expect him to come straight home with the money without meeting up with his friends and treating them. That lot wouldn't crawl out of bed before noon to search for a legitimate job, but they would throw something on and wash their faces for free treats. The best outcome was for him to show up at the bar with her half of the money intact.

Siu-lien and Boxer both worked at a dive called BaBa Bar near Chiang Kai-shek Memorial Hall Station. He was a combination bartender-bouncer for the rougher and younger crowd at the basement level. She poured drinks on the ground floor for the older men who still called her young lady.

Boxer shoved his right foot into a sandal and regarded Siu-lien in the sticky orange sunlight. She was still pretty, especially when you first saw her, like a colorful beach stone still wet from the tide. After you got it home and it was dry, you'd see that it was whitening in places and had a number of surface imperfections. You'd still keep the rock, though.

Siu-lien examined Boxer as he crouched to gingerly put on his left sandal. The strap was coming apart and the puckering leather was rubbing the skin between his toes raw. Boxer looked much older than 45, and Siu-lien noted that as he straightened up, popping sounds came from his bones. He sighed when finally erect.

"I'll see you tonight," he said. "I'll definitely leave your share of the money untouched," he added, gathering his hands together in a promise to her and a prayer that he could keep his word.

Siu-lien gave a grim smile and smoothed the sheet around her.

HOURS LATER, AT WORK, Siu-lien was wiping down the counter more often than she normally would have. She shouldn't have trusted Boxer. Every payday meant a night or two out with his friends, men only, or so he said. But the lottery win was bigger than a payday. It was practically a heist, one where Siu-lien, the victim, had little recourse. She hadn't filled out the back of the receipt. Boxer could have written in his name only. Siu-lien had paid for the cigarettes in cash, with her tips. If she had only used a card, it would have proven that the purchase was hers. Well, they weren't going to go to court over it. The judge could probably dig up enough on both of them to justify the state confiscating the funds. Boxer's record spoke for itself, and Siu-lien always regretted paying a fine for an "offense against sexual morality" instead of fighting the drummed-up charge. Back then, it had seemed the easier way, so that she wouldn't have to miss work, but the charge remained on her record. Siu-lien had thought it would be expunged, but now she didn't know if it was the cop or her public defender who had told her that.

She tried hard to remember, and mercifully that prevented her from being so furious at Boxer and herself that she wasn't able to work at all.

She half listened to the old men and half smiled. They didn't notice anything amiss.

"Miss, another round, please."

"Miss! Could you please read this email for me? I can't make the screen bright enough for me to see."

"You're so beautiful, young lady, why don't I see your boyfriend tonight?" asked one man who winked flirtatiously with the eyelid that wasn't drooping.

"He's not feeling well," Siu-lien said with a half laugh. Boxer was probably rip-roaringly drunk. His absence tonight also meant that Boxer had lost yet another job for sure. Nobody got a third chance at BaBa Bar, although the name implied that it was a lucky place. The bar's street address was 88. "Ba," the word for eight in Mandarin, sounds like "wealthy," and three of them in a row (including the sound in "bar") means "getting wealthy." A name like that kept superstitious Taiwanese coming in to drink.

Siu-lien wasn't getting wealthy. At nine o'clock, a retired army guy bought shots for everyone who admitted they were 65 or older. He made Siu-lien drink with them. She threw it back and grimaced. Boxer had to be tapping into her share of the money by now.

THEY WERE ONE PERSON short, so everyone had to stay late to clean. Siu-lien couldn't stand the sight of Old Chen bending down to move kegs, so she moved them herself trying to use her legs and not her back. It was hard to do even in her modest heels.

She took a cab home, and the streetlights flashed through her fluttering eyelids like passing thoughts. Siu-lien was hoping to find him in bed, passed out. She could forgive him then, no matter what else he'd done during the day.

The bed was empty, apart from the cold moonlight that pooled on his pillow. Siu-lien sat with one leg up on the sofa, driving the hard part of the armrest into her ribs, and checking her phone.

No returned texts, emails, or voice mail. Not even a butt dial.

She closed her eyes. Maybe someone had robbed him. Fat chance. He'd be the last man a thief would eye. He should have been the last man Siu-lien chose to eye.

God, why was she with Boxer? Had she settled for him only because he offered periods of relative stability, and made her feel loved sometimes? Or maybe just because they worked in the same bar?

If he came in right now with my money, she thought, I could forgive him. She crossed her legs and rubbed her feet.

SIU-LIEN AWOKE WITH A start about every hour. One time it was because someone dropped a set of keys on the hallway floor. Later she thought she had felt his touch on her cheek, but it was her own hand, probably brushing away a mosquito in her sleep. There were already two bites on her arms. She had asked Boxer to fix the window screen, but he hadn't gotten around to it. It wasn't a priority for him. He never got bit. He never bled.

Now Siu-lien was wide awake with anger, feeling both hot and cold.

Dim light in the shape of an elongated bug crawled to a corner of the ceiling. It could have been daybreak or streetlights. Siu-lien didn't want to know what time it was. A fresh level of disappointment in Boxer manifested as a cramp in her left side.

Siu-lien couldn't even cry. Not for the months of her life she'd wasted on Boxer that were more precious than the money, really. She'd have to get her share of the money, somehow. Even if she had to force Boxer to sell his blood plasma every two weeks. Was his blood even healthy enough to sell? Maybe that's why the mosquitoes avoided him.

Blood money. Hell, she was already bleeding money from paying for everything. Her share of the prize would've provided a cushion from rent increases. As a single person, she didn't qualify for subsidized housing, which required a family minimum of two people.

"Family," she said out loud.

She rolled onto her right side, a position she could never fall asleep in, and evaluated the possible paths to retrieve her money. Some weren't so legal. None were good. There were certain levels of humiliation associated with the start of each of them. The least unappealing choice also had the lowest probability of success: going to the police.

That damned Zhongzheng precinct was not even four blocks away from the bank that Boxer must have gone to! Siu-lien had gone to the cops at least five times over the last two years, and the first three times were to plead for Boxer's release after he picked fights with students at National Taiwan Normal University. The older cops didn't respect her because while she still had some looks, she was in her 50s, didn't have a husband, and worked in a bar. The younger ones were nicer or at least didn't openly scowl. The nerve. She was much smarter than any cop she had ever met.

She could have gone to a good college, but more than anything she wanted to be a singer. It seemed like a possible career path in the early '80s. The soldiers' sweetheart, Teresa Teng, was always on the radio. There were clubs everywhere. Siu-lien, as "Sue Teng," booked herself some late-night gigs singing in venues for veterans, the red-envelope clubs. There were no auditions, but the only pay was tips. At the end of the sets, teary older men nursing empty glasses would hand her red envelopes filled with cash.

Women who weren't good couldn't last a week, but Siu-lien was still in high school, and she was making more than her father. He hated what she was doing, most of all because she was serving mainlanders, but he grudgingly accepted a small wad of cash every month. Siu-lien thought she had a good hiding spot for her main stash until she noticed he was skimming from it. She moved out of the house as her father yelled and her mother turned her back.

The early '90s were still a prosperous time, and Siu-lien could barely fit all the red envelopes into her purse at night. A record producer had given her his business card, but when she called him, he wanted to have a meeting in a hotel room. He sensed her hesitation. "This is how it's always done," he said with a soothing laugh.

She hadn't fallen for that, but she did make the mistake of letting a boyfriend move in with her and do what he wanted. Soon enough she was pregnant. She could deal with the morning sickness and changes to her senses of taste and smell. When she began to show, however, she lost her singing gig, and couldn't find another job, not even answering phones.

The boyfriend had borrowed money from his friends and family. He had planned on marrying Siu-lien. He worked as a porter at Taipei Main Station, but talked about getting a good union job as a train conductor. They'd have a great family. When Siu-lien had given birth to a girl at the hospital, he'd put his name down as the father.

After they had settled back into her apartment, she spent time alone with the baby, wondering when motherhood was supposed to become fulfilling. The days only seemed to grow darker. He kept trying to get her to fix a date for their wedding; it felt like a life sentence was about to start.

When Siu-lien told him he had to leave, she couldn't believe the things he said. She chose to remember him for the sweet boy that he was deep down.

IT HAD BEEN A number of years since Siu-lien had seen her daughter in person, but she didn't have to imagine what Nancy looked like because that girl had been on TV. She had a celebrity boyfriend, Jing-nan, who operated a stand at the Shilin Night Market. What did it sell, dumplings? It didn't matter because he was known for his misadventures, not his food. Someone had tried to kill Jing-nan and he famously fought off the attacker with a cast-iron pot. After that, he was kidnapped by a crazy lady who held him in a basement, but he had escaped from that, too.

Nancy's boyfriend was a lucky guy, and now Siu-lien needed some of that luck. She had pointed out Nancy to Boxer when footage of the couple, taken by telescopic-lensed camera, appeared on TV after Jing-nan had once again cheated death. He had said that Nancy was "hot" and that he wanted to meet that celebrity guy someday. Boxer couldn't believe that Siu-lien knew people who were on television. It was the only time she felt that Boxer had acted carefully with her, before his aggressively insecure demeanor reasserted itself.

What was eating at Boxer, anyway? He was a boy whose role models were the men who pushed him around during his compulsory two-year military service. He reminisced often about the good times he had had with his army buddies. Sometimes it seemed he could only lighten up and laugh around other men. He had gotten his nickname because he liked to listen to his Simon & Garfunkel cassette a lot, and that song in particular. She couldn't imagine his scrawny body in a boxing ring. She couldn't imagine wearing his wedding ring now, even though he had dangled the idea a few times in the past and she had grabbed at it.

"Just kidding!" he would say.

Siu-lien got up and ran cold water over a hand towel. She lay down and placed it across her eyes. The sensation distracted her enough that she was able to sleep. Painful thoughts manifested themselves into sheer walls on all sides that swayed and laughed at her with an innocent cruelty that only children have.

WHEN HER ROOM WAS fully lit by the late-morning sun, Siu-lien rolled over the wet towel on the bed and picked up her phone. She still had Nancy's number listed as a VIP, even though the last time they had had a conversation was two phone models ago. Calling it a conversation was generous, too. It was more like an exchange of words, and Siu-lien's last words to her daughter were, "I never want to talk to you again!"

Before she could think it over and rationalize stopping, Siu-lien touched the number on the screen. The best tactic, she thought, would be to pretend that everything was fine between them and that she had never said what she did. With each successive ring she smiled harder.

CHAPTER 2

Jing-nan entered the apartment a little after midnight and worked his feet out of his shoes. He was 25 years old, with a trim build that spoke to a high-protein, low-carb diet. Jing-nan kept his hair just long enough so that the straight bangs nearly met his thick eyebrows. He had the longish face of an anime hero, but fatter, because he was human. As Jing-nan pulled off his socks he began to hum.

Nancy wasn't sure Jing-nan was aware that he was humming, and she wasn't certain if he did so on a regular basis, but the sound annoyed her now. She stretched her legs out over the wooden coffee table before folding them on the adjacent seat on the couch. Nancy had big ears that poked out of the coal-black tassel curtains of her shoulder-length hair.

Jing-nan slid his feet into house slippers and continued to hum. What song was it? It only seemed to have two notes. Maybe it was the bass line to New Order's "Temptation." That was one more annoying thing about Jing-nan. He always said he never quite liked that band, and yet here he was humming their song. Joy Division was his favorite band, for sure, but he never hummed their songs. Well, they *were* unhummable.

Nancy eyed the paper bag of unsold skewers in Jing-nan's right hand. They were her favorite late-night snack. It could never be truthfully said that Jing-nan was a bad cook, or that he forgot to bring her food.

But she wouldn't allow herself to smile. That phone call with her mom was still annoying the hell out of her, and she wouldn't feel better until she talked to Jing-nan about it. Nancy looked at him through eyes that had narrowed into two obsidian sacrificial daggers. She crossed her arms over her chest and each hand grabbed the opposite biceps.

As he approached, Jing-nan registered Nancy's irritation and did a quick mental check.

Was today an anniversary of a milestone in their relationship? How could it be? They'd only been together for half a year.

Had he done everything he said he would? Yes, to his knowledge.

Had he done something wrong? Impossible. He was at work the whole night, and there's nothing wrong with working.

Had he said anything that could be taken the wrong way? They hadn't had any conversations, text or otherwise, all day. Oh, that could be the problem.

Had he recently joked about something that Nancy took seriously? She was the one with the ribald sense of humor, so the answer was no.

Also, the ultimate Taiwanese danger sign—a slight smile—wasn't present. Such an expression indicates that the wearer is beyond the discussion phase of a dispute, and is already plotting your drawn-out humiliation and destruction.

Jing-nan breathed more easily now. Something must've happened to her, independent of his own action or inaction.

"Is everything all right, Nancy?" he asked. It was a question that could trigger blowback if he were wrong.

"No, everything's not all right," she said, bowing her head. When she looked up again she seemed tired. "My mother called."

Jing-nan had been set to hand Nancy her food when he froze. "Your mother," he repeated, his voice hollow as if his brain had just been removed for study. Jing-nan realized that this incident was very likely a most serious one. Nancy and her mother had never been close. Nancy's parents had split up when she was only a few months old, and at times Nancy grew up under the care of aunties, only one of them an actual relative. Nancy and her mother had gone without contact for years at a time, and the dry spell that just ended had lasted about three.

Jing-nan decided to let food lead the way.

Nancy watched Jing-nan do a tentative tightrope walk to her. He brandished the bag, which was marked with grease blotches that indicated the delectableness of its contents. She hadn't eaten dinner. She hadn't eaten anything since talking to her mother at ten that morning. It wasn't so much what Siu-lien had said or the insistent manner in which she had said it. Her mother's words were devoid of the apology Nancy was owed for years of neglect and dismissal. Worse than that, whenever Nancy heard Siu-lien's voice she became a little girl afraid of the big world, a little girl who always said yes to Mother.

Nancy was going glassy-eyed. Jing-nan moved the bag to just under her nose.

"Nancy?" he asked.

She emerged from her daze, wiped her face with both hands, and took the bag. "I'm hungry," she thought she said, but really it was a short grunt. Nancy removed a chicken skewer and spread out the bag to act as a plate to catch drippings. Suppressed hunger now flared up in her brain, and the only thought that wasn't scorched was that she had to eat that skewer. When she was almost done, she gasped, "Napkin."

Jing-nan jogged to the kitchen, returned with one, and anxiously unfolded it. With the last bite, Nancy closed her teeth and scraped the stick clean as she withdrew it from her mouth. She roughly wiped her mouth and balled up the napkin in a fist. Partially sated, Nancy felt she was now able to speak coherently.

"My mother wants you to get her money back from her boyfriend," she said evenly. Jing-nan sat on the edge of the coffee table, pushed his hands into hopeless-prayer position, and faced Nancy. She didn't seem to like her mother's suggestion, but Nancy's tone implied it was something he should do.

"Why me?" Jing-nan asked helplessly. "I don't know her, and I certainly don't know her boyfriend."

"You're sort of famous," said Nancy. "She thinks he'll listen to you."

Jing-nan ran a finger down the bridge of his nose. He was never comfortable with his nascent fame, but it tickled him nonetheless.

"Is he a dangerous guy?"

"He's only a danger to himself," said Nancy.

"Is it a lot of money?"

"One hundred thousand NT."

"Damn, so he ran off with her stash?"

Nancy hesitated. "Something like that."

"Should I do it, Nancy?"

"It would be a good thing if you did."

Nancy could still eat. She fingered the bag and counted

three more skewers before plucking one out. Folded intestines, a classic of Unknown Pleasures, Jing-nan's night-market stand. She wrenched off a bite and chewed. It was sweet and salty, with threads of spiciness binding the two, and not at all rubbery, like the fare from cheaper, lower-tier stands.

Jing-nan was smiling, happy to watch her eat. She didn't want to tell him just yet that they were scheduled to meet Siu-lien in the morning, and that Jing-nan was already committed to the deed. That was the worst thing about this. Not only did Nancy fall in line with her mother's demands—she had also compromised Jing-nan. She would be the worst spy ever.

For now she continued eating. He rose and ambled over to the reclining chair that he never reclined in.

Nancy watched her boyfriend drop into his seat, plug in earbuds, and get on his phone. He was sorting through Unknown Pleasures' social media to love, like, or challenge all the comments. He had to engage his customers as a business necessity, he had told her, but he sure seemed to get his kicks doing it. His online guise, just like his at-work persona, was carefree and fun-loving. In real life, Jing-nan was more serious, listened to a lot of music, and didn't talk much.

They actually met when she was working in a CD store and he asked to hear a pirated song from a rare official Joy Division release. At the time, she had pretended to be more interested in the band than she really was. She still hadn't dared to tell Jing-nan that she liked New Order, the successor band to Joy Division, better. It could change things between them.

But Nancy couldn't put off telling him something else.

She finished the skewer and waved an open hand at Jing-nan. He removed one earbud.

"Jing-nan, my mother wants to tell you more in person," Nancy said. "She's a little nervous because she's never met a celebrity before." He smiled and removed his other earbud in recognition that the conversation would go somewhere serious.

"I would never want to disappoint your mother, no matter how ambivalent or antagonistic you may feel about her," Jing-nan deadpanned. He swiped to the calendar on his phone. "When was she thinking of meeting?"

"Um, tomorrow morning at nine."

"Tomorrow, as in later today?" said Jing-nan. His face twisted with incredulity. "Actually, in a little more than eight hours, Nancy?" All the humor in his voice had dried up. Nancy stretched out and put a hand on his right knee.

"It's a major inconvenience, and, yes, it's true, she and I have never really gotten along. But if my mother was calling me, she had to be in a really desperate situation. You see that, right?"

Jing-nan nodded but the gesture lacked empathy. This year, how many people had he come across who had been in desperate situations? At least three, and trying to help them always led to some major personal crisis. For him.

Jing-nan unconsciously brushed his shirt above his abdomen. He literally had scars from acting on his good intentions.

"She's your mother," he said. "Of course I'll help her."

THEY WERE MEETING SIU-LIEN at one of the more expensive and less tasty breakfast places in Taipei Main Station. The menu included English and Japanese translations. It wasn't anyone's first choice to eat in, but the best places that had youtiao were table-share situations, and that wouldn't do at all. There were some personal matters to discuss. There's an old saying that delicate fare can be enjoyed when the conversation is bland, but that bland food was required in order to discuss delicate matters.

Jing-nan warily followed Nancy, who, led on by instinct, walked around the divided aisles to arrive at her mother's table. Siu-lien's depleted espresso cup held only skeletal foam.

"I'm so glad you both came," Siu-lien said as she rose. As is often the case with Taiwanese mothers and daughters, Siu-lien looked like an older sister to her daughter. The only giveaway was the grooves on either side of Siu-lien's nose. The mother and daughter were about the same height, and Nancy had her mother's ears, the only thing she was going to inherit.

Nancy had stopped just short of her mother's anxious reach, so Jing-nan stepped forward into the space between the two of them to make the snub less obvious. Siu-lien grabbed Jing-nan's right arm. He was a little uneasy about the immediate physical contact.

"I would do anything to help you," he declared to Siu-lien. She drew closer and held both his hands in a supplicating manner. Siu-lien's upper body was conditioned from hauling full kegs, and the strength of her grip surprised Jing-nan. She squeezed almost hard enough to crack his knuckles.

"It's an honor to finally meet you, Jing-nan," Siu-lien said, her voice breaking, perhaps genuinely.

"Please tell me what I should call you," said Jing-nan.

"Oh, just call me 'Siu-lien.' I don't care about formalities," she said with a laugh.

Nancy stiffened. She had resolved earlier to act as coldly as possible to her mother, and to only provide brief answers to her questions. She had agreed to bring her boyfriend, and now that task was done. But seeing her mother in person eroded Nancy's resolve. Siu-lien was older and sadder, and bore only a partial resemblance to the tireless and restless mother Nancy was still angry with.

"Hello, Mom," said Nancy.

Siu-lien sighed a burdened, matriarchal heave from a one-take soap opera about a once-mighty family's rapid decline. Why hadn't Nancy embraced her immediately? Her own daughter! Jing-nan, a stranger meeting Siu-lien for the first time, had come up and paid his respects first. Unbelievable. Still, she couldn't afford to alienate Nancy while she needed Jing-nan to get her money.

"My dear Nancy," said Siu-lien. She released Jing-nan, placed her arms at her sides, and looked at the air just above Nancy's head, waiting for her daughter to reach over and establish physical contact.

Nancy knew what her mother was expecting. That tilt to her head and slightly sideways stance was the posture Siu-lien would assume when she showed up at the door after months of being away. The old woman here still expected her kid to run up, give her a big hug, and say how much she missed her mother. Nancy seethed with resentment.

Siu-lien had indeed expected Nancy to relent. When it became apparent she wouldn't deign to even wave, Siu-lien brushed off her arms and returned to her seat. "Please sit down, you two," she said, pointedly only addressing Jing-nan.

Jing-nan took the seat opposite Siu-lien. Nancy remained standing. He smiled a little harder than was necessary, and smoothed back the hair on his head. Jing-nan was getting a preview of the neutral role he might be playing when Siu-lien was his mother-in-law.

Wait a second. Marriage? How could he be thinking about that now? There were so many things he wanted to have in place before he could consider proposing to Nancy. He needed to save enough money from the night-market stand, although he didn't know how much. He also needed a college degree so he could feel like a real adult, although he wasn't yet sure in what. And he certainly needed a wedding ring from Tiffany, even though that would be a drain on his savings, and potentially sabotage those first two points.

It seemed like life was a vicious circle sometimes. Everything interfered with everything else. The professional and personal, and the past, present, and future were all stuck together. How could he be expected to get anything done?

Jing-nan shifted and stowed his legs under his seat, dimly aware that Nancy was finally easing into the chair next to him. He gave her a reassuring smile, then turned to Siu-lien and bent his head in deference. "What can I do to help you?" Siu-lien closed her eyes and smiled.

Nancy pushed back from the table and her metal chair shrieked. "Well, let's order some food before we talk about things," she said. "Let's not make decisions on empty stomachs."

"Relax, Nancy," said Siu-lien as she turned her teacup counterclockwise. "I've already ordered for us. I got your favorite, dan bing youtiao." She leaned toward Jing-nan as if to convey a secret, although she didn't drop her voice. "She's loved it since she was a little girl. She ate it with hot sauce, too!"

As if on cue, a gangly waiter hustled in and set down a small dish of chili sauce so pungent the smell jabbed like a fishhook in Jing-nan's nostrils. Without breaking his stride, the waiter swished right and walked away from the table. Within a minute he returned with two plates and served them to Nancy and Jing-nan. Each featured a fried cruller covered with an omelet and then rolled into a browned flour pancake. Jing-nan regarded the dan bing youtiao and turned the plate 180 degrees, admiring the tidiness of the presentation, particularly the crisp edges of the omelet. He sniffed right at one of the open ends. The scallions in the pancake weren't freshly chopped or they weren't fresh, period. He scoffed at the citrus twist on the side. Why garnish this thing like a cocktail? Finally, why do we have forks? Well, if Siu-lien or Nancy didn't ask for chopsticks, he wouldn't bring it up.

Nancy removed the small spoon from the chili sauce and set it aside. She picked up the saucer itself and dribbled the sauce up and down the length of her dan bing youtiao. Jing-nan registered Nancy's movements and grunted lightly. He didn't like it when people seasoned their food before even tasting it, much less slathered on condiments that could be half sugar.

Why, he was going to do the decent thing and . . .

He turned back to find his plate missing. Jing-nan looked to Siu-lien as she finished dragging his breakfast to her side of the table with her left hand. Her right hand placed two sheets of paper in front of Jing-nan.

"I don't want you to get these dirty with crumbs," Siu-lien said, smiling minimally. "You should probably look these over before you eat."

One page was a map of the Wanhua district of Taipei, something he didn't need as he had grown up there. The other was a headshot of an unshaven man pretending to be happy about having his picture taken.

"So this is the guy," Jing-nan said.

"That's Boxer," said Siu-lien. She circled his face with a red fingernail that was greasy with Jing-nan's dan bing youtiao. "He's not a big guy. You could probably take him, if it came down to that."

Jing-nan placed his hands flat on the table. "I'm not a fighter, Siu-lien," he said. Her eyes showed no consideration of his words as she chewed.

"Jing-nan isn't a muscle-head," Nancy said to her mother. "You don't know what kind of man he is."

"You don't know what I know about men!" snapped

Siu-lien, as she picked up a fork and held it in a defensive position. Nancy hacked off a chunk of her breakfast and forked it into her mouth.

Jing-nan turned back to the map. Siu-lien had made a red "X" on Guangzhou Street, a few blocks to the west of Longshan Temple, a landmark he was intimately familiar with, as he had been dragged there by his parents countless times and pushed to his knees before the altars to ask for blessings and favors. Those goddesses and gods never came through. They were probably preoccupied with recovering from incense-smoke inhalation.

"Siu-lien," he asked, "is this where Boxer is staying?" He didn't mention that Guangzhou Street had a rather seedy reputation, in case it embarrassed Siu-lien, who was now taking her third or fourth bite of Jing-nan's dan bing youtiao.

"That's where I think he's staying," she said, as flakes from her mouth dropped to the plate. "He used to go there sometimes, up on the top floor. I don't remember the exact address, but at the street level there's a sign that says PURE LAND YOGA. It's really a place to party, though." She reached over the map and picked up the hot sauce. After dumping the rest of it on the plate, she asked, "You like spicy, don't you Jing-nan? I'm just going to eat a little bit more while you look that over."

Jing-nan ground his teeth as he considered ordering a replacement meal. It would seem a bit rude, since Siu-lien was paying, but she had swiped his plate, after all.

She was surely paying, wasn't she?

"Siu-lien, is there anything in particular that you think I should say to Boxer?" Jing-nan asked. Siu-lien finished chewing before speaking.

"I don't care what you say," she said. "It doesn't matter, either. Just ask for the money, and I guarantee he'll be so freaked out, he'll just hand it over. Other men in general scare him, and you've been on TV, so you have an extra edge."

"Are you sure," asked Nancy, "that Boxer won't be high on drugs and aggressive?"

Siu-lien straightened up. "He might be high, but when he is, he's very melancholy. His drug highs are personal lows."

"Mom, Boxer doesn't have any weapons, does he?"

Jing-nan felt his appetite ebb.

Siu-lien snorted. "He can't even cut a steak," she said.

Jing-nan folded the map and the picture of Boxer in half. "Well," he said. "No sense in wasting time. I'll go see him now." He paused to see if Siu-lien would offer to return his plate. Instead, she dug in her fork and paused.

"I agree," she said. "You should go right now."

"Mom, maybe you should go with Jing-nan."

Siu-lien raised her right index finger. "That is one more humiliation that I can't endure," she said, and lifted the fork to her mouth.

CHAPTER 3

Jing-nan got out of the train at Longshan Temple Station with waves of tourist groups from Japan, China, and the US. The ultimate destination was the 300-year-old temple, but the guides, who probably received some form of kickback, first brought their people through the underground mall that was mostly masseuses, fortune-tellers, and artists who presented factory-assembled jewelry and trinkets of machine-carved stone as items they made with the modest hand tools on display.

Jing-nan gave the tourists and their herders a wide berth as he headed for the exit, and felt distraught that shopping for this crap would be a memory they would take away about Taiwan. Even worse, these particular tour groups never brought people to his night market!

As Jing-nan emerged at street level, he found Guangzhou Street also packed with visitors streaming across the asphalt to Longshan Temple, whose ornamented roof spires reached for the sky like the legs of a colorful beetle on its back.

A cart nearby was selling Buddha boxes, speaker units the size of a travel alarm clock that recited prayers in a loop. It was the sort of thing that desperate people bought, and most locals headed for the temple were at their wits' end with their problems. Medication wasn't working, counseling wasn't working, the husband wasn't working.

Jing-nan eyeballed the cart of Buddha boxes. The woman selling them sized him up quickly as a noncustomer and didn't budge from her foldout chair. He craned his neck. The boxes were smaller and much more efficient now. When he was a kid, they required two double-A batteries. Now they only needed one.

He continued west on Guangzhou and stopped for car traffic. Chinese tourists were confused by the name of the street. After all, Guangzhou is a huge city in southern China that some Americans still call Canton. The Generalissimo, Chiang Kai-shek, in exile in Taiwan after losing the Chinese Civil War, renamed major streets after places on the mainland to bolster the morale of his fellow refugees.

For the majority of people in Taiwan who had never set foot in Guangzhou, it was just another name the mainlanders had changed.

Jing-nan came upon a row of storefronts filled with coin-operated amusements, and knew what he was in for. The arcades were crowded, even in the morning, with male pensioners who had nothing else to do with their disposable cash. Conveniently, on the upper floors there were a number of brothels, known as a-gong diam—"shops for grand-pas"—ready to take their money in larger increments than a coin-operated claw machine.

At the street level, quick-eyed greeters for the brothels were on the prowl for reluctant or unsuspecting prey. These women used a practice called la ke, literally "pulling customers," and dragged them in by the arm.

These were blocks that Jing-nan had steered clear of in

his younger days, and never happened to come across when he was older. The cabinets of the amusement machines were arranged to block off doorways and create perches hidden from the view of unbribed authorities and unwitting tourists who had strayed too far west from the big temple.

He checked the map provided to him by Siu-lien. Boxer's hideout was right in the middle of the sleazy stretch. Jing-nan straightened up and steeled himself as he crossed the street. He shoved his hands into his left and right front pants pockets, clutching his wallet and phone, respectively. The grabby ladies had sticky fingers, as well.

Jing-nan had barely made it to the curb when a woman in her early 40s stepped up and grabbed his left elbow.

"Hey," she said. "Let's go upstairs and have some fun." Jing-nan said nothing but walked faster. The woman kept up with him, never loosening her grip.

"Leave me alone, please," Jing-nan said as gruffly as he could.

"Stop, stop!" she cried. "My foot hurts!" Jing-nan could only sigh and stop in his tracks.

"Now will you let go of me?" he asked wearily. She now pulled his arm with two hands.

"You have to come with me, I think I'm hurt!" she cried.

That's it, thought Jing-nan. He was accustomed to breaking out of holds, as he and Dwayne play-wrestled nearly every night at Unknown Pleasures. Jing-nan had become quite good at horsing around, but he paused before his next move. He didn't want to hurt the woman, he just wanted to be free.

"You're embarrassing me!" said the woman. "Everybody's staring at us. Let's go!" A few people were looking, but they wore the dead expressions of caged zoo animals damned to watch groups of bratty kids running around.

Jing-nan dropped into a squat, using his body weight to

break the woman's grip, and then leapt up and ran down the street. The woman might have yelled something, but the laughing onlookers drowned her out.

When he was sure she wasn't following him, Jing-nan slowed to a fast walk and searched for the yoga place where Boxer was holed up.

BOXER TURNED TO HIS right side and wiped his face in his sleep. He was having a dream about walking through a field of tall flowers. Wet petals brushed against his face as he made his way forward. He wasn't sure where he was or where he was headed, but he was deeply unhappy.

Now he was walking through a swamp and sinking with each step. The sky had gone dark. Dammit, he could hear Siu-lien laughing. This was her plan all along.

Coughs rattled his dried-out throat. His eyelids fluttered from the pain, and the sunlight in his face couldn't be denied. Boxer forgot everything from his dream except for the sadness.

Well, the sadness was real.

He turned to his left side with the intention of going back to sleep but instead his mind replayed an imperfect recording of the previous 24 hours.

HE HAD PRESENTED THE winning receipt and his national ID card at the bank. The teller was a by-the-books sort of man in his mid-50s, a guy without the imagination to say much besides, "Hi, how can I help you?" or "Have a nice day." He hadn't said anything else in the entire course of the transaction. Not even, "That's going to buy a lot of fun!" or "Better not let your woman get ahold of this!"

A supervisor had come by to double-check the receipt, and nodded at Boxer before walking away.

Boxer had held himself by the wrists, unconsciously hand-cuffing himself, as he watched the clerk count out one hundred NT$2,000 bills. He took his sweet time doing it, too!

His eyes drifted to the back wall of the teller's side. A poster was promoting the Austronesian Cultural Festival, and the bank was a major sponsor. Who the hell's gonna show up for that? Boxer mused.

The teller was finally done counting. The stack was more money than Boxer had seen in a very long time, before his second jail term, which had made him vow to never again steal from people who were tourists from a territory that was an important trade partner of Taiwan.

The teller handed the bills over to Boxer on top of a letter-sized envelope. He had expected Boxer to count the notes once more, and then place them inside the envelope for safekeeping.

Instead, Boxer folded the entire pile in half so it bulged like an overstuffed sandwich. He shoved it into his right front pants pocket, pushing the pointy ends of his keys into his balls. Boxer nodded at the teller and staggered away.

"Have a nice day," the teller said, his voice hollow.

BOXER REMEMBERED WALKING DOWN the street, sur-prised by the large number of people off to work. He was never up early enough to see rush hour, and was elated that he wasn't caught up in the same rat race.

Look at me! I don't even have a real job and I have more money in my pocket than you! He kept one hand over each pocket: one to protect the cash; one to guard his empty wallet.

He was delirious from the adrenaline rush and lack of sleep. Boxer saw an empty bench and sat on it. He spent the next 15 minutes internally laughing at passersby while also being afraid of them. Some of them might know that half the money wasn't really his. Well, he hadn't run off with all of it yet!

He was suddenly hungry. Where did he want to go? He could eat anything he wanted. As is often the case with the foolish, he was suddenly overtaken by a childish impulse. Boxer wanted a giant shaved ice with every fruit topping— mango, strawberry, and kiwi!

Boxer hailed a cab to Ximending, a district that lit up at night with the young and trendy. He stopped the cab at a shaved-ice place packed with jet-lagged tourists. That place had to be good! The shop used frozen almond milk, not ice, making the dessert creamier.

Boxer had never tasted anything like it. He wasn't sure what he was tasting, actually. The shaved ice was topped with almond icing, freshly cut fruit, drizzled citrus syrups, and chewy chunks of mochi. The cloying sweetness alone was enough to wash all the traumatic memories from the slate of his mind. The bad things would resurface, as sharp as ever, he knew, but all the more reason to indulge now.

Halfway through his treat, Boxer's teeth ached. Sugar in solid, liquid, and gaseous forms saturated the soft tissue of his eyes, ears, nose, and throat. As his head began to throb, Boxer shoved his spoon into what was left, and tried to think.

The logical thing to do, he was able to discern, would be to go home and get some more rest before going to work tonight. Maybe even drink some water.

Boxer opened his mouth, maneuvered his tongue, and noisily sucked on a sore molar that gave off a sour taste.

Wait, why should he go to work tonight? Why should he go back to work at all? He could take this money and double the amount in a month by investing it with a loan shark. It was the safest way to make money because borrowers always paid up, usually on time. You have to invest money to make money, and to taste money, you couldn't waste money. Wasn't that from a '90s rap song?

Waste money. He glanced at his half-eaten shaved ice and shifted in his seat. Was he really done eating? The shaved ice hadn't been free, after all, and even though he was flush with cash and on a sugar high, Boxer was reluctant to abandon something that had some measure of value. He thought about getting more of it down when a group of English-speaking tourists came in. Hearing them reminded Boxer of his first term in prison, and he was spooked. It was time to leave.

He felt ashamed about not finishing his food, so Boxer decided to seek comfort at a bar that was managed by an old girlfriend. He had been in a few flaky relationships before, but this woman was special because she had been the one who kept breaking up with him, although she usually took him back when he begged her. This time he had money, so she was sure to be quite receptive!

He walked a few blocks over to Empress of China, a third-floor bar that used to be a red-envelope club like the one Siu-lien worked in years ago. It was a venue for homesick mainlander veterans where women sang sad songs about China. All songs about China were sad if you longed to be there.

A businesswoman had bought the club a few years ago and had intended to keep it going as such, but ended up converting it into a conventional bar and upping the mainlander-friendly decor. The walls were lined with anti-Communist propaganda posters and advance leases for land in the to-be-liberated China that had been sold to suckers. The decades-old memorabilia lent a kitschy factor to the bar, and the only people offended by it were those few who genuinely believed Chiang Kai-shek could have taken back the Chinese mainland, with US forces in a supporting role. Not many of the people in that demographic could handle the walk up the spiral stairs, anyway.

Boxer noticed that Empress of China's ground-floor door was propped open with a chipped cinder block. He was just in time for the booze delivery. How opportune.

Boxer lumbered up the stairs, which wound so tightly he felt like his body was almost turning in place. The sugar high was gone and had left him shaking. Anxiety weighed on him. Boxer knew he was risking everything that he had now—his woman, his job, and his windfall—and yet his feet kept going. Once he reached the top, he knew he'd end up going on a free-fall bender.

Bee Bee would be happy to see him. Well, she'd definitely be ecstatic that Boxer could finally pay her back, and with interest. She would never have seen this coming. He sure didn't. If he didn't have any money, this would be the last place in the world he'd want to be, but now, he was compelled to come. Money was power, and it was strong enough for him to find the courage to do the impossible.

As he made the last turn in the stairwell, he saw her refilling glasses of water for the two men who had been carrying up crates of liquor. Bee Bee was wearing a black short-sleeve blouse with red trim and a black skirt that ended above her knees. Her long curls of hair reached down to her daringly low neckline.

The men, stout human moles, were overtly staring at her breasts and ass. She accepted the attention. These men were of use to her, after all.

In fact, she kept her face neutral-to-pleasant until she spotted Boxer.

Bee Bee frowned like the protagonist at the beginning of the ultimate revenge scene in a kung-fu film. She slammed the pitcher down on the counter, and water sloshed to the floor.

The two men could see the tension in the scene and warily watched Boxer as he approached.

Boxer gave a stupid little wave with his right hand.

"Hi, Bee Bee," he was able to say, his voice boyishly high. She said nothing and he stopped in his tracks. "I'm here to pay you back. I have money." Bee Bee's eyes twitched.

"You have money?" Her tone ridiculed him. "You mean someone's about to give you some, or you need to borrow a few hundred NTs to get back a thousand, right?"

Boxer lifted his right foot and stomped it with confidence, the overgrown toenails aimed generally at Bee Bee.

"I have it right here," he said. He squirmed as he worked the bills out from his front pocket. He walked up and dropped the wad on the counter. The money flipped open and fanned itself out, relieved to have oxygen again.

Everybody including Boxer stared at the money in disbelief.

Bee Bee pounced on it and began to count out what she was owed.

"Did you steal this?" she asked, without stopping or looking at Boxer. "Wait, I know you must have. Tell me who you stole it off of!"

He laughed bitterly. "This money is legit," he said, wiping his mouth. "I won it in the lottery. Got the receipt from buying some smokes, if you can believe it."

"I don't believe anything you say," said Bee Bee. After recovering her money, she twisted the bills into a roll and tucked them into the waistband of her skirt.

"How much did you win?" one of the men asked Boxer. The subservient tone was annoying.

"I won a lot," Boxer snapped. The man was immediately quiet and Boxer trembled slightly, marveling at how much power the money had given him over people. Rich people felt like this all the time! He turned to Bee Bee. She remained wary and seemed almost afraid of him. The fear in her face made her beautiful. Yes, he could even compel her to follow his will. But that could wait.

"Well, then," said Boxer. "Drinks are on me!"

BOXER PINCHED THE BRIDGE of his nose. Thinking about the hours after that were fuzzy and vaguely irritating. The two men hadn't stayed long, and Boxer remembered giving them small tips and calling each of them "brother." He recalled getting into a cab with Bee Bee, and heading down to Guangzhou Street in Wanhua to see if his key still worked in the old crash pad, where he was now continuing to languish.

They drank from bottles Bee Bee had grabbed from the bar. She had drugs on her, too, didn't she? It wasn't candy crumbs they were licking off the palms of their hands. Boxer had a dim recollection of quickie sex with Bee Bee, and then falling asleep. He woke up later when she apparently returned with some prepared meals, and chewed his way through a reheated pork cutlet that was dry and too salty.

He fell back asleep and woke up feeling dissatisfied, still hearing Siu-lien's echoing laughter from his dream. The morning was undeniable, as was his betrayal. Boxer's heart flooded with regret.

There were so many things he should have done with the money, including putting it in a bank—hell, he was right there!—or at least giving Siu-lien her share. Well, wait. How much was left? Boxer rolled out of the bed and pulled himself along the floor as if his lower body were a fish tail. He reached the wall, crawled under the desk, and grabbed his pants. The pockets felt worryingly flat. He turned them all inside out, and some bills fluttered to the floor.

Shit, how much was left? Did Bee Bee take even more

when she went to get the food, and keep the rest? No, wait, had he bought drugs in the lobby, from a messenger?

There was a knock at the door. That couldn't be Bee Bee. Maybe it was her boyfriend. Was it Siu-lien? Goons sent by Siu-lien? Drug dealers returning to rip off a mark who was now high? Cops dropping by for a shakedown?

He shoved his legs into his pants, nearly falling over in the process, and flung all the remaining money under the bed. If he was overpowered and searched, they wouldn't find anything on him.

Whoever it was, Boxer was determined not to be easily taken. He grabbed a wire hanger from the closet and approached the door.

CHAPTER 4

The door had no peephole, but it was adorned with three chain locks that looked more decorative than defensive, and none were chained at the moment, anyway.

More knocks came, steady and persistent. The visitor knew Boxer was in, and knew what they wanted from him.

Boxer decided his biggest advantage was the element of surprise. He threw open the door with his left hand. His right hand was raised, ready to strike with the hanger.

In the doorway stood a man framed with too-bright sunlight, giving him the dramatic appearance of a just-landed movie alien backlit by studio lights. Boxer shaded his eyes with his left hand and saw a look of concern, not anger, on the man's face. He was holding folded sheets of paper.

Boxer didn't lower the hanger just yet. The visitor could be one of those Holy Joes who go around the red-light district trying to save souls. But he did look somewhat familiar.

"Who are you?" Boxer asked, unable to contain his curiosity. In any case, he should have cleared his throat first. Boxer's voice was thick with phlegm and worse, sounded whiny.

The man bowed his head and rubbed his nostrils before

speaking. "My name is Jing-nan," he said. "I'm a friend of Siu-lien's daughter. She asked me to come here to see you. Siu-lien, that is." Jing-nan knew from reading a book about body language that wiping your face was a sign of insecurity, but he couldn't help it. His nose felt tingly, and he touched it again.

Boxer took a step back. Now he could place the man. That famous guy who was dating Nancy, Siu-lien's daughter, who had nice tits. Maybe this was a fortuitous visit! He threw the hanger aside.

"I was just straightening up," said Boxer, motioning for Jing-nan to enter. Boxer's words were a lie on every level. Nothing was straight in the room, not even the floor. The place was a mess and Boxer's life was a mess, and he was completely useless at cleaning, fixing, or otherwise improving anything. Boxer stepped quickly to the rumpled sheets on the floor and did a quick search for any drug paraphernalia left out in the open.

Jing-nan wasn't used to entering homes without removing his shoes, but in this case his instinct was overruled by a sense of unease triggered by the smell. The odors of a decomposing rug soaked in alcohol and wall-length stretches of mildew, along with a whiff of urine, nearly caused him to gag. Out of politeness, Jing-nan tried to maintain a friendly smile while breathing through his mouth. He also tried not to stare at the mole on Boxer's chin. Or was that a scab?

Boxer, satisfied that nothing incriminating was in open view, sat on the one chair in the room. A bra was hanging on the back of it, but he didn't seem to mind. Boxer gestured for Jing-nan to sit on a part of the mattress partially covered with a sheet.

"I'll stand," said Jing-nan. Now that it was clear Jing-nan wouldn't stay long, Boxer became a little desperate to detain him as long as he could. He had never met anyone from the TV before, and the famous guy was standing right there in front of him!

"Can I get you some water?" Boxer asked, though there were no cups in the room.

"No, please, I wouldn't trouble you," said Jing-nan. Despite the noxious atmosphere, he was starting to get hunger pains. Jing-nan never skipped breakfast, and now he was becoming too feeble to stand this unhealthy environment and execute the task at hand. How would one ask for money that was owed? The direct route was probably best with someone who was clearly impaired and compromised.

"Say, Boxer, Siu-lien tells me that the two of you have decided to share something." Boxer crossed his legs and covered his crotch with both hands.

"Share? Oh, yes, we . . . we won a prize. In the lottery. I went to the bank yesterday to cash in the receipt." Jing-nan looked at him expectantly.

"That was two days ago," said Jing-nan. Boxer wobbled before continuing.

"Of course, two days ago. Well, I've opened an account and deposited most of the winnings for safekeeping. I didn't want to do something stupid with it."

Like hell there's a bank account, thought Jing-nan. But he nodded, anyway.

"But I do have some money now for Siu-lien," said Boxer. He lifted himself out of his chair and slid to the floor. He crawled under the bed and pulled out all the bills. He quickly flattened them out and sorted them. They came out to NT$21,500. Now that was a good amount of money! Boxer presented the wrinkled bills to Jing-nan with two hands, and Jing-nan accepted them with both his hands, as well. It was a most respectful transaction.

"Thank you, Boxer," said Jing-nan. Not all the money was there, but he was surprised that it was that easy to get Boxer to produce any money at all. Jing-nan considered capitalizing on his fame more often.

"Tell Siu-lien that I'll give her the rest soon," said Boxer. "It's just a matter of setting up the bank account properly. It takes at least a day for the money to settle before I can withdraw some more."

Jing-nan resisted calling out the prolonged lie, and then realized he was in an awkward position. Siu-lien had wanted her full share. Now that Jing-nan hadn't recovered it all in one swoop, did Nancy's mom expect him to continue hounding Boxer for the rest? He certainly didn't relish the thought of returning to this dump.

It didn't seem that Boxer had the initiative or will to pay Siu-lien on his own, however. Anyway, it was about more than just getting her the money. Jing-nan's rep was on the line, and he had to show the ability to get it done.

"I'll come back tomorrow," said Jing-nan with a slight edge in his voice. "The bank account should be straightened out by then." Boxer broke out into a sweat, but made a pathetic attempt at chuckling.

"I won't get a chance to go to the bank today," he said. "Come back in two days. Everything will meet Siu-lien's satisfaction, I promise." Jing-nan nodded and made his way to the open door. It was great to breathe fresh air again. Boxer hadn't accompanied him to the door, but Jing-nan was glad the common courtesy wasn't observed. "You want this door open or closed?" Jing-nan asked.

"Close it," called Boxer.

JING-NAN WALKED BACK THROUGH the makeshift open-air stairwell and felt a dull sting in his nasal passage, a sure sign rain was coming. He looked up and saw dark clouds at the side of the sky, billowing like the heads of charging lions.

He scampered down the concrete stairs, hoping to get to the MRT station before the deluge. Jing-nan dashed down the block, avoiding the side where he had shaken off the woman earlier. Although thunder rumbled through the sky several times, not a drop of rain fell. It was like that sometimes. Other days, when there was nothing but sun in the sky, rain could suddenly materialize and soak the tourists, sending them running into the nearest bakery for shelter and carbs.

Jing-nan texted Nancy as he paused near the station entrance.

I HAVE SOME GOOD NEWS AND SOME BAD NEWS, NANCY.

BE AWARE THAT I'M WALKING WITH MY MOM, JING-NAN.

BOXER GAVE ME SOME MONEY AND I WANT TO GET IT TO YOUR MOTHER.

I'M TAKING HER AROUND THE NTU CAMPUS. IF YOU'RE FREE TO COME BY IN THE NEXT HOUR OR SO, WE CAN MEET UP SOMEWHERE.

OF COURSE!

Jing-nan disliked the burden of obligations not related to his business. It had always been this way, ever since he was a child working and yawning at the night market. He thought he'd be free to live his own life once he went to UCLA in America, but tragedy had reeled him back across the Pacific Ocean to Taiwan a few years ago, dropping him right back at his family's indebted business at the Shilin Night Market. He was ashamed about being an orphan, although it wasn't his fault, and he was forced to work at his family's stall with all the adult worries that had plagued his parents.

Somehow, while he was flailing, he'd managed to make the best of it with the only family he had left, longtime employees Dwayne and Frankie the Cat. The rebranded Unknown

Pleasures also had a high profile on social media, mostly because Jing-nan was fluent in English, and he had the band Joy Division to thank for that. He had studied especially hard to learn the subtleties of the lyrics by singer Ian Curtis. To understand a song such as "Digital," one had to know the literal meaning of the word to appreciate its binary construction, and the figurative implications of an encroaching new world of social alienation with each technological "advance."

And yet one also had to retain a sense of humor in the face of things. Light amusement went far online. It made followers hungry for more.

But it was Jing-nan who was now starving, to the point where he wouldn't be able to truly enjoy the act of eating. He picked up a prepackaged, refrigerated curry pork-cutlet sandwich on white bread from a nearby FamilyMart. Maybe he should post a selfie with the sandwich, captioned, "If I can't get to Unknown Pleasures, I'd rather eat this than any other night-market food!" Naw, there could be blowback from the other vendors. Anyway, why help publicize FamilyMart?

He wolfed down the sandwich cold before catching the train to National Taiwan University.

CHAPTER 5

Nancy and her mother stood outside NTU's electrical-engineering building. Siu-lien crossed her arms and defiantly regarded the bricks in the building's facade.

"I was very good at math, you know," she told Nancy. "In grade school, the teacher would divide the class into two lines and call us up to write down and solve a problem at the chalkboard, two at a time. The slower one would have to sit down. I was always the last one standing by myself. Everyone else took ruler slaps."

There she goes again, thought Nancy. Building herself up when she feels insecure. "What grade was this, Mom?"

"Third grade. Fourth grade, too," said Siu-lien. "I was naturally talented. I instinctively knew the right answers."

"My best subject was biology," said Nancy. "I never really liked anything before studying the lives of bees."

"Umm," her mother hummed, as if she were hearing this for the first time. It may have been. Their relationship was mostly empty spaces. It was structured like a honeycomb but not as sweet, and many cells were sealed off and inaccessible.

"Maybe you should go back to school for math," said Nancy.

Her mother snorted. "Go back now? So people can laugh at me?"

"No one's going to laugh at you. We never stop learning."

Siu-lien sliced the air with her right hand. "I wouldn't be able to respect myself."

Nancy shook her head. Siu-lien still harbored the hope she'd somehow make it as a singer. Nancy blamed shows like "Asia's Got Talent" that include older contestants who think they've "still got it!"

SIU-LIEN HAD SENT NANCY to live with "aunties" for months at a time, and once for a period that overlapped two Lunar New Years. Siu-lien would send letters listing reasons for the separations. She had told Nancy that it was going to be easier for her to find an apartment by herself, that she didn't make enough money to house and feed the two of them, and that Nancy would be going to a better school in whatever neighborhood the current aunt was in.

Nancy was a child with a studious temperament, and was able to budget free time despite elementary cram school. Every public library she visited had resources to find assisted housing for single parents and children, although the shame of doing so seemed to be the biggest societal barrier.

Money wasn't really a problem, anyway. Nancy knew her mother was sending substantial checks to her aunts. She was meticulous enough to grab the mail first, hold her mother's unopened letters to the light, and literally see through the argument that Siu-lien lacked funds. Nancy deduced that her mother was probably living with someone who didn't know about her or want a kid in their life. It saddened her.

The young Nancy was also well aware that she wasn't

going to the best schools. Most teachers didn't encourage her, and even the cram teachers chastised her for showing off.

Nancy never told her mother any of that, to this day. She also never asked Siu-lien the real reasons for their separation. There couldn't possibly be any good answers.

Without saying anything to each other, the two women backed away from the building and continued down a wide pedestrian path.

NTU, generally accepted as Taiwan's top university, had an international reputation, and about one out of every six students was from a foreign country. People who didn't get into NTU grumbled that their spot was taken by a rich foreigner, who paid nearly five times as much in tuition fees as the Taiwanese citizens.

Groups of students were putting up flyers to publicize Austronesian Festival events that were going to be held in campus venues. The notices emphasized amazing food in ample supply.

They continued walking in silence, and Nancy averted her eyes whenever people came near. She worried that she would see a friend, which would force Nancy to introduce her mother. Nancy felt a sharp pain in her right hand and realized she was making a tight fist and digging her fingernails into her palm.

"What building do you spend the most time in, Nancy?" asked Siu-lien.

"Let's go somewhere else," said Nancy. They were walking south, by Nancy's design, away from her biology building.

"Maybe there are some fun places to hang out off-campus. Do you want to go there?"

"Not really."

"Have you heard from Jing-nan?"

"No."

It brought Nancy minimal pleasure to register Siu-lien's disappointment with the brief answers to her questions. But this only made Siu-lien stop asking questions.

Nancy had never told Siu-lien about her boyfriend. The only reason her mother knew about Jing-nan at all was because of his profile in the media. Others knew about him, as well. About once a month, someone in the street would ask for a selfie with him. To his credit, Jing-nan always made it a point to talk about Nancy, and to pull her into the frame when cameras were clicking.

She learned that Siu-lien had first heard about Jing-nan secondhand from several friends who had cared for Nancy when she was a child. They came into the bar and showed off screenshots from Jing-nan's first misadventure. "That's your baby and her boyfriend," they yelled at Siu-lien and all the other patrons. After that, Siu-lien turned the bar TV to the news programs at the appointed hours, in case Nancy and Jing-nan popped up again. Every other month, it seemed, there they were.

NANCY AND HER MOTHER came upon a vending machine and they paused.

"Do you want something to drink?" asked Siu-lien as she dug through her purse. Nancy was thirsty but was determined to resist a treat from mama.

"I'm fine, Mom," she said. Siu-lien raised an eyebrow, swiped her MRT card, and selected a mango-flavored aloe drink. Nancy watched her mother twist off the cap and relish the first mouthful.

The day seemed to be getting hotter by the second. Siu-lien slipped on a pair of shades. She couldn't drink from a bottle and walk at the same time, Nancy remembered from her past behavior. Siu-lien paused to fill her mouth, continued for several steps, and then stopped again to swallow. It was like walking with a robot toy that needed to be wound every minute. God, was she swishing the chunks of aloe through her teeth?

"Mom," Nancy said, unable to mask the disgust in her tone. "We're going to meet up with Jing-nan." This time Siu-lien stopped in her tracks out of surprise.

"So you *did* hear from him?"

"I'm waiting to get another text from him to see where we can meet."

Her mother lifted her shades and glared. "*When* did you hear from Jing-nan?"

"A little bit ago. I didn't want to bother you because he doesn't have many details, anyway."

Siu-lien let her shades drop back to her nose. "Well, he failed to get the money, or else you would have told me."

"Hey, he managed to get some of it."

"How much?"

Nancy narrowed her eyes. "I don't know." Siu-lien felt an ache in her head behind her eyeballs. That bastard Boxer had finally gone too far. She closed her eyelids and tilted her head back in anguish. Because she had shades on, it looked to Nancy like Siu-lien was reveling in triumph.

Just when Nancy's temper was about to boil over, her phone jolted with a new text from Jing-nan saying he was already on the train. Nancy told him to meet them at the bookstore near the campus. She planned on browsing books while letting Jing-nan deal with Siu-lien.

Suddenly, Siu-lien moaned and put her hands on her head.

"Mom," said Nancy. "Are you all right?"

"I feel like I have a migraine!"

Nancy led Siu-lien to an empty bench and guided her to sit at one end. It was the first time she had seen her mother so pale.

"Something bad is happening," Siu-lien said softly.

Nancy tossed the aloe drink and bought a bottle of water from a vending machine. They waited it out for a while as Siu-lien slurped down water.

She's only going to get older, Nancy thought, and she really needed the money that Boxer stole. Nancy began to regret the hard feelings she had toward her mother, but they didn't soften.

JING-NAN ARRIVED AT THE bookstore as Siu-lien was sitting by herself, reading the back of a DVD case, her shades pushed to the top of her head. She had a lingering headache from her swoon, but the sight of Jing-nan revived her.

"What do you have there?" he asked her.

Siu-lien tossed the DVD aside and looked directly at Jing-nan. "Was Boxer alone when you saw him?" she asked.

"Yes."

"How much did he give you?"

Jing-nan handed the cash to her with both hands. "I think that comes to 21,500," he said.

Siu-lien fingered the bills. "That's right," she immediately pronounced, pushing the shades back on her nose.

"Um, where's Nancy?" asked Jing-nan. He watched his warped reflection in her shades smile crookedly.

"She's in the can," said Siu-lien. "So that was all the cash he had left, huh?" Jing-nan crossed his arms, feeling unappreciated.

"Well, I didn't search his body."

"Why not?"

"For one thing, that would only escalate things. On top of that, he didn't look very clean."

"I'm not surprised. Was he even dressed?"

"I really caught him off guard. He wasn't wearing a shirt when I saw him."

Siu-lien made a sucking sound of disgust.

"Boxer picked up all these bills from the floor. His pockets actually looked pretty empty."

"This is really it, huh, Jing-nan?" she said with resignation.

"He did say that he had put most of the prize money in a bank account," said Jing-nan, "but he was probably lying. He didn't seem to believe it himself."

Siu-lien's shades wiggled. "Bank account," she spat. "The guy doesn't even own a personal seal to stamp the forms, what bank would take his business?"

Jing-nan tried to sound a hopeful note. "Maybe most of the money's somewhere else, if it isn't in a bank."

Siu-lien began to crack her knuckles one by one. "The money's with *someone* else."

Nancy was coming down the stairs when she heard her mother's distinctive knuckle-cracking. Siu-lien was getting ready to fix someone.

Nancy rushed downstairs. "Jing-nan," she said, "looks like you got the money back."

"Only some," he said, shaking his head.

"He did terrible," said Siu-lien. "Jing-nan got almost nothing back!"

Nancy whirled on her mother. "At least he tried! He didn't have to do anything for you."

Siu-lien folded the bills and stashed them in her purse, lest Nancy try to snatch them away.

"He would've tried harder for you," said Siu-lien.

"Please listen," said Jing-nan, making an effort to maintain an even tone. "I did all I could. You think I should've threatened to kill him?"

Siu-lien removed her shades and tapped the tips of the

arms against the back of her left hand, considering the measure.

"Maybe that's too far," she said, "but you could've offered to take a selfie for the rest of the money he was hiding."

"I'm sure Jing-nan got all the money Boxer had left," said Nancy. "Anyway, it's your fault you didn't hold on to the receipt in the first place."

"How dare you talk to me like that," Siu-lien whisper-threatened. "I'm the victim! And I'm also your mother!" Siu-lien turned from Nancy and found herself face-to-face with Jing-nan.

He looked directly into Siu-lien's eyes. This was somewhat difficult for him. You didn't confront peers and certainly not elders. But Jing-nan wasn't seeking to challenge her. He wanted to understand Siu-lien, and he wanted her to understand him.

"You are definitely the victim," said Jing-nan. "I told Boxer I'd be back tomorrow." He saw that it was about a lot more than just the money. She wanted Boxer back, as flawed as he was. Jing-nan turned to Nancy. She seemed exhausted and it was only the middle of the day. "Nancy," he said, "are you all right?"

She seemed startled to hear her name. "Jing-nan, I'm fine. I was just wondering what Boxer did with the money." That was a lie, because she was really remembering being young and feeling the impatience in Siu-lien before she could hand off her child to another aunt.

"I'll tell you what he did," spat Siu-lien, but contrary to her words, she cut herself off and said no more.

After waiting a moment, Jing-nan said, "Well, it's entirely possible he'll have more money tomorrow."

"Will he even be there?" asked Siu-lien. "He's probably rowing a boat to China right now."

"Mom," said Nancy, "Boxer doesn't have a lot of ambition. He'll either be in that room or back with you."

Siu-lien made a sound that could have been revulsion or smug satisfaction.

"I have an idea, Siu-lien," said Jing-nan. "I have some time before I have to get to work. Why don't I go back now to see Boxer and try to get him to come with me to Unknown Pleasures? I'll promise him free food, and then you can confront him out in the open."

Siu-lien shifted her jaw as a thoughtful look appeared on her face. The public humiliation aspect appealed to her. "That's not a bad idea," she said.

"Don't go to too much trouble, Jing-nan," said Nancy.

"Nonsense," said Siu-lien. "He has the time!"

JING-NAN GOT OUT OF the train at Longshan Temple, but something odd was in the air this time, apart from the smell of concrete and soil after a brief rain shower. Rivulets ran down the nearly empty sidewalks. He walked down Guangzhou Street and saw a few police vehicles and zero grabby prostitutes. He didn't exactly love cops, but he appreciated their presence when their focus wasn't on him. As he got closer to Boxer's building, he saw that the entire street had been taped off. A few passersby were standing around, shading their eyes and trying to figure out what was going on. He approached a man and woman wearing straw hats against the hot sun that had emerged after the rain.

"What happened?" Jing-nan asked them.

"About half an hour ago, they took a body out of that building," said the woman. "I think it's a prostitute." That was Boxer's building. Jing-nan hoped he had nothing to do with it.

"This street used to be really dangerous," said the man. "I hope we aren't backsliding."

Jing-nan could have told them he grew up not far from this very spot, but he didn't want to get into an involved conversation right now. That was something he did for work, not for free.

He called Nancy to tell her it was a bust, and he headed to the night market without thinking for a moment that the little life that Boxer had led was over.

THREE FLOORS UP FROM where Jing-nan had been standing, Captain Huang stood in the back room of a brothel, staring at a monitor in disbelief. He was watching footage captured by the brothel's street-level closed-circuit camera, Taipei's top crime-fighting tool. They were mute witnesses to assaults and worse. For the most part, CC cameras were fairly reliable for catching a perpetrator after a crime was committed. Great for people who have suffered property damage. Not so great for murder victims.

Captain Huang was the head of the Shilin precinct, just north of Jing-nan's night market. He had been called to Wanhua by the precinct's head detective, who had done his military service with the captain. The detective had been securing and reviewing surveillance footage in the area, and recognized the person entering and leaving Boxer's building.

A police informant and drug dealer had heard there was a guy with a lot of money looking to party. The informant had pushed open the door of the apartment and found a body with the head split nearly in half.

"You little motherfucker," Captain Huang growled at the screen. He paused the digital recorder and tapped the untrimmed nail of his right index finger against the pixels of Jing-nan's neck.

Jing-nan was fairly well known by the public, but the city's police knew that Captain Huang was no fan of his. The captain in fact put a big bet on Jing-nan in the monthly celebrity death-pool game that many cops played on a password-protected site.

"I'm going to nail you like a fucking calendar!" Captain Huang thundered. "And your stupid night-market crew, Dwayne the cannibal and Frankie the Cat!" The captain checked his phone and plotted to hit Jing-nan and Unknown Pleasures when they were busiest, for maximum public humiliation.

CHAPTER 6

Frankie the Cat sat up in bed, pulled his phone out from under the mattress where it was clamped, and shielded the screen with his right hand. It was 4:58 A.M., two minutes before the alarm would go off. He was disappointed. He usually rose one minute before.

Frankie slipped out of bed without disturbing his sleeping wife, stood on the floor, and placed his arms at his sides. He exercised his toes by lifting one at a time by about a centimeter while staring at the commercial-grade hotel shades that were blocking out the glow of streetlights. In his mind's eye, Frankie saw images playing on the darkened screen. A group of thirty young men, some just boys, running barefoot across a field, through a shallow, rocky stream, and over a hot sandy beach. Which one was he? Maybe all of them.

They were the orphan brigade and supposedly varied in age from 15 to 20. Some of them were younger, and nearly all were undocumented refugees. The story the government pitched to the international media was that they were the sons of men who were killed by the Communists during the Chinese Civil War. After undergoing training on the Nationalists' bases on Taiwan, the orphans would lead the charge to retake the mainland. Buoyed by revenge, the boys surely were a deadly spearhead.

Frankie finished with his toes and silently dropped flat to the floor, chest down. He began to do push-ups on his fingertips and continued to think about the others. A part of his mind was always thinking about them, but his memories were particularly vivid in the morning, sharpened by his dreams of being with his compatriots. Some of them, like Frankie, were sent to prison under the martial-law era without ever being formally charged and released, sometimes decades later.

Frankie did 88 push-ups, his rod-straight body dipping like a manual stapler in use. Then he swung into a sitting position and ran his fingers over his palms, which bore raised impressions from the planks of the wooden floor. He weighed the Chinese belief that one's fate was predetermined, and that life was a matter of connecting dots already fixed by the universe. Well, many Chinese ideas didn't play out so well in Taiwan these days, and even the mainlanders were seeing their youngest generation act like this island was their real home.

What was "home" but where you slept, anyway?

Frankie turned, pressed his back into the floor, and began to do crunches, matching each elbow to the opposite knee while alternating sides.

ALL OF THEM HAD been gung ho about going to war. Each of the orphans had trained with live ammunition, and no one flinched when a shot was fired off. Their hearts were steeled and their minds were thoroughly washed. They were better than any Communist soldier. Hell, they were better than any Nationalist soldier, too!

After about a year of training, they were marched out

before a group of foreigners with cameras and instructed to do some maneuvers. Some pictures were for *Life* magazine, they were told. In the following months, their fortunes turned. The commander was replaced, and soon after they were disarmed and relegated to run more and drill less.

Finally the orphan brigade was disbanded, and its members were reassigned to cleaning and kitchen duties in the veteran soldiers' barracks. Frankie and the rest of his brigade went from being the literal poster children of the Nationalists' propaganda machine to plain orphans again.

In the barracks, they were at the mercy of the actual soldiers, who had fought in China and retreated with the Nationalists to Taiwan. The orphans were hazed and bullied by the older men, who were ashamed to be alive and freeloading in military housing while not being allowed to fight to free the mainland.

The veterans also resented that the brigade had been portrayed as young heroes in foreign media, photogenic whelps who had never even been on a battlefield, never taken a bullet, never seen their best friend blown to pieces.

FRANKIE WAS CROUCHED DOWN, cleaning the tile around the squat toilets, when they came for him. A man who weighed 250 pounds sat on Frankie's back. The other soldiers stood around and laughed at Frankie, expecting the teen to crumple.

Instead, Frankie swerved on his feet and the heavyset soldier tumbled off, landing with an arm in the not-quite-clean ceramic basin. Incensed, the man scrambled to his feet and tried to slap Frankie's head but kept missing. The boy spun away faster than a top. The soldier was particularly galled that Frankie had never even looked up, nor stopped scrubbing the tiles.

The onlookers now laughed at their fellow veteran. The big man grew winded and confused by his fruitless effort, and he chuckled bitterly as Frankie began idly whistling.

"Listen, boy," said the soldier. "I'm sorry I was trying to give you a hard time. I'm just kidding around." He extended a hand. Frankie rose and shook it, but on the second shake, the soldier headbutted him. Frankie reeled backward, and the soldier tried to laugh out loud but found that he couldn't because a toilet brush was shoved into his mouth and the bristles were poking into his nasal cavity.

Frankie then kicked the soldier in the balls. As the man fell on his back, Frankie straddled his stomach, yanked out the brush, and scrubbed the soldier's eyes.

Fifteen minutes later, both Frankie and the soldier were standing before the desk of a senior officer. The sergeant was in his 50s and had seen combat against the Communists, the Japanese, and then the Communists again. He noted the stooped soldier's face, which was rubbed raw and bleeding. Frankie stood at attention and seemed unaware of the red mark on his forehead from the headbutt.

"That boy got the better of you, soldier," spat the sergeant. "When I heard all the screaming, I thought I'd find you beating the crap out of him. Instead, you were switched around. Maybe that's how it should be!" The soldier was moved to Frankie's cot and tasked with cleaning toilets, while Frankie was transferred to bunk with the regular troops.

Frankie became the hero of both wings of the dorm, and nobody picked on the orphans anymore. However, the demoted soldier was now bullied by the men who had fought by his side. The final humiliation was when they forced him down to his hands and knees to shine Frankie's shoes while the teen stood in them. Frankie had felt badly about it, and insisted that the whole episode stop, but nobody listened to him, not even the disgraced soldier.

The soldier hanged himself that night in the bathroom stall where he had accosted Frankie only a week before. An investigation was launched. The sergeant who had promoted Frankie was reassigned, and Frankie's file was pulled out for thorough examination. The dead soldier's uncle was the Minister of Development in the Executive Yuan, and the politician wanted some goddamned answers and the proper punishments meted out. Apparently, Frankie's older brother had remained in China. That was reason enough to set up Frankie as someone with Communist ties and sympathies.

The investigating officer hated reds even more than the norm because he had been a Communist when he was young, and concealed his past by overcompensating. If he had had his way, Frankie would be in front of a firing squad. Frankie's file, however, contained a picture of him saluting with a torn shirtsleeve to an amused Chiang Kai-shek. Why was the Generalissimo smiling? The officer held the photo under the bare bulb of his desk lamp. He could make out KILL MAO tattooed on Frankie's arm. Frankie was no commie, and because Chiang was in the photo, there were bound to be many other prints elsewhere.

A death sentence wouldn't do. But Frankie's older brother remained behind enemy lines, and on top of that was a college graduate. The mark of a fully accredited Communist! The officer's head throbbed as he considered where he would send Frankie to prison. Someone had to pay for the soldier's death, not just because the cake-eating politicians wanted revenge— troop morale would be hurt otherwise. Even worse, there could be talk of the soldier's ghost walking around, moaning about injustice, and looking to harm anyone it came across.

No civilian court would convict Frankie on the charge

of having Communist sympathies, but Taiwan was under martial law. There was no need for direct evidence, stated charges, or even trials—only sentences to be pronounced, and served by the designated guilty parties.

Frankie was apprehended by military police and brought to Green Island. He was shocked when he was told that he was sentenced to serve time for his brother, who was aligned with the "bandits" in China. Frankie wished they had simply told him that he was being punished for the soldier's suicide.

The island's prison was overcrowded with legitimate criminals and political prisoners, so Frankie was placed in an improvised cell that had been blasted out of the volcanic rock itself. It wasn't more than a hole with a steel grate on top. The cell wasn't quite so bad, though, Frankie mused. He labored all day like the others, pummeling stone into gravel that was supposedly shipped to be used in the garden of one of Chiang Kai-shek's residences.

Yes, the labor was bad, but his cell wasn't. He was usually dead asleep in it, anyway. Jing-nan had asked him about the cell being flooded with seawater, but that had only happened eight or nine times, during some bad storms. It was a nice, quiet place. On top of that, it was surprisingly warm and well-lit, and you certainly couldn't say that about most of the other cells.

HIS EXERCISES COMPLETED, FRANKIE rose from the floor. He unfurled a pair of drawstring linen pants and stepped into them. He unrolled a linen shirt, put his arms through it, and let it hang open. He put his phone in the shirt pocket and silently left the bedroom, closing the door behind him.

He drew a mug of hot water from the heater on the kitchen counter and dropped a scoop of dried tea into it. Frankie watched the leaves unfurl across the water's surface like miniature dragons. The tea was a gift from a fellow orphan who now, strangely, lived peaceably in China and operated a plantation near Yunnan, which had been a Communist stronghold in the civil war. Frankie smiled into his mug. His reflected face played upon the trembling surface of his tea, at times looking mirthful, mischievous, or bitter.

Frankie inhaled the fragrance of burned flowers and baked soil. It reminded him of childhood, smelling the country air in the mornings, with fires from the previous night's battle still burning. He sipped the tea and savored the light oily essence sliding across his tongue. This is what China tastes like, he thought. It spoke of bottled-up emotions, self-denial, and rigidity.

Frankie drank in the tea and felt the warmth extend to his extremities. He pondered why he continued to be vibrant when so many of his peers were tired, breaking down, and dying. Green Island friends, from unrepentant, hardened criminals to the less so—nobody is completely innocent, after all—complained about being too old to meet up for tea or stop by the night market. They couldn't believe he was still working, and on his feet all night, at that.

Well, his orphan-brigade compatriots had proved to be the harder lot. The ones still alive were leading robust lives. Cancer had claimed a few over the years. Suicide was the leading cause of death.

FRANKIE HADN'T CONTEMPLATED SUICIDE while locked up, but he had considered the suicide mission of braving the ocean to swim to freedom from Green Island to Taiwan proper. It was 33 kilometers between the two islands, a doable distance for someone who had trained for imagined missions to strike the coast of China. But with all of Taiwan under martial law, he'd be swimming with bull, tiger, and great white sharks from his cell to a huge prison island, a heavily patrolled land of curfews filled with informants and secret police.

Besides, he had no family in Taiwan. Who would he be swimming toward? Even if he had managed to make the journey, he'd be living on the run to evade capture.

One day, after a full shift of labor, Frankie was waiting to be marched back to his cell when two unfamiliar officers took custody of him and brought him to the administrative office. He was aware that it was his first time there since he had arrived at Green Island a decade before. They locked Frankie in an interrogation room, and he shivered in the air-conditioning. He saw that he wasn't alone. On the other side of the room, a heavily tanned, middle-aged prisoner regarded him warily. There was something familiar about him, though. The two men stood and silently approached each other. Frankie suddenly sneezed, as did his reflection. He stepped to the two-way mirror, noting first his straight posture and then his skinny face. His cheeks looked like two overbaked chicken thighs—no fat left in them.

The lock rattled and Frankie turned to square his shoulders with the door. A sweaty man in a suit entered, smiled, and did a series of supplicating mini-bows endemic to creatures set for a lifetime of bureaucratic work.

"Hello, Mr. Lee," said the man. "Guess what? You're leaving Green Island today. The government has declared that you are indeed a true patriot."

"What?" was all Frankie could say. The man wiped his forehead and nose.

"It's been determined that your brother had arrived in Taiwan quite a number of years ago. He hadn't remained on the mainland, after all." He gave a stupid and apologetic smile. "Bit of a funny mix-up. Well, not *funny*."

Frankie mechanically took hold of some objects the administrator handed him while staring at the room's open door.

"As far as leaving the detention facility," said the man, "there's a boat in a few minutes, if you're ready."

Frankie left with the change of the guards. It was an odd role reversal. The guards huddled in the back together, subdued, as Frankie stood watch over them. One offered him a cigarette.

Frankie landed in Taiwan proper with the clothes on his back and three envelopes in his pockets. One contained his official release document, which failed to mention his imprisonment. It only stated that his citizenship in the Republic of China was fully restored. He hadn't been aware that it had been revoked.

The second envelope had a wad of cash, more generous than was normally provided to a released prisoner, due to Frankie's military service. The last envelope held contact information for his brother.

Frankie made his way north, to Taipei, hitchhiking with a combination of civilian and military trucks. The last ride was with a group of soldiers headed to the Shilin Night Market. They pulled their overloaded jeep onto a gravel road and the six mainlanders staggered out to the closest stand. The food was good, but the soldiers made fun of the people running the stand, a family of benshengren hicks who couldn't speak Mandarin fluently. When the soldiers were done eating, they patted the man who had served them on his head and walked away without paying. Frankie stayed and tried to pay the bill with the last of his money.

Jing-nan's grandfather wouldn't accept it, however, so out of frustration, Frankie said, "Well, you'll have to let me work here, then." That was more than four decades ago, and Frankie stayed through the deaths of Jing-nan's grandfather, grandmother, mother, and father. Now, the night market was five times the size it used to be, and the gravel roads were all paved over. Most of the customers were foreigners who didn't speak Mandarin or Taiwanese, and couldn't tell and didn't care if you were a mainlander or not.

OVER THE YEARS, FRANKIE'S friends—as they changed to walk the straight and narrow, or rose up in the ranks of criminal organizations—married and had children, and tried to encourage Frankie to do the same. Surely he had girlfriends, right? Hey, Frankie, are you dating anyone? You cook, right? Women love men who can cook! My sister-in-law's a match-maker, she can find you someone!

He would smile, light a cigarette, and say nothing. Years went by, leaving scars on the kitchen wall where calendars were taped up and torn down.

One morning, about 15 years ago, a woman showed up at his doorstep with two suitcases. He invited her in and after some hesitant conversation, Frankie was able to glean that her name was Linh, she was from Vietnam, and she was married to Frankie's brother Chun-chieh in Kaohsiung in southern Taiwan.

Chun-chieh had gone to Vietnam on an excursion to find a bride. He was in his 60s and Linh, who was a seamstress, was nearly a third of his age. The marriage broker had told her that Frankie's brother was a rich Taiwanese business-man who wanted her to live in his mansion. If she married him, she would live in luxury, and he would send money back to her family every month. A deal was struck, and Frankie's brother gave Linh's family money up front as a goodwill gesture.

In Taiwan, Linh found that she was a servant, expected to cook and clean everything. Also, Chun-chieh wasn't rich or a businessman. He was a low-level manager at a supermarket, and refused to give Linh money for groceries or anything else. The refrigerator was packed with unsalable, nearly spoiled meats and produce from the supermarket. Yet he complained when his meals were comprised of oddly shaped components that had their moldy parts hacked off.

He had given her beatings, too, and they became more frequent after his work hours were cut back.

A few days before, in a drunken rage, Frankie's brother had vowed to kill or divorce her. She took refuge, as she had many times, in the bathroom, and waited for the old man to pass out. Then she emerged and took money from his wallet. She retrieved the cookie tin in the back of his files, which Chun-chieh thought was a clever hiding place. Inside, Linh knew, was her national identity card, and searching among the rest of the items in the tin, she found Frankie's Taipei address scrawled on a cardboard flap. She had made her way to Frankie's, and now she was here.

He told Linh to sleep in the bed while he would take the couch. In the morning, Frankie with both hands presented her an envelope of money, half of his savings. Linh refused it, saying that she had renounced her Vietnamese citizenship to apply for Taiwanese naturalization, a years-long process, and was stateless. She couldn't rent an apartment or get a job on the books.

Frankie thought about his own story, of when he had fallen through the cracks and had nothing and no one.

He told Linh to stay with him as long as she needed to. Over the next few weeks, they found help from Taiwan Is Our Home, a citizens' rights organization for recent immigrants. They managed to get Linh's marriage annulled. A year later, Linh and Frankie were married, and both sleeping in the bed.

FRANKIE REVIEWED THE LIFE that he lived every morning, and it was as much a part of the morning ritual as his workout and tea. One last step. He pulled out the center drawer of his work desk to glance at an envelope tucked in the back, the third one he had received upon his departure from Green Island. It was still sealed after all these years. No reason to open it today, Frankie thought.

He glanced at the clock. It said 8:00 A.M. He called Dwayne to wake him up.

CHAPTER 7

Dwayne swung out his right arm frantically and missed the phone by a mile. He was still caught up in one of his baseball dreams, stomping his feet in the batter's box, with two strikes, two outs in the bottom of the ninth. Dwayne was the team's last hope. He had to hit a grand slam or the season was over.

The pitcher had been brushing him back from the plate, but he couldn't let himself be hit and get on base that way. Jing-nan was up next, and of course that guy would pop out.

The home crowd out there had turned against Dwayne for some reason. At first, they had taunted him by making savage animal sounds, mocking his Aboriginal heritage. Those racist Han Chinese bastards! He was going to show them! Now they changed their taunts to sound like a giant ringing phone. What a bunch of unimaginative idiots!

The pitch was coming, straight across the plate. Dwayne put all his weight on his back leg and swung as hard as he could.

Dwayne's arm lunged again with the second ring. His hands grabbed the phone and pressed it to his ear before he was fully awake.

"Dwayne." Frankie's voice through the speaker was patient and knowing. Dwayne woke up with a snort. "Time to go to the gym, Dwayne." Dwayne stretched all four limbs and ended a yawn by clenching his teeth.

"I swear, Cat," said Dwayne, "you're calling me earlier every day."

"No," said Frankie. Dwayne's tone softened to one of whining.

"I can't wake up this early when I go to sleep so late."

"You tell me to wake you up," said Frankie. "Want me to stop calling?"

"No, no, no, please don't stop. You know, I've been reading those murder-mystery stories after work," Dwayne continued to plead. "How am I supposed to sleep after?"

"Maybe you should read something boring at night, Dwayne. Try news about stocks."

"No. That might make me start worrying about money and give me insomnia." Dwayne took a gulp of water from a cup on his nightstand, and noisily sucked his teeth. "How are you doing, Frankie?"

"Fine."

"Well, don't worry about me, I'm awake now."

"Are you sure you want me to call tomorrow?" He asked the same question every morning.

"Of course, Cat." This was the closest they came to saying "I love you" to each other.

Dwayne rolled out of bed, stood, and gasped in the heat. He lived in an apartment that had been illegally added to the roof of a residential building. It had no insulation, so it was chilly at night, and hot as a toaster when the early morning sun hit the corrugated metal exterior walls. At least he didn't have any leaks when it rained.

It wasn't shabbily built, and none of Dwayne's few visitors

were aware that the one-bedroom apartment was constructed after the landlord and builder had cut through some red tape by making it a cash transaction and not notifying any regulatory body. It looked like any other of the hundreds of thousands of legal and illegal additions in Taipei.

Dwayne skimmed his latest emails and checked the battery level on his phone. He yanked out the lamp cord before recharging. Dwayne never had more than three items plugged into any of the power sockets. Electrical fires had brought many illegally built housing additions—along with their residents—to fiery ends. Dwayne sweated every night over the possibility of a fire overtaking him while he slept. He kept a dry-chemical extinguisher under the bed and a smaller one in the bathroom, in case he had to make a last stand in there against a rooftop-wide blaze.

Dwayne pulled on a T-shirt, shorts, and yesterday's socks. Why work out in clean underwear and socks? He walked to the living room, lifted the shade of his only window, and surveyed the city's profile against the light-gray sky. There was always a chance of rain, no matter how much sun there was. Even if the view was flat-out bleak at times, he still loved to look up at the clouds. It was the same sky his ancestors had seen, had prayed to, and had cried out to in anguish and ecstasy, minus the occasional plane or helicopter.

Dwayne pushed himself away from the window frame and veered toward the coffee table. He picked up the television remote with a sense of trepidation. Just check the weather, and don't get sucked into some trashy story that's going to plant you on the couch. That would mean no gym and another day the flab won out.

He lifted his shirt and stared at his stomach. No one could honestly say he was fat.

Besides, Dwayne was absolutely going to make it to the

gym today. He had promised Chen, a friend from church, that he'd be there. They were going to spot each other. But first, Dwayne needed to know the weather. He could check on his phone, of course, but then he could be lured into catching up on emails and social media, wrecking his plans.

He clicked on the television, which was preset to the weather station. The screen immediately filled with the smoke and garish flames of Dwayne's apartment-fire fears. But it was a forest somewhere in America that was burning down. He covered his open mouth.

"Holy Mazu!" he whispered through his fingers, taking the name of Taiwan's top Daoist deity in vain. Flames flicked between the trees, looking like wet strips of yellow, orange, and red papaya. After the segment was over, Dwayne desperately checked all the other cable channels to see more shots of the fire.

Twenty minutes later, Dwayne texted his friend Chen, saying that something had tied him up, but he would definitely be at the gym tomorrow morning. Chen replied immediately with a curt, "Sure." Dwayne felt guilty, but was immediately distracted by a commercial for a new white-meat chicken sandwich at McDonald's. "That looks gross," Dwayne told the ad, his mouth pooling with saliva.

Now that the workout was off for certain, he might as well eat. Dwayne went to the fridge and pulled out a pack of wheat buns from the freezer. Most people just popped them in the microwave, but that only heated up the already dehydrated buns. Steaming was the proper way to prepare them.

Dwayne poured only about three centimeters of water into the bottom pan of the steamer. The trick was to keep the pan shallow so the water boiled faster, and anyway steaming was a fairly quick process. He leaned against the wall and eyed a televised roundtable discussion about the merits of President Tsai Ing-wen's personal style.

Tsai was part Aborigine, as she had some Paiwan blood. Dwayne thought about other people of Aboriginal descent who were making it in mainstream society. His pal Chen was one of them. The guy was doing marketing for some tech company, and sometimes he traveled the world. He'd eaten sausages in Germany, cheeseburgers in America, and steaks in Brazil. Dwayne had never even been on a plane. Hell, he'd never even been to the airport.

Well, the things that he had accomplished in life couldn't be measured by conventional standards. Had Chen ever kneed a gangster in the nuts before? Had President Tsai ever knocked out two thugs who were trying to beat down a friend?

He settled down in front of the television with a cup of hot tea and a plate of wheat buns drizzled with condensed milk. Dwayne picked one up and watched the liquid dribble onto the plate. He was almost 40 years old and here he was with the same breakfast he was eating back in elementary school. His teachers might have been right that he lacked maturity and ambition. Well, at least he had been capable of altering the comments they wrote to his parents, so he wasn't lacking in creativity!

Dwayne drank a mouthful of hot tea and felt the bun melt away between his teeth.

He slid lower on the couch, and thought about how he had let down his friend Chen. The elders had always encouraged younger generations to uphold each other, and Dwayne had blown it, yet again.

Chen was the opposite of Dwayne in several ways. He had gone to college and had a day job at an accounting firm. Chen pushed for more-inclusive hiring practices at the company, and was volunteering for the upcoming

Austronesian Cultural Festival. That thing was coming up soon, wasn't it?

Dwayne finished his breakfast, not even paying attention to the TV ads. What was it that his grandfather had said? The stories are in the songs and dances, and they only made sense when holding hands and participating in them. You couldn't simply watch and listen. The culture was in your movement, and your own voice. Dwayne was young, then, and wouldn't sing or dance with his grandfather because he thought it was something for girls. The look on his grandfather's face was the first time he had seen someone look sad in the soul.

Dwayne's father had abandoned the old ways to get a job in a factory, working at night. That was a time when the family was supposed to be together, his grandmother had admonished.

See, Dwayne wasn't to blame for not being connected with his culture. It was his father who had caused the break.

As a teen, when his eyes were just starting to open, Dwayne grew to hate his father for not teaching him how to be Amis. A father who didn't know who he was couldn't pass anything down to his son. When he finished high school, Dwayne left his family and turned down a potential college baseball scholarship to live in what he thought was an authentic community in Taitung County in the south, ancestral lands of some of the Amis. Dwayne thought he'd live among his people and soak up the culture. Instead, it was just a facade, a place designated as a "folk center" that made money by doing shows for bussed-in school groups and tourists.

Dwayne put his hands on his knees and cracked his neck. How angry he had been, back then. Mad at the fake village, his father, the mainstream Taiwanese society that had erased him, and the world. Not necessarily in that order.

Dwayne fought in bars and nightclubs, and because he usually won, he found employment as security in those venues. Seeing the same trouble night after night—the sort of bullshit he himself used to cause—put him on a path from breaking up fights to breaking the cycle. He joined a Presbyterian church after seeing a flyer in the men's bathroom of all places. Nearly everyone there was Aborigine, and at the end of the service, people gathered, joined hands, and began to move. It was the most powerful thing Dwayne had ever experienced, and he could feel his grandparents.

Not long after he started attending church regularly, Dwayne joined a small group and went to the Shilin Night Market to hang out. Coincidentally, they stopped by the stall run by Jing-nan's grandfather. Frankie and Jing-nan's father were also working that night—along with a 10-year-old Jing-nan. Dwayne noticed the grandfather behind the stall, struggling to pick up a rack of just-washed bowls. Dwayne jumped in and lifted the rack to a shelf for drying.

Jing-nan's father shared a glance with Frankie before asking Dwayne if he wanted a job. Dwayne said okay, even though he had no idea what the salary was. It was a more innocent time in Taiwan, and its island culture enforced mutual trust and dependency between people—even between boss and worker.

Dwayne started out with the muscle jobs, washing pots and sharpening knives, while Jing-nan spoke English to make the tourists feel at ease. Dwayne graduated to perfecting the secret sauces directly under the watch of Jing-nan's grandfather. Well, more like refining the recipes. The elderly man told Dwayne many times how to make the five-generation-old stew base and the basting sauce from a recipe of the Ming Dynasty's royal court. The instructions were never the same twice.

Dwayne had many shortcomings. His memory, however, was perfect. But he could only nod and continue listening to Grandfather Chen's variant recipes with apprehension, pressing his fingers over his trembling lips lest he speak out.

Jing-nan's grandfather stopped coming to the stall about a year later, and Dwayne eventually settled on what he believed were the best recipes, based on his own taste buds. Most importantly, the grandfather had approved of Dwayne's cooking with a hearty handshake, the most physical affection he had ever shown anybody.

So, 15 YEARS LATER and I'm doing essentially the same thing, Dwayne mused, although there had been a few changes. Ingredients were different, and so was Unknown Pleasures' menu. Sometimes Frankie, who was the chief procurer of the stand's basic ingredients, wasn't able to get something crucial. One night they ran out of sesame oil, and Dwayne made his own. He roasted sesame seeds in a wok, pulverized them, and then mixed them with cooking oil over heat. Finally, he strained a bottle from the concoction and presented it to Frankie, who smelled it and gave one of his big smiles.

Work indeed had its creative moments. And apart from the cooking itself, there were those recent insane adventures with Jing-nan.

Dwayne stood up and stretched. What to do in the hours before work, now that he had bagged the gym? Well, it probably made the most sense to settle in and play video games. It would give more meaning to his workout tomorrow, which he would no doubt make. Besides, he best stay indoors because he still had no idea what the weather was going to be.

CHAPTER 8

Dwayne arrived at Unknown Pleasures at five in the afternoon with his right hand wrapped in a bandage.

"Wow," said Jing-nan, "you punch a wall or something, Dwayne?"

How the hell did that scrawny punk guess correctly? What a lucky little bastard! He's going to live to be 120!

Dwayne had been trying to get past the mini-boss in one of the higher levels of the video game *Radiant Silvergun*, but he hadn't been able to do it, not even with the cheat code for infinite lives. He had managed to restrain himself from taking out his frustrations on the controller of his Xbox. But after he was just a pixel too close to an incoming missile—resulting in his spaceship exploding right when he was about to win—he had to hit something. Dwayne had opened his closet and punched a sidewall through a rack of clothes, thinking they would cushion his hand. One suit jacket, however, had a small metal plaque in the chest pocket, a token of thanks for taking part in a church mentoring program for at-risk youth.

"Jing-nan," said Dwayne with equal amounts of exasperation and menace, "if you really have to know, I hurt myself at the gym. The weights in a machine weren't locked properly and they slammed on my hand."

"I'm sorry that happened, Dwayne," said Jing-nan with measured sincerity. "Your injury isn't going to interfere with work, is it?"

Dwayne flexed both his arms. "It's not that bad," he said.

"Because, you know, I saw some schoolgirls around here that I could ask to do your job tonight . . ."

Dwayne pointed at Jing-nan's nose. "You'd better not start with me . . ." he warned.

"Dwayne," asked Frankie, "what sort of machine was that?" He took out a pocket comb and ran it over the right side of his head.

"What machine, Cat?"

"The one that hurt your hand. I can't think of anything in a gym that could hurt you that way."

"It was one of the triceps machines, if you must know. The thing was broken," said Dwayne.

"I thought you said it wasn't locked properly," said Frankie.

"Well, I didn't examine the mechanism too closely because I was hurt at the time, Frankie. Maybe you should investigate what happened."

Frankie slid his comb into a back pocket. "I will. Now, which gym was this?" he asked.

"Well, it doesn't even matter," Dwayne said. "I don't care anymore." He noisily dragged a plastic crate of washed cilantro, chives, and chili peppers across the floor and onto a workbench. Frankie tossed Dwayne a pair of latex gloves.

"You should wear these so you don't get those bandages wet," Frankie called out. Without a word, Dwayne slipped on the gloves and began to chop vegetables with a cleaver large enough for a horror film. His focused, work-ready face resembled that of a deep-sea fish waiting for a victim to snap up.

Jing-nan turned his attention to what the stall would be offering tonight. It had to be something sticky for eyeballs, in the social media sense. As he did most nights, Jing-nan pondered the ultimate questions: What would tourists visiting Taiwan believe was authentic, and what price point would they be willing to pay for a bite of this authenticity?

One thing he learned early on was to keep the samples behind a window. Unknown Pleasures' lighting threw enough glare onto the glass to foil people who wanted to post online without paying.

Foot traffic tonight was great. Jing-nan didn't even have to step to the front to rope people in. In one sense, he wasn't that different from the la ke women at the brothels. Jing-nan thought about seeing Boxer that morning, and hoped the guy would scrape up some more money the next time they met.

So many people were crowding around Unknown Pleasures that the people waiting at the front were pressing up against the glass displays. As soon as he could, Jing-nan stepped around the counter with a rag and a bottle of cleanser. He wiped away smudge marks until he saw himself crouching in the glass. A familiar, scowling face with baggy eyes swam up next to him. Jing-nan wished he could wipe that away, too.

"Jing-nan!" Captain Huang declared in triumph, as if a manhunt were over. Jing-nan crossed his arms defensively. Both Frankie and Dwayne discreetly monitored the officer's actions.

The captain didn't come by Unknown Pleasures too often, but when he did, it was to wind up Jing-nan. It annoyed Captain Huang that someone within his precinct was a minor celebrity for outwitting criminals.

For a guy who enjoyed engaging with people, Jing-nan

certainly hadn't made many friends in the police department. After escaping a few weeks ago from a kidnapper, Jing-nan had given some Zoom interviews, thinking that almost any publicity was always a positive. During one conversation that was posted online, however, Jing-nan openly rolled his eyes or twisted his mouth whenever he mentioned the police. He had made sure to say that many cops were good. But that didn't matter when the video went viral. The takeaway for the viewers who worked in law enforcement was that Jing-nan, the guy with the stand at Shilin Night Market, thought they were shitty at their jobs.

For Captain Huang, it was one more thing to hold against Jing-nan. The captain already had a history with Jing-nan's uncle, Big Eye, who lived in Taichung, a two-hour drive southwest from Taipei. Despite the distance, Big Eye had some influence and financial interests in Taipei outside the conventional legal channels.

Depending on whom one asked, Big Eye was either a small-time gangster who owned legitimate businesses, or a big-time gangster who owned legitimate businesses. Big Eye himself simply said he was an entrepreneur who liked to lobby in unconventional ways for a better operating climate. This included co-opting the services of high-ranking people in law enforcement to assist in various endeavors that Jing-nan could only contemplate with his eyes squeezed shut.

"Still looking for my uncle?" Jing-nan asked Captain Huang's reflection. "He's not here." The captain grabbed Jing-nan's shoulders, pulled him up roughly, and spun him around so they were nearly face-to-face. Captain Huang was about three inches taller.

"No, no, you're the one I want," the captain said. "I want you to come down with me to the station to see this very interesting video I have." Jing-nan threw up his hands.

"Are you still mad about that interview? I was tired, I didn't know what I was doing. I put up an apology video, and almost no one watched it. I have nothing against cops in general, as you know."

The captain was unmoved. "No, I don't know, Jing-nan," he said before continuing with a raised voice. "But I don't care about this bullshit from the past right now. I have you on camera leaving the apartment of a murdered man. And I also know you returned to the scene."

Jing-nan shifted his stance as he tried to read Captain Huang's poker face. At the mention of murder both Frankie and Dwayne laid aside their instruments and crossed their arms. The line of 10 people at Unknown Pleasures turned to the right to see what exactly was happening. Captain Huang recognized that these tourists understood only rudimentary Mandarin, so to help them out, he pointed at Jing-nan and said in English, "This man is a murderer!" They gasped.

"That's a lie!" Jing-nan said in English. In Mandarin, he snapped at Captain Huang. "I have no idea what you're talking about."

Captain Huang swept his arms in a grand gesture. "Take a walk with me, then. I'll explain everything to you."

"Am I under arrest?"

The captain conceded he was not.

"Well, to hell with that, then. I'm staying here. I have a business to run."

Captain Huang leaned against the counter and wiped his fingers on the glass that Jing-nan had cleaned so carefully. "If you come with me voluntarily, Jing-nan, I'll let your staff keep Unknown Pleasures open. If you don't come, I'll get some of my boys over here, and they'll buzz around your lousy little shack all night. Might be bad for business. It's up to you."

Jing-nan followed the captain as he left for the precinct.

"I'll be back soon, you guys," he cheerily called out to Dwayne and Frankie. Dwayne stared back in disbelief. Frankie, as always, smiled. To the tourists, Jing-nan said in English too quickly for Captain Huang to pick up, "The cop's mad because my car's in his parking space."

AT THE PRECINCT, CAPTAIN Huang brought Jing-nan into his office and shut the door. The floor tiles were heavily scuffed as if the desk were roughly slid around on a regular basis.

One wall was adorned with four certificates of merit.

"Don't you know four is an unlucky number?" Jing-nan asked as he sat across from the desk in a metal chair with worn fabric upholstery.

"I make my own luck," the captain replied absently as he clicked through items on his computer. "All right, here we go. A little something a colleague in the Wanhua District spotted." He turned his flat-screen monitor until it faced Jing-nan directly. "These are timestamped from this morning." The captain hit a key to maximize the top window and tapped the space bar to begin the video.

Jing-nan watched two clips showing him casually walking into and exiting a building. That was when he visited Boxer, but Jing-nan didn't want to say that. He knew to say as little as possible unless he had a lawyer present.

"So what?" he asked the captain. "You brought me down here to watch myself walk around?"

"Wait," said the captain. "One more from just a little while ago." He cued up a clip, only a few seconds long, that showed Jing-nan standing behind a taped-off barrier, arms crossed.

Captain Huang swung his monitor back into position, put his hands together, and leaned toward Jing-nan.

"Hey, listen," he said quietly. "Just tell me that you killed Boxer."

Boxer! Jing-nan felt a sudden itch along his arms, and couldn't help but scratch himself with both hands.

"He's dead?" asked Jing-nan.

Captain Huang clapped slowly. "Oh my god, you said that as if you didn't know! Jing-nan, you're this year's contender for the Golden Horse award. Best leading actor! Well, at least best supporting actor. You only have one line, after all."

Jing-nan considered explaining why he had gone to see Boxer, and that he had seemed to be maybe drunk or high. He decided to say nothing, however, because the captain would build a case against him with any information. He was just fishing for anything now. Maybe it wasn't even decidedly a murder yet. Boxer had obviously consumed drugs and alcohol. He could have popped one more pill, overdosed, and died.

Damn you, Boxer, you're dead and you're still causing trouble!

"Won't talk, eh?" asked the captain. "C'mon, Jing-nan, we've known each other for years, and right now it's just me and you here. When you write your confession to me that you killed Boxer, I'm just going to file it. No one else will ever see it. Nothing will happen to you. I promise."

"That's a strange thing for you to say inside a police precinct, Captain," said Jing-nan. "That would be a strange thing for you to say pretty much anywhere."

Captain Huang stared hard enough at Jing-nan's face to see through to cavities. "I'm gonna level with you, Jing-nan. No one gives a shit about that guy, and he probably deserved to have his head caved in."

"Head caved in!" said Jing-nan.

The captain continued. "Boxer was a drug addict and a

shiftless loser. I know you have a connection to him, Jing-nan. Boxer was the boyfriend of your girlfriend's mother. In a way, that makes him your father-in-law.

"Boxer never contributed anything to society," Captain Huang went on. "No one's going to miss him. Not even Siu-lien, I'll bet. She's probably relieved he's gone." He cracked his knuckles, leaned back in his chair, and sleepily waited for Jing-nan to react. But the night-market vendor remained mute.

"All right, forget the written confession. Just tell me you killed Boxer. I won't charge you with any crime, I promise. I only want to be sure that there isn't a murderer on the loose. If I know you did it, I'll find some way to classify this as a suicide."

"Didn't you say his head was beaten in?" asked Jing-nan. Captain Huang held up his left index finger and jerked open a drawer with his right hand. He fished out a photo and held it in front of Jing-nan. At first, it looked like a cherry pie that someone had stomped, but in fact it was a grisly close-up shot of Boxer's head. Jing-nan recognized only the mole on the chin. The officer withdrew the picture.

"We can say he ran headfirst into a wall," said the captain.

"You've got to be joking."

Captain Huang raised an eyebrow at Jing-nan. "What did you use on him, Jing-nan? A hammer? Tell me how it happened, just to satisfy my own curiosity. You didn't leave any fingerprints or footprints, and there's not a scratch on you that I can see." Captain Huang tilted his head. "I'll be honest, Jing-nan, I didn't think you had it in you to kill so efficiently."

"I didn't do anything," Jing-nan shouted. He instantly regretted the outburst, and stood to leave. Captain Huang leapt up and grabbed Jing-nan's right arm.

"What the fuck were you doing there in the first place,

and why did you go back? I know that Wanhua is your old haunt, but I didn't think you enjoyed the drug and prostitution areas." Captain Huang pushed Jing-nan back into his seat. "Yeah, we found traces of ketamine and meth in Boxer's blood. We also know there are drug couriers who deliver door-to-door there. We let them play their games a little bit, and in exchange they give us information."

"I didn't know that, but it makes sense," said Jing-nan.

"My sources tell me Boxer won big in the lottery, but you already know that, right? That little bastard went on an alcohol, drugs, and sex spree. When we found him, he didn't have a cent on him. You didn't happen to take any money from him, did you?"

"I still have nothing to say," said Jing-nan.

"You sure you're not holding out on me?" the officer asked. "Maybe you killed Boxer and you clean forgot. Moment of temporary insanity, perhaps? We all have them."

To prove his point, Captain Huang handcuffed Jing-nan's right wrist to the metal tube armrest with one hand. He patted Jing-nan's chest and retreated to his desk. The captain picked up his phone receiver, pressed a single number, and then hung up. Jing-nan tested the chain but it was solid. Only then did he realize his chair was too heavy for him to lift. He leaned back and spotted the camera in the corner of the ceiling behind Captain Huang's desk.

"Don't be concerned about that thing," said the captain, "it hasn't worked in years. It's purely ornamental at this point. You see, we were required only to install them, not keep them in working order."

Someone knocked on the door. Jing-nan hoped his ordeal was coming to an end, but the captain opened the door a crack and then smiled. The door opened wider, and a man of average build entered and locked the door behind him. His face was neutral, clean-shaven, and unexceptional. He could be a composite of men in their 30s.

"This is my friend Li," said the captain. "He's quite knowledgeable."

"Yes, I know a lot about orthopedics," said Li, his voice barely above a whisper as he put his hands on Jing-nan's left arm. "For example, I know that this appendage isn't supposed to bend this way." Li twisted Jing-nan's arm, bringing the outer elbow to the chin.

"Goddamn fucking shit!" yelled Jing-nan as a fiery pain burst in his left shoulder. The captain hit play on a recording of New Year's fireworks and turned up the volume. Li maintained the hold.

"We could do this for a while, Jing-nan," said Captain Huang above the din. "It makes sense for you to confess now."

Li released Jing-nan's arm and moved to where Jing-nan wouldn't be able to reach him. Jing-nan worked his shoulder and elbow.

"Doesn't leave a mark, does it?" Captain Huang said. "Not detectable in a medical examination, either."

"Perhaps it's time to move to the fingers," Li said, raising his voice above the fireworks.

"Wait," said Jing-nan. His captors smiled. Jing-nan opened his left hand and slapped himself hard on the forehead. "Is it red?" he asked.

Li looked scared. "Just a minute, now," he said in his normal voice, as he moved to restrain Jing-nan. But the night-market vendor managed to punch himself hard in the face two times. The nose wasn't broken, but Jing-nan could feel a stream of blood running into his mouth. Not bad for a rightie.

"Oh, my god!" said Li. He ran out the door and slammed it behind him.

"You crazy, stupid piece of shit," said the captain. "Only a maniac would hit himself." He walked over to Jing-nan and unlocked the handcuffs. "Now don't do something really stupid, like take a swing at me. They'll take you out of here in a coffin."

"I just want to leave," said Jing-nan, sputtering blood as he spoke. "I didn't kill Boxer."

"Yeah, fine, you didn't do it." He wouldn't even look at Jing-nan. "I swear, though, if I find out that you're lying, I'm going to make you pay for making me go through the trouble!"

Jing-nan watched blood dripping onto his lap. Nobody's going to buy my food if I look like this, he thought. "Captain, would you mind if I washed up in your bathroom?" he asked.

"Go ahead," said Captain Huang. He opened the door, stepped out, and pointed down the hallway. "Three doors down, you can't miss it." Jing-nan made his way out, nearly walking into a beat cop who couldn't help but stare. "Hey," the captain said, "he came in like that. I didn't touch him." The beat cop turned and walked away quickly.

In the bathroom, Jing-nan looked himself over in the mirror. Blood was dripping from his left nostril, and a barely noticeable bruise was forming on his left cheek. He washed his face with cold water and tended to his nose. He wet a paper towel and managed to clean the blood spatter off his shirt collar and pants.

Jing-nan stopped by the water fountain for a drink to clear his head. Boxer was murdered, and not too long after Jing-nan had visited him. It sure didn't look good. He wiped his mouth and was struck that he hadn't mourned the loss of Boxer.

Jing-nan didn't see Captain Huang on his way out of the precinct, but he did see a cleaning woman entering his office with a bucket loaded with spray bottles and rags.

CHAPTER 9

Nancy stopped typing on her laptop to eye her ringing phone. Jing-nan. What timing her boyfriend had. He always seemed to call right when she was just about to start a burst of writing. If she took this call, how long would it take to get back into the zone?

She swallowed her anguish and answered. "Hi, Jing-nan," Nancy said with false cheer.

"Nancy, listen to me." Her grip on the phone tightened. She could tell he had something serious to say. "Boxer's dead."

"Boxer's dead," she repeated.

"Yes, remember when I told you someone had died in that building and I couldn't get back in? I hoped Boxer wasn't involved, but it turns out that he was the one who was killed! He was murdered, and the cops think I did it. Captain Huang dragged me into the station. He has a video of me entering and leaving the building."

Boxer? Dead? Nancy glanced at the notes on her screen that were long lines of letters. She tried to picture Boxer's face and couldn't, even though she had met him several times over the years. His voice, though, she could recall, and his coughs. Nancy had vaguely disliked him, but that was more about how she felt about her mom than anything else. What did he do to get by, anyway? She had a vision of him from the back, shirtless and perched by her mother's open refrigerator, a monkey who had figured out how to open the door, looking for hangover-friendly food.

Now, Nancy was ashamed that she was so indifferent to his death. Nancy had cried when a goldfish she had won at the night market had died, but she couldn't even manage a single sob for her mother's longtime boyfriend.

What if she couldn't cry when her mother passed away? That would be terrible, and maybe a fitting end to their relationship.

"Are you there, Nancy?" asked Jing-nan.

"Jing-nan, I'm shocked," she heard herself say. "Why do they think you killed him?"

"All I know is that he was beat in the head with something. Captain Huang thinks I did it, just based on the surveillance footage. He was talking crazy, saying that if I admitted to killing Boxer, he wouldn't even charge me with the crime because I did a service to society."

Nancy's eyes drifted back to her laptop screen. How the hell was she supposed to write now? Something big and horrible had happened, and Jing-nan was right in the middle of it. Again.

"I'm so sorry for you and your mother," Jing-nan said to fill the silence. "Boxer didn't seem that bad a guy."

Nancy closed her laptop. "Jing-nan," she said, "how can the police suspect you? You're the last person in the world who would kill anyone." She paused before adding, "Especially considering everything you've been through."

Jing-nan, who was making his way back to Unknown

Pleasures, turned sideways to allow tourist couples entwined in each other to pass. The night market was getting more crowded, and the demographics were in favor of the foreigners, people who held hands and kissed in public.

Jing-nan switched his phone to his right hand. Meanwhile, his left shoulder was still bugging him. He wondered if he should tell her now about how Captain Huang had tortured him. No. Jing-nan was already hitting her with more than enough information. He didn't want to completely freak her out.

"You're right," Jing-nan said tersely into his phone. "I wouldn't murder anyone. I'm the guy who's always trying to stay out of trouble!"

"Of course you're innocent, Jing-nan," Nancy said. "The silver lining to this is that you're going to be even more infamous."

"My Instagram could blow up again," said Jing-nan. He was soon approaching Unknown Pleasures, and noticed that a line had formed. That was good and bad. Customers were always good, but a long wait wasn't. "Nancy, I have to go, but could you tell your mother about Boxer? If the cops haven't called her first, that is. Please tell her I'm so sorry."

They said quick and clumsy goodbyes. Nancy tapped her right knee with her phone. Fifteen minutes ago she had the will to pull an all-nighter to finish her paper. No chance of that now. She began to think about how she would break it to her mother.

"Mom, are you sitting down?" No, that wasn't it. Siu-lien would be annoyed if Nancy implied right off the bat that she was taking a break at work.

"Hey, Mom, something terrible has happened!" That was too shocking.

Nancy picked up her phone. Maybe she should just wing it. Dial her mother and just say whatever came to mind.

Nancy found her mother in her recents list. Siu-lien's entry had no priority markers, and was simply labeled "M." Nancy's finger lingered over the screen as her eyes fell upon her closed laptop. She thought about her obligations beyond the university.

Boxer's death was something she should tell her mother about in person. Nancy looked down at her T-shirt and sweatpants. She had to put on something a little more presentable in order to go to a bar, even one as down-market as the one that Siu-lien worked at.

Siu-lien deftly picked up a hammer from under the counter and shook the claw end of its rusty head at the unruly customer's eyes. He went cross-eyed with fear and shrank back down to the cowardly middle manager that he was.

"What did you call me, you motherfucker?" she yelled. The two men who had been sitting on either side and laughing with him went mute. He slid to the back of his stool and held up two open hands.

"Hey now, please calm down, miss," he said slowly. "I was just kidding!"

"Say you're sorry!"

"I'm sorry!"

Siu-lien turned the hammerhead sideways. "You see that dried blood on there? That's from the last man who called me a bitch!" She feigned a thrust at the man's face, and he fell to the floor in fright. His onetime companions roared with laughter as he scrambled and stumbled his way out of the bar.

Siu-lien tossed the hammer back under the counter. She never actually had to use it on anything but nails. Something was always falling apart. The "dried blood" on it was hot sauce from a burger she had been eating on the sly earlier that night.

Siu-lien wiped her hands. Most people didn't cause trouble. The average customer was just trying to fake another persona, a more carefree one. Alcohol fed the illusion, and the jukebox, stacked with hits that won't die, provided the soundtrack.

Siu-lien regarded a woman in the bar who looked about 30 and was talking to a man who was at least five years younger. She was managing to hold his attention with her overly painted lips. Two women at the far end of the bar were folding black drink napkins into mustaches, holding them up to their lips, and cracking each other up.

Other people in the bar had a money angle. An unlicensed financial advisor in his 40s who worked the uncertain people in the corners was always trying to push stock tips. Right now, he was pointing out the performance of his portfolio on his phone to two men. "If you had bought this Internet stock when I was telling everyone two months ago, you'd be a millionaire by now!" he was probably saying. Siu-lien knew his pitch cold.

Now a woman in her early 20s walked in the door. She looked a little lost. What was her game? Actually, thought Siu-lien, she looks like my daughter, Nancy. Siu-lien froze, and then quickly came around the bar.

"Hello, Mom," Nancy nearly shouted. An old Rick James song was thumping the walls.

"Nancy, what are you doing here? What's wrong?"

"Mom, can we go talk in the bathroom?"

The stalls were occupied in there, but at least there wasn't any music or bar conversation, so Nancy spoke softly to her mother by the sinks. The cops hadn't contacted Siu-lien, and her grim expression barely changed upon hearing that Boxer was dead.

"So Jing-nan killed Boxer!" Siu-lien said.

"No, of course not!" Only her mother could annoy her that quickly. Nancy hadn't even mentioned yet that Jing-nan had been brought in for questioning, and she wasn't about to mention it now. It would only embolden her mother. Nancy looked into Siu-lien's narrowed eyes. There wasn't a trace of sadness in them. "Mom, aren't you sad Boxer's dead?" Siu-lien turned to face the mirror and fixed the collar of her shirt.

"I was sad for long enough when Boxer was alive," she said to her reflection. "I tried to stop wasting any of my emotions on him years ago." Nancy crossed her arms.

"You're not surprised he's dead, then, are you?"

Siu-lien shrugged. "It was bound to happen sooner or later." She turned slightly to look at her daughter in the mirror. "Did they find any more of the money?" Nancy had to believe that her mother's callousness was just an act.

"I think the money's probably all gone, Mom. Gone for good."

Siu-lien sighed. "Now that's something to be sad about."

CHAPTER 10

Captain Huang sat at his desk, watching more video recordings of the entrance to the building that Boxer had died in. The coroner's report wasn't in yet, but the woman was an old friend. She'd already given him the toxicology report, and told him that Boxer had been dead for a couple of hours, tops. There was no way Jing-nan could have killed Boxer in the morning, during his visit. The captain had thought he could shake fruit out of Jing-nan's tree during their talk, but there was nothing there.

Damn, it was really one of the dumbest things he'd ever seen, a suspect punching himself, but the captain had to admit it ended up being a clever move. Now that the Jing-nan route was probably closed, what was left?

There was footage of that woman who went in with Boxer late last night, but she hadn't even been there two hours. She was the bartender of Empress of China, Bee Bee. She had probably just waited for him to pass out and taken his money. It would be impossible to prove theft, of course, because she could say that Boxer gave her the money. Bee Bee would be a logical person to interrogate, but Captain Huang would leave it up to the Wanhua precinct to handle or ignore. The latter was probably the wiser course, but hey, it wasn't his problem.

You never wanted to step on anyone's toes. The only reason Captain Huang was involved was because the Wanhua boys had recognized Jing-nan, and respectfully notified the captain since the Shilin District was his turf.

Captain Huang licked his index fingers and smoothed his eyebrows.

Who the hell killed Boxer? Really, why bother, even if the motivation was revenge? The guy was probably a year or two away from stumbling drunk in front of a truck. What about money? Well, Boxer hadn't managed to hold on to any in the end. Maybe he should be the new mascot for the lottery. The captain amused himself by imagining the picture of Boxer's crushed face on the poster. He really wanted to forward the image around to his fellow jaded cops, but you couldn't do that anymore since one idiot accidentally sent a tasteless joke to the family of a victim.

His mirth drained away, and Captain Huang covered his face. He needed to sleep more. He needed to sleep, period. He was under pressure right now from the mayor's office to encourage a restaurant and a bookstore to drop complaints against five kids accused of shoplifting and destroying property. The unruly high school students in his district at Taipei American, Taipei Japanese, and Taipei European Schools were all a pain in the ass with their petty crimes and group brawls. So their parents were stationed in Taiwan for work, and they didn't want to be here. Why couldn't those rich spoiled fucks all go back to where they came from? When he was their age, he was already a man with a job.

He toyed with the table flag of the Republic of China. It used to represent China. Now it represented people almost no one wanted to have diplomatic relationships with. His grandfather had fought under that flag. Against the Communists, then against the Japanese, and then the Communists, again. That man, Lieutenant Huang, brought his wife and two boys over to Taiwan on one of the last boats that made it over. A ship behind them took on water and sank, but they couldn't stop to pick up the survivors. No time and no room.

Captain Huang sat back and stretched his legs. The media always portrayed mainlander families as being well-off or otherwise privileged. To hell with that. His family had had it hard. The desperate trip over was just the start. They had no money, and the lieutenant had no marketable skills, other than following orders. So maybe it was fortunate that his grandfather had died in that sad accident at the side of the road, early on in the Huang family's sojourn in Taiwan. That was how fate worked. The life insurance payout and his grandfather's pension helped them get their laundry business off the ground.

When Captain Huang turned 12, his father told him that the lieutenant had killed himself, and that the MPs had removed the hose from the scene. The disclosure was accompanied with an admonishment to never commit suicide because a man who felt useless simply needed to work harder.

He grew up with hands chafed from constant handling of wet clothing. Captain Huang even learned how to take apart and fix washers and dryers. Most of the time, problems were solved by simply greasing the pulleys and replacing the belts. His upbringing had much in common with Jing-nan's in that the two men grew up working at their family businesses when their friends were reasonably free to play games and get into trouble, outside of cram school.

Captain Huang shut down his computer. He usually didn't bother, but a memo had gone around. There were concerns over hacking, and computers in sleep mode were vulnerable. Captain Huang had heard that hacking had tipped the presidential election in the United States, and if something like that could happen in the world's strongest democracy, well, a little police outpost in Taipei had to do everything it could to defend itself against cyberattacks.

The computer was taking forever to shut down. Part of the problem was that the precinct was using an older version of Windows because one of its database programs wasn't compatible with the latest operating system.

He stood with his right foot on the floor and rested his left knee on the seat of his chair. Captain Huang watched dots spinning in a circle next to the status caption "Shutting down." The screen should have gone dark by now, but something wouldn't let go.

He thought about how he had treated Jing-nan, not only tonight, but always. Why am I so mean to him? Captain Huang wondered. He didn't understand his anger. Something about that night-market hawker just got under his skin. Jing-nan was just too happy-go-lucky. He was just too happy, period, especially when he put on that fake cheerfulness to call over the white people to buy stuff. Yes, that's what Captain Huang found irritating. Jing-nan's whole shtick displayed a total lack of self-respect. That was no way for a real man to be.

And then the computer screen finally died. Captain Huang stood up straight and brushed off his shoulders. He picked up his briefcase, and slung on the shoulder strap. Nine-thirty P.M. Now the dilemma at the end of any good 12-hour day: Pick up something to reheat from the FamilyMart and head home, or go to a restaurant and maybe get caught up in drinking too much?

Captain Huang took the stairs to the precinct's garage

and walked out a side door. The spring on the hinge was so tight, he had to put his shoulder to the door to get out, and it slammed shut behind him with a bang. Captain Huang didn't flinch, but a sausage seller on the sidewalk jumped nearly three feet into the air.

"Fuck, that sounded like a gunshot!" exclaimed the sausage man. He called himself Chen Rong, after the famed painter of dragons in ancient China. The little cart was named "Dragon Sausages," after all.

"That sounded nothing like a gun," said Captain Huang, before adding, "and you know it." Chen smirked, dropped to his knees, and turned on the gas burner.

"How many do you want tonight?" he asked the cop, who went with the option for immediate food.

"Five," said Captain Huang. "You know how I like them."

"Yeah, burned," said Chen. A flame burst under his blackened wok. He rolled a few sausages into it, and an evil sizzle filled the air.

The two men shared knowing smiles. They each knew what the other knew. A number of years ago, Huang had had an affair and his wife left him, and not even his closest colleagues knew either of those two details. Chen was once one of the big bookies when da ja le, one of those numbers games, was huge. He walked away at the top of his game, having settled all his payments to his winners and the relevant cops. Chen's sister was the woman whom Captain Huang had had the affair with.

"You heard about that murder of the guy in Wanhua District?" Chen asked. "It's all over the news." Captain Huang turned aside but continued talking with Chen without making eye contact.

"What about it?" he asked.

"That guy was a fuckup. His name was Boxer, and he used

to be a pickpocket." The cop sucked his teeth bitterly. How much of this shit was leaking out?

"All the same," said Captain Huang, "Boxer had done something. He had been spreading money around pretty thick on his last night on earth." Now it was Chen's turn to be stumped. Boxer usually didn't even have money for cigarettes.

Boxer had been a numbers runner for Chen for a few years. He was good because he was too cowardly to rip off his employer or the players, and fear of reprisal kept him moving quickly. A former cop who had been in the numbers ecosystem, and was now with a network that sold club drugs, had texted Chen with some details of Boxer's death. In any case, Captain Huang probably didn't know how Chen knew Boxer.

"He was spreading money, huh?" Chen said stupidly. Captain Huang sensed that he had won this particular exchange of clandestine info.

"That's right, Chen," he said.

Chen picked up a pair of tongs and idly pushed around the sausages. He searched his memory for instances of seeing Boxer with cash, but Chen could only recall images of the guy fumbling with pocket change at a vending machine.

"Chen," asked Captain Huang, "you were a part of that whole, ah, socio-economic group that Boxer was a part of, huh?"

"I was only a supporting character," Chen offered. He picked up a glassine bag and whipped it open. Captain Huang swept his tongue over every tooth, readying his mouth for a meatfest. Chen lifted the sausages into the bag. "You want any sauce or chili powder on them, Captain?"

"All I need is a skewer and two napkins," said Captain

Huang. He took the bag from Chen with hesitation. "How's my credit?"

"It's always good." The cop couldn't resist making a dig.

"You've had a lot of practice keeping numbers in your head, huh?"

"You've had a lot of practice getting food without paying."

"A man's got to eat to live," said Captain Huang.

CHAPTER 11

Captain Huang tore through his sidewalk meal, and without covering up his sausage breath he stopped by the ramen restaurant to see if they were willing to drop the charges against the Taipei American boys. He presented the school's offer to add the restaurant's logo to the orientation packet for new students. The proprietor responded by banning the captain from the premises. It wasn't the first time he had been rebuffed harshly, but it was the first time by a woman brandishing a knife, and angry enough to potentially use it.

He should work on his cop memoir, but not tonight. Normally, the captain would be headed home at this point, but he found himself in a cab racing the opposite way, to a bar. He may have a drink or two, ultimately, but mainly he wanted to talk to Boxer's longtime girlfriend, Siu-lien. He hadn't told her about Boxer but if Chen was any indication, Captain Huang was sure that she had found out through Jing-nan or another way. Who knows? Maybe he could jar a clue loose from her. After all, if Boxer's death went viral in the media, it would require some investigation.

The underclass of Taipei wasn't formally organized, but

it sure was efficient at spreading and sharing reasonably accurate news. Captain Huang was also certain that Siu-lien would be at the bar, not at home. Grieving Taiwanese people throw themselves into work. It's the most comforting activity they know.

Captain Huang looked out the cab's window and saw tourists walking against the light. He wanted to write them jaywalking tickets so badly his fingers twitched. Then he noticed that the driver was looking intently at him in the rearview mirror.

"Hey," Captain Huang called out. "Are you looking at me?"

The cabbie coughed and turned back to the road. "Sorry," he said. The apology was heavy with resentment. The cop leaned forward and eyed the photo license on the dashboard. Name wasn't familiar.

"I don't need your 'sorry.' Just tell me why you were staring at me."

"I've seen you before."

"Yeah? When?"

The cabbie cocked his head and cleared his throat. "When I came down to the police station about five years ago. You had arrested my brother."

"Who's your brother?"

"It doesn't matter. You were wrong to arrest him."

"What, he was innocent or something?"

The cabbie hunched over the wheel and tightened his grip.

"You know what?" he called back to his passenger. "He was guilty. But you didn't have to rough him up."

"'Rough him up'? I've never done anything like that!" Captain Huang caught himself shouting, and applied restraint before continuing. "I don't go around hurting people. I'm a professional."

The driver cracked a shoulder.

"My brother had one eye bandaged during his trial. That injury came from you." Captain Huang sat back. Now he remembered. He was a truck driver caught red-handed illegally dumping barrels of chemicals into a pit that was going to be the foundation of a shopping mall. The dirtbag wouldn't even give up any names. Even after Captain Huang—with the aid of an interview contractor, such as Li—did his best to encourage him.

What had happened exactly? The driver had tried to bolt from the interrogation room and Captain Huang had tripped him. Or had he thrown a chair at him? Things had happened so quickly, a surveillance camera, had one been engaged, wouldn't have caught everything.

The arrest was shortly after the Kuomintang was swept back into power. Relations with China were better, and land development was on the rise all over the island. Corners were being cut, and bribery was rampant. Money didn't trickle down to the cops, though, at least not to Captain Huang's precinct.

"Your brother was clumsy and hurt himself," said the captain. "If you guys don't believe me on that, just sue me and the whole police department, huh? He didn't even get any jail time! He destroyed the environment, and he only got a fine!"

The cabbie didn't reply as they came to a stop at a crosswalk bustling with tourists. Foreign money was bigger than ever, and it seemed that some shops and restaurants weren't meant for Taiwanese. There weren't even Chinese characters on the signs. Anyway, the prices alone would have kept them out. Everything was getting more expensive, and salaries weren't keeping up. And the pay the cops were getting? Forget it!

Captain Huang had never accepted bribes. Not that any of the offers were that generous. The fat years, the old-timers said, were in the '80s. The money on the side would be more than your salary, and it would also include perks like nice dinners and drinks with young girls. You could do anything you wanted to back then, the retired cops would sigh. This whole transition to democracy meant less freedom and fun for law enforcement.

Finally the taxi pulled over to the sidewalk. Captain Huang paid in cash. No more words were exchanged.

The captain walked briskly down the sidewalk. This was not a flashy block. It was filled primarily with office buildings of Taiwanese companies. It was about 10:30 P.M., and still many windows above remained lit, mute testimony to unpaid overtime. The consolation was a free dinner. In fact, some bosses would passively demand that their employees stay late by handing out menus in the afternoon and asking people what they wanted for dinner. Anything among the cheaper dishes, anyway.

Those so-called professionals were paid well but lived like cowards. Why, if Captain Huang had had the grades and money to go to college, he'd be a boss, not an employee. That was the way to do it.

He nearly tripped in a poorly lit section where the sidewalk suddenly rose half a foot in elevation. A concrete ramp to ease the transition was crumbling, and made the sidewalk even more dangerous.

The bar was at the end of the block at the intersection of two streets that used to be crowded with number runners taking orders from office workers. They and their betel nut–juice stains on the sidewalks were ruthlessly removed from the streets long ago.

Their unsavory locale, the bar, however, soldiered on. Captain Huang put his hands in his pockets as the sign for BaBa Bar came into view. He was old enough to remember the old name of the bar, Foremost, which was a play on "Ilha Formosa," the name Portuguese sailors had called Taiwan centuries ago. It meant "Beautiful Island" in their language. He wished it were still called Foremost. It was subtle and dignified. The name BaBa Bar was an embarrassing and kidlike name, and it cheapened the dive bar that much more.

Captain Huang hadn't wanted the cabbie to drop him off directly at BaBa Bar. Why clue in anybody who didn't need to know about where he was going? The move had already paid off, because the driver had proven to be someone who had it in for him. What if he had taken pictures and started a rumor that Captain Huang patronized holes in the wall?

NANCY SAT AT THE bar and observed her mother serving drink after drink. How could she smile and carry on in the face of the double tragedy of losing her boyfriend and a stack of money?

Nancy didn't like BaBa Bar's vibe or the lingering looks from some of the men. She didn't trust anybody there, except for Siu-lien, sort of. Yet for some reason, she couldn't bring herself to leave. Maybe she needed to make sure that her mom was all right. Maybe Siu-lien needed a hug. Maybe Nancy needed a hug from her. Nancy sipped her lemon-flavored seltzer water and tried to stay small.

She felt a tap on her left shoulder. Nancy was the last one to have noticed Captain Huang. When Billy Idol's "White Wedding" ended, the bar was silent.

"Nancy," he said, with overtly faked friendliness, "I saw your boyfriend a few hours ago. That's why you're here, huh? I thought you and your mom didn't get along, but I guess you guys have patched things up. As best you people can. Ah, of course, this sort of explains why Jing-nan was over at Boxer's to begin with. You needed someone to keep an eye on the lottery money."

Now someone tapped the cop's shoulder. He turned and met Siu-lien's enraged eyes set in her relaxed face. The woman was holding a hammer, the handle end pointed at his guts.

"What do you want, Captain Huang?" she asked, emphasizing the last two words. What did it matter? Everyone there already knew he was a cop. Not a dirty one, but one that liked to play dirty. One of his favorite tricks was pretending to write something on a pad, and then throwing an elbow into someone's back or side.

"It's so nice to see you, Siu-lien," he said. "You want to be careful with that hammer. Swing it the wrong way, and that could be a charge for assault."

"Oh my," said Siu-lien. "Well, if I touch you with this, it will purely be an accident."

Captain Huang widened his stance and crossed his arms.

"Look, I came down here because of Boxer, and all. I wanted to look in on you, Siu-lien. Sort of a wellness check." Both knew that was a lie. Captain Huang's heart was calloused from years of experience with the lower classes, and going through a divorce. His heart was barely supple enough to pump blood.

"It's not your job to make sure I'm all right," she snapped. "You'd better just watch out for yourself." Captain Huang held up his hands. He could see that the low-key wringing of information from her that he had imagined wasn't going to happen. Neither was a courtesy drink and courtesy refill. He licked his lips before continuing.

"I just thought that you might be a little unstable," he said, adding loudly, "since Boxer's dead." Patrons gasped. Siu-lien teetered on her feet. Now everyone knew he was dead, and there was no way she could carry on as usual at the bar.

"I'm fine!" she declared. She grabbed her daughter by the arm and pushed her way out.

"It's a shame about all that lottery money," Captain Huang called out to her. "Something went wrong, that's why Jing-nan had to go back to Boxer, right?"

When Siu-lien reached the door, she turned and yelled, "Fuck you, Huang!" Nancy cringed and followed her mother out to the sidewalk. The captain was ready to respond in kind, but he took note of the dirty looks from the crowd.

"Why did you provoke her?" a man in sweat suit asked.

"All I wanted to do was simply talk," answered Captain Huang. He raised his right index finger before continuing. "Now, you should make sure that you don't provoke *me*, punk." The man was about his height, but as he drew up his sleeves, Captain Huang saw that his arms were muscular and bore tattoos of dangerous animals with leering faces. The cop wondered why a vicious-looking anthropomorphic tiger would also need to wield a handgun. Captain Huang lifted his chin and narrowed his eyes to slits. Lowlifes like this only understood one thing. He pointed at the man's throat.

"A little bitch with tattoos is still a little bitch." Before the tattooed man could respond, a thin middle-aged man stepped between them and let out a full-throated laugh at Captain Huang, revealing teeth coated in a yellow-brown patina from cigarette smoke and cheap alcohol. He also had a particularly bad case of halitosis. Captain Huang waved away the smell and focused on the thin man's familiar face. Ah, it was Arlen Chen, a columnist at *Taiwan Now*, one of the country's most prominent queer-loving liberal rags.

"Oh, my, Captain Huang!" said Arlen. "Don't you recognize a great artist when you see one? This is Ming, the most famous sculptor in Taiwan. Known around the world!"

"Famous artists don't come to shitholes like this," said

Captain Huang. "You think Michelangelo would drink with you scumbags?" Arlen laughed hard again, unleashing another stink cloud.

"BaBa Bar is where the artists come to be together, and you're one of us, Captain!" Ming held out his arms and went in for a hug. The captain jumped to the side to dodge the embrace.

"Aw, he's not really a captain!" said Arlen. "He's just another flatfoot trying to get free drinks!" Some people began to laugh. Captain Huang shivered with anger, but he knew it was time to leave, and that doing so quickly and quietly would be best.

He breathed in deeply and walked steadily out the door, imagining that he was tossing live grenades behind him. The bar became so loud and lively that Arlen Chen was forced into the bathroom to call a friend at the left-leaning cable station who was always looking for tabloid stories.

CHAPTER 12

Around 11 P.M., a crowd gathered at Beefy King's monitors. It was a sign that Uncle Bing, the guy who ran the steak stand, had found a news item salacious enough to switch away from the menus on his flat-screen monitors. As Taiwan's cable stations reveled in sensationalist "stories," there usually wasn't a dearth of material for Uncle Bing to sift through when he felt business was flagging.

He also broadcast the audio from the show through Beefy King's public-address speakers to bring in more people. A slow drumbeat and minor piano chords were a tipoff that tonight's story was tragic, and not about yet another celebrity caught exiting a love hotel with an intern. The audio wasn't mixed to be blaring at a night market, so the music drowned out the narration. "Murder" and "money" were the only words discernable from down the alley, where Unknown Pleasures stood.

Jing-nan drew a chain across the front of the stall, and he, Frankie, and Dwayne decided to head over to Beefy King to get a look. But they knew. Jing-nan had told Frankie and Dwayne about the lottery money, and Captain Huang trying to extract a confession through torture. Neither was surprised. Frankie had examined Jing-nan's nose without comment.

"Maybe it's not about Boxer," said Jing-nan as they made their way over.

"What else would be making the news now?" asked Dwayne, as the three came upon the monitors showing Boxer's picture, accompanied with hyperventilating text. "Wow, he looks awfully young there."

"That's an old booking photo," said Frankie. "Probably the only picture of him they could find right away."

"What a waste of all that money," said Dwayne. "What a shame."

Uncle Bing, a middle-aged man in his "Got Beef?" T-shirt as always, came over and shook the television remote control at Jing-nan. "How come you found trouble again?"

"What are you talking about?" asked Jing-nan, suspecting exactly what Uncle Bing was talking about.

"Just wait for the program to repeat!" Uncle Bing continued walking through the crowd. "Hey, you! You're too skinny! Order a steak!"

The program began to show a sweeping shot of the exterior of BaBa Bar.

"That's where Nancy's mom works," said Jing-nan.

"Boxer worked there, too," said Frankie.

The camera cut to Arlen Chen being interviewed on the sidewalk outside the bar.

"Terrible, terrible news," he said, his booming words rattling the plates of those dining indoors at Beefy King. "I feel terrible for his girlfriend, Siu-lien. Everybody in this place respects and loves them so much."

The screen displayed a picture of Siu-lien that was also a booking photo taken a number of years ago. A narrator said the news program couldn't find her for comment.

Jing-nan cupped his hands around his face and hoped that Nancy had gotten in touch with her mother before any of this broke. It was the closest this atheist would come to praying.

"Hey, Jing-nan, you're on," said Dwayne.

Indeed he was. They were showing a clip of his muted talking head under a voice-over from an incredulous male narrator: "It is said that Chen Jing-nan, the owner of the famed Unknown Pleasures stand at Shilin Night Market, might have been the last person who saw Boxer alive. Chen, who is well-known for his death-defying brushes with violence, is connected to the late Boxer, word has it. We tried to reach Jing-nan, but he hasn't returned our calls." Jing-nan's phone was set to silence unknown callers, a status that wasn't going to change anytime soon.

Uncle Bing stepped up to Jing-nan. "You have to go to the temple and straighten it all out! Ask Mazu for help, and apologize to Lord Guan!" The news of Boxer's murder must've made people hungry, and Uncle Bing's face dripped with sweat from the surge in business.

Frankie bent his head toward Jing-nan. "Let's go," he said.

Mazu, the all-powerful sea goddess, was one of Taiwan's most popular deities, easily recognized by her beaded veil. She supposedly caught bombs dropped by Allied bombers when Taiwan was a Japanese colony, and Japan was at war with the Allied powers. Lord Guan was a legendary general from the Three Kingdoms period of China, a patron saint for both cops and criminals because he symbolized justice, not merely the written law.

But neither Mazu nor Lord Guan could do anything for nonbelievers such as Jing-nan.

He did a final cleanup at Unknown Pleasures with Frankie and Dwayne. Some gawkers stopped by, no doubt lured in by the story, but Dwayne chased them off by gruffly telling them the stand was closed.

JING-NAN LEFT THE NIGHT market immediately. Frankie smoked his final cigarette of the night, watching the clouds of smoke thin into wisps as the lights of the night market died. He tapped his thumb on the side of the cigarette filter. Some ashes swirled from the lit end and were quickly swept away.

"Hey, Cat, smoking's bad for you," said Dwayne. "Haven't you heard?"

"As long as you have good thoughts, nothing bad will happen," Frankie said.

But Frankie wasn't having good thoughts. He imagined Boxer's last hours alive. He hadn't known the man, but he knew people stuck in that lifestyle. Part-time schemers who never amounted to much because they wouldn't even commit to a life of crime. Guys who couldn't meet your eyes or take their hands out of their pockets. Then when someone like Captain Huang came along and slapped 'em around a few times, they'd give up their own mothers. You couldn't count on them for anything.

LIKE A TRAINED SEAL ascending a podium, Captain Huang hauled himself up on his elbows at the counter of a bar friendly to law enforcement. He was about to top a retired cop's story about the thief who called the police when someone stole his car while he was robbing a store.

The captain looked up and down the counter, but the man was gone. A lot of people were gone. Had he fallen asleep, and only now woken up?

"Are you all right, Captain Huang?" asked the bartender. The man wore a bow tie and a measured smile.

"Yeah, yeah," said the captain.

Ordinarily, a detective could safely move a case like Boxer's to the back burner, and then let it slip into the trash can. That guy got what he had coming, everybody would say. But in the last few hours of his stupid life, Boxer had to win that big lottery prize and claim the money.

Captain Huang had received a forceful email after leaving BaBa Bar, passed down from the top of the chain of command. The government had to publish the names of the major lottery prizewinners, and journalists profiled the lucky stiffs and ruined their lives.

Indeed, if Jing-nan had confessed to killing Boxer, Captain Huang would have had to renege on his vow not to do anything. The stupid bureaucracy would have forced him to break even a promise he meant to keep. With that scenario in mind, and in his inebriated state, the captain had sympathy for how Jing-nan was dragged into the investigation.

For a victim, Boxer was lucky in one way. It was too late to ruin his life. Captain Huang read one headline on his phone: MAN MURDERED HOURS AFTER CLAIMING BIG WIN. That'll make more people want to play.

Shit, Boxer wasn't even his case, but his buddy Lieutenant Chang in the Wanhua precinct had been desperate to make it go away. That desperation only intensified with the breaking news about the murder. Now the case wasn't going to disappear until they pinned it on someone. The lieutenant had shot over a few frantic texts after Captain Huang forwarded that email from the bigwigs.

Wanhua had been set for major rezoning, something akin to the Disneyfication of Times Square. The captain had seen *Taxi Driver*. If a seedy place like that could become a moneymaker, Wanhua could also be washed clean.

Another text slid across Captain Huang's phone. Lieutenant

Chang again! The developers were calling him at home, yelling for the murder to be solved immediately.

Captain Huang had done all he could. Dead end. Was he also supposed to trek over to Wanhua and harass its denizens? That was a job for the Wanhua boys, and from what he'd heard, they were pretty good at it.

He slapped the back of his phone with disgust. Captain Huang looked up, caught the eye of the bartender, and pointed at his empty glass for another Asahi Super Dry. A responsible place would have stopped serving him. This bar, however, had respect for the contours of the law when the line had to be drawn. The bartender set down a fresh coaster and replaced Captain Huang's glass with a just-poured pint.

He suddenly became aware of how quiet the bar was. Not many people tonight. All cops were afraid for their jobs when a murderer was about. They didn't want to be traced to a bar when the case got worse, or if it got solved. Cowards, thought Captain Huang. A man should never be too scared to drink.

"Let me pay something," Captain Huang said to the bartender, meaning a tip. The cop shifted in his seat as he fished in his pocket and drew out two coins. "Does that work?" The man nodded and smiled. His manner was so supplicating, it made Captain Huang suspicious. Had he spit in the beer? Or worse?

Screw it, the cop thought, I'm a little too sober after that nap. He tilted the drink into his mouth.

NANCY HAD TO PUT some effort into keeping up with Siulien, who was practically skating down the sidewalk with angry determination, and would have flattened anyone in the way.

"Mom," Nancy interjected a few times without receiving a reply. "Mom!"

"What?" Siu-lien finally answered, without looking at her daughter or breaking her stride.

"Where are you going?"

"Home!"

"Do you want me to come with you?"

The question surprised Siu-lien. "Sure! Yes, of course! You can help me."

"What do you need help with?"

"Throwing out old trash!"

SIU-LIEN HEAVED ASIDE THE sliding door to the bedroom closet with such force, it derailed and stood tilted. She reached in with both hands and yanked out shirts on their hangers.

"Nancy," she called out. "You empty out his desk drawers. Anything that's not worth money should be thrown out!"

Nancy opened the top drawer of Boxer's desk. There were some knickknacks packed tightly into the shallow space, stuff a prepubescent boy would collect: glossy ceramic ashtrays, plastic toys from fast-food restaurants, and low-denomination foreign coins.

"I don't know much about this stuff," said Nancy, "but some of it could be valuable." Siu-lien walked over and frowned at the meager belongings.

"Nonsense!" she declared. She reached down for the wastepaper basket and tossed in the ashtrays, smashing them to pieces.

"Maybe we shouldn't do this yet," Nancy called out over the din. "What if the police need to search for clues in his stuff?" Her mother stood up and wagged her right index finger at Nancy.

"Listen, girl," she said, "when the police come, they don't look for clues. They look for things to steal and confiscate them as 'evidence.' I'd rather throw it all away!" Nancy opened her mouth but didn't know what to say. Her mother was obviously more experienced with police searches. "If you don't help me," declared Siu-lien, "I'm going to do it myself, even if I cut myself on something and bleed to death!"

Nancy nodded. "All right, Mother, I'll help you." She dug out the coins and set them on the desktop, and dumped out everything else from drawer.

It became easier to toss things as they went on. Siu-lien put on a Stray Cats playlist to erase any dreariness from their task, and the rockabilly beat animated the proceedings. Nancy was moving along at a brisk pace until she lifted a binder and some photos tumbled out of it. She bent down and picked them up.

Three of them featured Boxer sitting at tables, presumably in bars. None captured him sober, but he looked happy in them, or at least satisfied. The fourth was a black-and-white photo of a tanned and shirtless young boy smiling hard. Boxer seemed to have handled the photo a lot, as it was heavily wrinkled.

"How old is Boxer in this photo?" Nancy asked her mother.

Siu-lien grabbed it. "Who cares?"

"It's probably his only childhood picture."

Siu-lien grunted and put the photo in the sock drawer where she kept her other mementos. "I guess his ghost will haunt me if I toss it out. I don't want some evil spirit trying to ruin my life. I already have enough evil people trying to do that, like goddamned Captain Huang. I wish he would just die!"

Nancy was glad she'd kept it. "Mom, I think before we throw out his stuff for good, we should go to the temple. We should say a prayer for Boxer, and wish his soul a safe passage."

Siu-lien crossed her arms. "He never in his life went to any temple, unless he was cornering someone to borrow money from," she said. "Why should we visit the gods on his behalf?"

Her skin was glistening and her eyes were bright with resentment.

"Think about Boxer's soul," said Nancy. "It will need all the help it can get to move on. Maybe in this life, Boxer wasn't so great, but that's no reason to hold that against his spirit. Besides, Mom, you said you don't want to give Boxer's soul a reason to come back and haunt this place, do you?"

Siu-lien wriggled as if a light electric current had just run through her body. "You're right," she said. "I don't want that. Where can we find a temple at this time of night?"

"We could go to Cixian Temple," Nancy said. Cixian was the temple that sat in the middle of the Shilin Night Market.

"That's a Daoist temple," said Siu-lien. "We should find a Buddhist temple."

"Don't worry," said Nancy. "They have a Guanyin idol, and the Goddess of Mercy is exactly the one we need to pray to." As a show of approval, Siu-lien stopped the music.

THE NIGHT AIR SMEARED across Captain Huang's nose. He reeled and nearly fell over. God, what was that smell? Could it be stinky tofu gone bad? Could something already fermented like stinky tofu go bad? He shrugged to no one as he shuffled down the street.

Was he going the right way? How many drinks did he end up having? The boy behind the counter kept pouring them. How could he not finish them? Not doing so would've been rude, and a real man had manners. Captain Huang waved his right finger crazily in the air so that people a block away would know he was making a point. Captain Huang never forgot how to behave properly, all right?

He should probably hail a cab home. He knew he was being followed. It was just a sense that someone in his line of work developed, like how farmers can feel rain coming even on a sunny day. He turned around and began to walk backward, his reversed steps confident if not stumble-free.

"Okay, I know you're after me," he said as he evaluated three dark shapes behind him. He deduced that two were stationary objects because they were shorter as he continued walking backward. The one in the middle seemed to be advancing.

"Ha, you've given yourself away," Captain Huang meant to say, but instead he only mouthed it through a yawn. The rush of oxygen made him forget. He turned around and resumed walking forward. A vision of a truant child somehow crossed his mind. Those goddamned international students!

"I'll forgive you if you leave now and don't cause any trouble for the next week," Captain Huang said or thought. "I know who your parents are, don't forget!"

In one of his earliest assignments as a beat cop, back in the late '80s, he was charged with going to the local video-game arcades and ice-cream parlors to chase out the kids the night before the big math exams. The importance of those test scores couldn't be underestimated. They were tabulated on an international basis. Each year, Taiwan, the Republic of China, had ranked in the top five countries, counting as a Cold War propaganda win against the People's Republic. Japan was almost always number one.

The benshengren were just brainwashed about the Japanese. All those decades of colonization just brainwashed them into loving the Japanese. Some even thought they were related to those dwarf pirates!

"I was never the smartest in class, but I for sure never thought I was a Jap," said Captain Huang. He didn't care who heard. He didn't care about anything. The sidewalk tilted and he began walking down an unlit alley.

Suddenly he couldn't breathe. He tried to put a hand to his mouth to clear his airway but touched a wrist that seemed to be made of stone. I am being choked to death, Captain Huang thought. How strange. He fought it for a little while, but then gave up because the entire situation seemed so ridiculous. He let his arms fall to his sides.

Near the end, he saw Lord Guan appear. You've come, Captain Huang thought. It was his last before he tumbled backward forever into the darkness.

CHAPTER 13

Siu-lien had changed into a long-sleeved blouse for temple etiquette. It also offered a degree of protection against all the tourists they had to work around both at the Shilin Night Market and at the temple itself. Did people visiting Taiwan have to stop and film everything, anyway? Nothing was really that amazing, and not everything was meant to be preserved and remembered.

Nancy and Siu-lien smelled something in the night market that was sweet, fried, and slightly spicy. A woman about Nancy's age was dramatically looping spiced honey over a rack of freshly fried chicken fillets.

Nancy had thought about stopping by Unknown Pleasures while they were here, for a bite and some conversation. But Jing-nan was always distracted, like he'd rather be working the crowd than talking to her.

A sharp sound from the fried-chicken stand startled her. The cook was swinging a midsize cleaver, chopping fillets into strips and then cubes. She whipped open a glassine bag and scooped chicken cubes into it.

Without a moment's delay, Siu-lien bought the next bag.

Nancy planned to steal a cube or two, but after catching a whiff of the chili powder the cook dashed into the bag, Nancy ordered her own, with some chili powder, too.

Siu-lien and Nancy walked to the temple eating two cubes at a time out of the bag with their wooden skewers. Neither had had dinner. Giddy, the two laughed together like they hadn't in years or maybe ever.

"It's just enough honey," said Siu-lien.

"It really supports the taste profile," said Nancy. She realized she was using one of Jing-nan's phrases. Now she felt a little bad that she wasn't going to see him. Well, the uptick in her relationship with Siu-lien was worth it.

They tossed their empty bags and dirty skewers at the first intersection, and Siu-lien stopped to buy a small bottle of water.

"You should swish some water around," Siu-lien said as she handed it to Nancy. "When you pray, your mouth shouldn't be dirty." She produced two moist-towelette packs from her purse. "For your hands."

Tourists mobilized under the rows of red paper lanterns covering Cixian Temple's approach obscured the temple entrance. Mother and daughter advanced, saying "Excuse me," in English. It wasn't a very big temple, and the roof seemed to be supporting more dragons and divine figures than was tasteful. But Shilin Night Market first arose to cater to its worshippers, so the temple was the seed from which everything grew. Even if most of its visitors these days weren't there to worship, the gods inside were still receptive and potent.

Siu-lien tossed her wipe into the trash on the threshold and belched.

"I'm letting it all out now, Nancy," she said. The two laughed and walked past ribbons of smoke streaming from burning joss sticks planted in two large brass censers.

They entered the temple through the dragon door and

bought a pack of incense from a tired woman behind a counter. Charms and souvenirs were also for sale at inflated prices for the truly desperate Taiwanese and the exchange-rate-advantaged tourist.

A few Americans were talking loudly and making videos. Siu-lien and Nancy watched in amusement as they exited through the dragon door—a major faux pas. The saleswoman lowered her head and sighed.

"You should put up a sign in English," Nancy said.

"They don't read signs, anyway," said the saleswoman.

Siu-lien and Nancy made sure to pay respects first at the temple's main deity, Mazu, who was known by various titles including Goddess of the Sea and Mother of Heaven. This particular Mazu idol wore a beaded veil made from black seashells hanging from the brim of her crown.

"Mazu has been very good to me," Siu-lien whispered. "I don't like to bother her unnecessarily, so I will only thank her now."

Siu-lien lit three sticks and held them in her hands as she bowed intensely several times. Nancy stood next to her mother and bowed with about half the enthusiasm.

Siu-lien and Nancy continued through the temple, going down the right side first. At every altar, they each lit one stick and bowed three times.

They reached Guanyin's image and knelt on cushions before the Goddess of Mercy. Siu-lien began to mutter to herself, and her breathing became labored. Nancy couldn't imagine the heavy thoughts she was having right now. What would Nancy do if Jing-nan died? Oh, it was too horrible to think about. Nancy focused on sending positive thoughts about Boxer to Guanyin.

Just to cover their bases, they sought out other deities in the temple who could help.

Siu-lien was excited to find an altar to Dizang, another Buddhist deity. One of his supposed powers was entering the underworld and helping deceased loved ones rise out and achieve nirvana.

"I think we need this guy!" Siu-lien said.

Dizang's rendering was lifelike. The staff that he used to force open the gates of hell gleamed with power, and the wish-fulfilling jewel borne in his left hand seemed to wink. The bodhisattva's face was calm and smiling. All will be well, it seemed to say. That was the big difference between Buddhist and Daoist idols. The former looked like they understood human problems and had empathy for mortals. The Daoist deities demanded a certain level of respect or there'd be consequences.

Siu-lien and Nancy located cushions and knelt once more.

CHAPTER 14

Jing-nan woke up feeling hollow. Things were amiss, for sure. He had a certain sense that was getting far too familiar, a sheen of guilt that came from knowing that someone was dead, and that he was indirectly responsible for it.

There was something else, too. A late-night text from Nancy saying that she was going to spend the night with her mother. The message was cold and informational, but Jing-nan wrote back that he was sorry for everything, and that he hoped things would be better soon. They never wrote that they loved each other, and there was no smiley face or even a kiss emoji in the exchange.

Jing-nan turned on his side. He scrolled back through their conversations in recent days. Well, Jing-nan himself didn't exactly write the warmest messages. A few days ago he had told Nancy that he couldn't wait to try out a coarser grind of pepper for one of the beef stews. Jing-nan even mentioned that he was upset about a bad review from someone whom he had treated especially nicely. Seeing that last message again brought Jing-nan right back to that moment.

HE SHOULD HAVE KNOWN that she was trouble right from the start. A young girl who wore the uniform of the Taipei Municipal Zhongshan Girls High School—a selective and prestigious public school—asked Jing-nan if he licensed the intellectual property of Joy Division for his stall. That was her opening question. Right away she was trying to challenge him. She wasn't joking, either. The girl didn't laugh at all when Jing-nan casually replied that the former members of the band who were still alive and the estate of Ian Curtis should be paying him a promotional fee.

It had been early in the evening, a little after 5 P.M. She was part of a group getting a quick snack between the end of regular school and the start of cram school at 6 P.M. Kids making the transition didn't usually come all the way into Jing-nan's part of the night market for food. They stuffed themselves at the sidewalk vendors closest to the cram schools, for time's sake. She must have corralled her friends for a cab ride in order to eat at his stand.

What really got Jing-nan was that he knew that she loved the food. They all did. You should have seen how clean they picked the skewers and the way they drained the stew bowls dry. She had written a bad review for Unknown Pleasures simply to be mean. Oh, and it wasn't one of those easily dismissible, hyperventilating one-star reviews. She had given three. She had damned his place with the faintest of praises. The food was "mostly adequate" and it was "good for when you're in a rush." He remembered her face when she was saying a smug little goodbye. Her online avatar wore that exact look: she knew everyfuckingthing.

Jing-nan got out of bed and regarded the emptiness of the mattress in the gauzy morning light. Why hadn't he told Nancy about the bad review, apart from saying it was stupid? Maybe she would've appreciated hearing about the encounter if he had told her a little more. He dressed quickly and stepped into the kitchen.

Nancy used to tell him little stories about her lab. Some were a little funny, but then they began to blur together, probably because he paid less and less attention to them. One day, he wasn't sure when, she had stopped.

He breakfasted on the reheated chicken skewers that he had brought home for Nancy last night.

They didn't tell each other little things, anymore. Maybe they would begin to talk less about everything. They could end up as one of those older couples that dined in silence. Actually, there was little danger of that. They almost never ate together. Maybe they were at a point where something terrible happens—such as the death of Siu-lien's boyfriend— that makes them put everything on pause and meaningfully reconnect.

Just not quite now, though. Jing-nan moved briskly, picking up bags and stepping into his morning sandals for his trip to the day market for fresh ingredients. He psyched himself up to find one outstanding ingredient that could create a special entrée that would go viral on social media.

He threw open his door to find three men blocking his exit. One, wearing a ballcap, was on his knees, about to insert what looked like a thin screwdriver into the door's keyhole. Another was in the back, a big man in a suit that made him look like an approachable mountain. Sandwiched between them was Big Eye, Jing-nan's uncle.

Big Eye had changed slightly in the months since Jing-nan had seen him. His uncle was trying something new with his hair, which was growing out and pulled back in sort of a ducktail. A casual blue cotton blazer streamlined his frame. Big Eye's face, which usually wore an expression of slight pain, lightened up.

"Ah, Jing-nan, so good to see you!" Big Eye boomed. "We didn't know what time you woke up, so Whistle over here was going to let us in without waking you and causing an annoyance!"

Whistle stood and touched the brim of his cap while sliding the tool up his coat sleeve. It clacked against something metallic.

Nothing was said of Gao, the big man, and Gao said nothing.

"Please, all of you, come in," said Jing-nan.

"Sure it's not a bother?" asked Big Eye, although his menacing tone suggested he didn't care if it was. "Anyone else here, dear nephew?"

"No, it's just me." Gao was the last to enter and closed the door firmly.

"Good to hear," said Big Eye. He removed his shoes, and Jing-nan did the same, now that his departure was delayed. The two moved to the middle of the living room while Gao threw the door bolt. He and Whistle remained by the exit, an acceptable place to keep their shoes on.

Big Eye picked up the TV remote, turned it on, and jacked up the volume on a morning show that was debating if the latest government agency appointment was an act of "cronyism." Two people calling in branded each other a traitor and yelled while the host called for calm. Amid the din, Big Eye leaned into Jing-nan and spoke softly.

"I'm not going to take up a lot of your time, here. I heard about Boxer's murder, and I know he was the boyfriend of your girlfriend's mother. And considering the closeness of your relationship with him, that also means that I'm in the party of the victim, as well." Big Eye moved his arms in an arc to draw the figurative big tent. "I understand you had seen him earlier that day."

"I didn't know Boxer at all, Big Eye," said Jing-nan. "That was the first time I ever saw him."

"You don't get what I'm saying," snapped Big Eye. "The point is, I'm affiliated with the group that was wronged. Look, I know the guy who oversees Guangzhou Street in the Wanhua District. I asked him to make things right. He personally went down and beat the shit out of the dealers who work the building where Boxer was murdered." Big Eye reached into his blazer and pressed a stack of Polaroids into Jing-nan's hands.

"What's this?" asked Jing-nan.

"That's proof of how sorry Wood Duck's gang is for Boxer's death. They took his money for drugs, and it contributed to the end result."

Jing-nan sorted through the pictures. Two young men were on their knees on a concrete floor in the first few pictures, which showed progressively growing numbers of facial bruises. After the sixth picture, one man was on his side, bleeding from his mouth, and the other was face down, hands visibly tied behind his back.

"Fuck!" shouted Jing-nan.

"What's wrong with you?" admonished Big Eye. "Using such foul language in the morning!"

"What's wrong with me? What the hell are these pictures? Are these guys dead?"

Big Eye chortled. "No, no," he said. "You think I'm dumb enough to walk around with evidence of two murders? It's just a beatdown. A warning."

"Thanks for ruining my day," said Jing-nan. He held the photos out for Big Eye to take back, images down.

His uncle stepped back. "Whoa, I don't want 'em back. Give 'em to Siu-lien."

"Are you crazy, Big Eye? She's already had enough of a shock with Boxer's murder!"

"Look Jing-nan, Wood Duck, who heads a very powerful clique in Taipei, wants to show contrition. This is how we apologize. We show that we punish our wrongdoers in the name of justice."

"Maybe, in the name of justice, Wood Duck can give the money back to Siu-lien."

Big Eye laughed in his face. "You have it all wrong, Jing-nan! We would never cheapen a human life by equating it with a certain amount of money! We're not the government!"

"No, you're not," said Jing-nan. His arms dropped to his sides, and the Polaroids slipped to the coffee table.

"You show her those pictures today," Big Eye said.

The TV boomed with a preview of the next segment and showed the old mug shot of Boxer.

SIU-LIEN WORE A POKER face as she thoroughly examined the pictures. Nancy, seated next to her, reeled in horror after a quick glance.

"Jing-nan, why are you showing my mother this garbage?" Nancy chided him.

Jing-nan didn't know what to say. Doing this task for his uncle had only further harmed his relationship with Nancy. He sipped more coffee. The three of them were seated in a dining court in the Xiaofu complex on NTU's campus. It was almost nine in the morning, and the tables were nearly full.

Ordinarily, someone mourning a loved one would be wearing a burlap armband or a patch of burlap somewhere, the modern equivalent of dressing entirely in burlap, which is rough on the skin. Back in the day, one had to show how much the death was causing one to suffer with arms, legs, and face rubbed until bleeding. But Siu-lien hadn't worn a scrap of burlap. She didn't have any, and she and Boxer were never married.

"You said you had something serious," Nancy went on. "I

had no idea how terrible it would be!" She straightened up and accidentally kicked him. "Sorry," she said curtly.

Jing-nan couldn't remember Nancy ever being this angry with him before. Even when her life was in danger, she had never lashed out at him. Perhaps it meant that her relationship with her mother was improving.

"I really didn't want to do this," said Jing-nan. "But, you know, my uncle . . ." He marveled at how weak he sounded. A little boy who did what he was told.

Nancy started, "Jing-nan . . ."

"Nancy," said Siu-lien, "it's okay. Don't worry about it." She turned to Jing-nan. "Tell Big Eye that I accept Wood Duck's apology."

"Mom, we should probably call the police!"

Siu-lien shook her head. "You don't understand," she said. "Not even those young men who were beaten would complain. They knew the risks." She touched her right ear. "Anyway, it's not really that bad. They didn't even get their teeth knocked out or arms broken. They did worse in the old days." She opened her pocketbook and slipped in the pictures. "These comfort me more than visiting Cixian Temple last night because I know there was punishment."

Jing-nan's eyebrows shot up. "You were at the night market?" he asked.

"We both were," said Siu-lien.

"You didn't tell me you were there," Jing-nan said to Nancy.

"I didn't want to bother you," she said, her face heating up. "It was a little after 10, and I thought you'd be too busy."

"I was busy then," said Jing-nan. "But I did leave a little after 11."

"You left Unknown Pleasures early?" asked Nancy.

Jing-nan nodded solemnly. "I was having a hard time focusing after meeting with Captain Huang."

He wanted to tell her about seeing himself on the Beefy King monitors, but he stopped himself. For one thing, Siu-lien's presence gave him pause. For another, it just seemed like a stupid thing to talk about.

"Mom, you should thank Jing-nan," she said. Siu-lien was focused on her phone. "Mom?"

Siu-lien looked up, her face pale. "There's been another murder," she said.

DWAYNE WALKED DOWN THE street, tired but also restless, his gym bag slung over his shoulder. He had an old set of earbuds on, ones that were okay to get dirty or break during a workout. Dwayne was walking with a swagger, as if he were listening to tough-guy lyrics and thumping beats. He wasn't listening to metal or hip-hop, though. Instead, Dwayne was listening to an old A-Mei album, and he had reached the ballad about a love that never was. Dwayne began to wonder about a certain girl he never had the guts to ask out, and one day never saw again. What was her name?

He put a bounce in his step that sent his gym bag thumping against his back. Dwayne entered an alley, a shortcut that took him by a neighborhood playground. He liked to flex his arms to get a reaction from the three-year-olds, and their nannies.

The alley opened up into a brightly lit walkway through a green space, of which the playground was the centerpiece. But it was empty. The concrete turtle that usually stoically bore several children on its shell was naked and alone. The three swings hung limply, forlorn and forgotten.

Where was everybody? Was there some Han Chinese holiday that required the presence of kids too young to read or talk? How odd.

Dwayne continued, entering another alley, one too narrow for Taipei's diffuse morning sunlight to penetrate fully.

Everything looked aqua green. Or was it aqua blue? One apartment building's facade was completely covered with creeping vines. The only giveaway that a house was somewhere underneath was a camera with a call button poking out of a bunch of leaves. Dwayne had a childish impulse to ring the bell and run, but he wanted to conserve his energy for the gym. Besides, he didn't want to make all Aboriginals look bad in public with a dumb prank.

Nobody was around to witness him, though. Not a single person fixing their bike or a grandpa washing his feet and watering his plants with a hose. It was so quiet he could hear birds cooing.

"This is weird," Dwayne said out loud. The alley bent slightly, and Dwayne saw a large and somber group of people gathered at the end. What was going on? He picked up his pace. Everybody in the neighborhood seemed to be there. Dwayne finally reached the back of the crowd and shuffled sideways until he found someone short to look over.

A small tent had been set up on the ground and a few police officers, some in uniform, stood guard.

"Excuse me," Dwayne asked the older woman standing in front of him. "Can you tell me what happened?"

"Someone's been murdered," she said, almost gleeful to disclose horrible news. "A police officer!" She touched her earrings and their presence reassured her.

A middle-aged man in a suit standing next to her added, "It wasn't just a police officer, it was a high-ranking officer, Captain Huang." The man was dazed, making his demeanor somewhat giddy.

Dwayne's skin burst into goose bumps. He crossed his arms to cover them up, and breathed through his mouth. Sweat was running down his back.

"Excuse me," he nearly whispered, "did you say Captain Huang, the guy from the Shilin precinct?"

"Oh, yes," said the man.

"It was," said the woman.

A strapping man in his 20s two rows up turned around. "I'm with the Volunteer Police Force, and, yeah, the victim was *that* Captain Huang," he said.

Dwayne swayed slightly. How could it be? Just last night that lousy cop had dragged Jing-nan down to the station.

Wait. There was no way that Jing-nan could've killed him, right? Dwayne thought it through. He did leave the night market earlier than usual, which he never did, and who knows where he went. Maybe he was so angry he somehow followed Captain Huang, and murdered him here, only a matter of blocks away from Dwayne's house? Maybe Jing-nan was guilty of both murders! It was just like the murder mystery stories he'd been reading: the last person you'd suspect was really the killer!

Then Dwayne shook himself off. No way did the kid pull this off. Jing-nan was even a little squeamish about handling the butcher knife. Jing-nan couldn't hurt anyone.

"They're still examining the captain?" Dwayne asked the volunteer cop. The man smiled, making him look like a body-building college student.

"The corpse is long gone," he said eagerly. "But they are still looking for clues in the immediate area. I wish I were working on this, but I'm off this week." He shook his head. "Strange timing for my break. Two killings in two days! I heard that last night, they found a print from a ballerina's shoe in Captain Huang's blood."

"Ballerina shoe?" asked the older man. "I thought it was a dog's footprint."

"It was definitely a woman's shoe," said the cop.

"I thought they found a bullet casing," said the older woman.

"A bullet casing!" said the cop.

"I didn't know there had been a gun!" said the older man. "The murderer must be an American!"

Dwayne lost his taste for the conversation. He nodded to the three and moved along the row, looking for an opening so he could get to the gym. Two uniformed cops called on the crowd to step back. Both sidewalks and the street itself were closed off. How could he get to the gym now? Maybe he shouldn't go at all. It would probably be bad luck to go after being so close to where the captain's spirit had left his body.

Oh, Jesus, I should pray for Captain Huang's soul, thought Dwayne. I didn't like him, but everyone deserves God's love and forgiveness. He bowed his head and prayed for the captain. It made him feel better.

Dwayne broke away from the crowd and pulled out his phone to cancel yet again with his gym buddy Chen. He walked back through the murky alley.

Dwayne considered stopping by the small Mazu shrine on his block to light a joss stick for Captain Huang. He was conflicted. A Christian man shouldn't be offering incense to an idol. Dwayne told himself it was all right to burn incense as long as he didn't bow to Mazu. He would admit to calling upon Mazu for things a Western god wouldn't understand, such as help in selling certain types of skewers when Dwayne had made too many. He knew she wouldn't stand to see food go to waste.

Dwayne exited the alley and emerged into the sunshine, set on heading to the Mazu temple, when he smelled something freshly baked that was buttery and just a touch salty. He'd have to see what it was.

CHAPTER 15

Frankie the Cat was pouring a second cup of coffee for his wife.

"Thank you," said Linh. She had short hair that allowed her angular face to be seen fully. Linh picked up the cup, put her elbows up on the table, and blew the coffee cool.

"This coffee is from Vietnam," said Frankie.

"Oh, I've been there," said Linh. "Do you have a pen pal in Saigon?"

"An old friend of mine is doing some business in the country."

She sipped some. "It's very good. Yes, I can taste the land, the people, the mornings, and the nights." Frankie smiled. He reached for a steamed bun, tore it in two, and put the halves on his plate. Ah, this one's curried beef. There was something pleasurable about picking up a bun not knowing what was inside. Every meal should have some surprise and delight. A chicken skewer never fooled anyone at any point in its production or consumption. It had no other possibilities. A steamed bun, however, could be beef, pork, chicken, egg, stewed vegetables, or even red-bean paste.

He bit into a bun half and slurped some of the excess curry. "This is so good," he said.

Linh tore off another piece of her steamed bun, capturing a nugget of curried chicken from the filling in the center. "These came out well," she said.

"Maybe you could freeze these," said Frankie.

"They die a little when you reheat them," said Linh.

"No, I mean, you could start a company, put these in boxes, sell them in supermarkets."

"Maybe I should open a stall at Shilin Night Market, right next to you. I'd give you a real run for your money."

"You don't want to compete against me," said Frankie. "I don't take any prisoners." She laughed.

"Ah, I'd just watch you all night." She checked her phone and frowned. "Would you mind if I take the rest of these in to work with me? We have a meeting right at the beginning of the day."

Frankie began to wrap them up even before she had finished speaking.

Linh was one of the officers of Taiwan Is Our Home, the organization that had helped her years ago. The nonprofit didn't pay very much, and Linh always made a far bigger breakfast than the two of them could possibly eat so that she could bring leftovers in to her staff.

Frankie was well aware of what she was doing, but he chose not to comment on it. She never wanted any acknowledgement of her generosity; to do so would imply that there was the possibility she could have deviated from her duty to be kind. It was the same reason some cabbies and waiters took offense when tourists tipped them. The extra payment implied that their work is so unskilled that exemplary service isn't usually included.

Frankie was the same way as Linh. Early on, she had given up thanking him for taking her in after she had run away from his brother's place. She knew the brothers hadn't seen each other in years. Frankie had said once that it was a blessing that he never again had to speak with someone as terrible as his brother. He left it at that.

One thing Frankie did like to talk about, though, was solving mysteries.

"Frankie, I read about Captain Huang's murder this morning," said Linh. "He used to give Jing-nan a hard time, right?" Frankie pushed back his seat. He had read about it on his tablet.

"Yes, that's true," said Frankie.

"Who do you think killed him?"

"It's hard to say. Captain Huang made a lot of enemies over a long time."

"Did Jing-nan think of him as an enemy?"

Frankie snorted. "Jing-nan doesn't have 'enemies.' He just has customers and noncustomers. Oh, and a girlfriend."

"Didn't an old friend of his try to shoot him?"

"In a way," Frankie conceded. "Really, though, that episode was just a cry for help. On the part of the friend."

"Captain Huang's murder doesn't seem to bother you. If the police can't even protect themselves, how can they protect all of you at the night market?"

"He wasn't killed anywhere near the Shilin Night Market, and anyone who makes trouble long enough can't protect themselves—not even a captain."

"Two murders in two days, Frankie. Are we becoming New York?"

"It's too hot and humid to be New York." Frankie tapped the table with all his fingers and stood.

Linh chugged the last of her coffee while Frankie finished packing the buns into a bamboo basket and placed it in a tote bag. She touched his neck and kissed his lips.

"I love you," she said.

"Love you," he whispered.

WHEN DWAYNE TEXTED HIS friend Chen to say that he was bagging out on the gym again, Chen suggested that they meet up later at the Hope Project, a nonprofit center that included a café and gift shop operated by trainees. It was the opposite direction from the crime scene, so there was little chance of the way being blocked. Unless there was another murder.

Dwayne checked the latest news on the homepage of his browser app. MURDER EVERYWHERE: ARE WE BECOMING NEW YORK? the top headline read. Dwayne snapped his phone off and walked down Xinyi Road. He entered the lobby of the Hope Project, which was incorporated into a mixed-use condo by the developer as a concession to the city in exchange for the speedy processing of the building permit.

The center housed several different organizations that had common goals to help marginalized people participate in Taiwan's capitalist and democratic society. In fact, the clients of the nonprofits that staffed Hope Project's café were learning the pros and cons of the service industry by experiencing customer abuse firsthand.

Dwayne waited in line at the Hope Center's café, three people behind a woman who was complaining that her decaf latte from yesterday had kept her awake all night. Listening to the woman go off made Dwayne glad that customers were mellower at night, already beaten down by their day jobs or jet lag. People disgruntled by their purchases at Unknown Pleasures could always be placated with an apology and a replacement skewer. Jing-nan's grandfather had a policy against refunds, and it remained the driving policy at the stall.

The woman behind the café counter kept her head down

and made supplicating noises. She had given the customer a refund and a coupon good for a new drink, and still the woman wouldn't relent.

"I watched my clock all night, and I'm someone who needs rest," the customer growled.

"You seem to be doing just fine with no sleep," Dwayne heard a familiar voice say.

Outraged, the angry customer turned around, revealing herself to be a minor politician that Dwayne recognized from TV. "Who said that? Who dared to talk to me like that?"

"I did," said the woman directly in front of Dwayne. Wow, it was Frankie's wife, Linh, whom Dwayne had met a few times.

"Ah," said the politician. "Your Mandarin is as bad as hers! You're a foreigner, too!"

"At least we're not assholes," said Linh.

"Why don't you go back to . . ." The politician was stumped because she wasn't sure what country to name.

"Why don't you go back to China?" asked Linh. The politician was from a mainlander family and liked to talk up the supposed ancestral ties of people on both sides of the strait.

Other customers snickered, and the politician's face turned red. She whipped her shoulder bag around and stomped away.

"Linh," said Dwayne, "you handled yourself well."

"Dwayne!" she exclaimed. "Oh, my! I don't think I would've been so bold if I knew a friend was here. I'm so embarrassed!"

"I wish I had my phone ready to record it!"

"You wouldn't dare!"

"Can I help you?" asked the woman at the counter. It was Linh's turn to order. "Actually, I should really say 'thank you.'" Then she said something to Linh in Vietnamese, which Dwayne didn't understand.

His phone jumped. It was a text from Chen that said he wasn't going to make it to the café. Was that a revenge move for Dwayne missing the gym two days in a row? Maybe he should have mentioned that the latest murder all over the news was the reason he was blocked today. Anyway, it was nice to run into Linh and catch her star performance.

Now Linh was speaking to him, and he pulled himself away from his phone.

"Dwayne, this café is run by Vietnamese and Aboriginal people."

"That's the best kind of partnership," said Dwayne. "Maybe we should work here, too, then!" Linh laughed and handed him a cup of coffee. "What? No, you can't pay for me! Frankie will kill me."

"It's free," Linh whispered. The barista nodded.

They walked over to the side to fix their drinks.

"Are you gonna hang out here?" Dwayne asked Linh.

"I have to go upstairs," said Linh. "I work here!"

"I see," said Dwayne. He paused to look at a poster on the wall behind the stirrers. It was promoting a troupe of Australian acrobats, the Flying Wonders, as part of the Austronesian Cultural Festival. Someone had added a handwritten note in marker: INCLUDES ONE PAIWAN!

"Looks interesting, huh?" asked Linh.

"I've never liked show-offs," said Dwayne. "How much is it, anyway? Aw, two thousand bucks? No way!"

"I don't know how the whole festival can go on when there are so many murders happening."

"I hear ya," said Dwayne. "It's a real shame. I will say, though, that we get one thing each year, and I'll be damned if I let anyone take it away. I'm a big supporter of the free and cheap things, anyway."

After Linh left, Dwayne found an empty seat at a dirty

table. Why didn't people clean up after themselves? He blew away a patch of sugar and blotted a spill with his only napkin. How could he complain, though? The coffee was free.

Someone at the next table over was watching the news on their phone. There was that Captain Huang who was murdered. It was creepy seeing his headshot. Dwayne prayed again, mainly to comfort himself.

Dwayne turned on his phone and tried to log into the café's Wi-Fi. The login page featured a screenshot of the acrobats. Man, they were pushing it hard. Accepting the terms of the Wi-Fi service caused a short clip of the troupe in action to play. Dwayne knew right away who the Paiwan acrobat was. The Amazing Mazy, as a subtitle read, was a woman who was balancing on one foot on the seat of a bicycle that was coasting backward in a big circle. Wow, maybe it would be worth the price of admission to support her.

The next performer was introduced as Umaq with the subtitle, "Taiwan's Paiwan Wonder," and Dwayne winced with guilt that he had thought the woman had been the Aborigine. Umaq, a young man, danced across a tightrope. Dwayne forgot his embarrassment as he watched the man leap in the air and land safely on the rope. The camera pulled back to reveal there wasn't a safety net.

To do something like that, Dwayne mused, you'd have to not give a shit if you died.

He sipped coffee and tapped his news app. The top stories were the back-to-back murders. In death, Boxer and Captain Huang were linked forever in the archive of online stories. Maybe now they were bunkmates in hell.

The paragraphs about Boxer's murder in the seedy part of town were filled with salacious details, and the parts about the captain outlined a storied hero who'd lost his life in the unworthy endeavor of trying to find Boxer's murderer.

One story claimed to have an unnamed source in the police department who said that whoever killed Captain Huang had to be strong because his head was nearly snapped off.

Dwayne unconsciously flexed his arm and chest muscles. If the murderer ever came after him, Dwayne would show him. Whose neck would end up broken?

He shifted in his seat. Well, he'd have to hit the gym regularly, and then he'd be ready. He drank more coffee.

FRANKIE SET DOWN A tray in front of an elderly man who seemed lost but wasn't particularly distressed about it.

Frankie bowed slightly to the man and asked, "Would you mind if I sat with you for a little bit?"

The man regarded Frankie, smiled, and gestured at the empty spot across from him at the cafeteria table. The man was friendly in his actions even if they didn't demonstrate any particular recognition of Frankie.

Frankie took a seat and placed two cups of tea on the table between them.

"What is this?" the man asked Frankie.

"It's black tea, from Yunnan. Try it, you'll like it."

"It smells good." The man picked up the cup with both hands and slurped the tea. "Strong taste," he said approvingly.

Frankie placed a pineapple cake in front of the man. It looked like a big, fat fried mahjong tile, and its surface was golden and crumbly. The two men could both smell the excessive amount of butter that had been baked into it. Frankie cut the cake in half, revealing the filling of shredded candied pineapple.

The man reached for a piece, but hesitated when Frankie held up his hand.

"Just, um, if you would, sir, please have a bit more tea," said Frankie. "To clear your palate."

The man nodded and took a large sip of tea. A degree of

awareness about who Frankie was came into his face, but then his eyes focused on the pineapple cake.

"Oh, we're sharing this?" he asked.

"Yes," said Frankie. "Please, after you."

The man smiled like a little boy and bit off a third of his piece. He chewed and breathed in deeply through his nose. The man was eating the cake that he had tasted in his youth. He finished with another sip of tea to rinse his mouth.

"That's very good," the man said.

"It's the best I can find," said Frankie.

"Did you know people eat pineapple for luck because the word sounds like 'bring forth'?" he asked Frankie.

"In Taiwanese it does," said Frankie. "In Mandarin, it doesn't."

The man was startled for a second. "You don't understand," he said. "You're a mainlander!"

Frankie couldn't suppress his smile. "Yes, I am."

"You're Frankie!" the man said, prompting Frankie to nod slightly. Worry came across the man's face. "We're out of uniform! We're going to get in big trouble!"

"We're on a leave. It's okay, Lieutenant Yang," he said.

"Where are we?"

"This is a recreation center," said Frankie. "We're here to relax before we have to report back."

"How are we doing?" Lieutenant Yang said under his breath.

"It's not looking good, to be honest," said Frankie, "but we still have a chance."

"As long as we stay disciplined," said the lieutenant.

"Yes," said Frankie. "It could take years."

"We'll retake the mainland with patience. There will be opportunities whether the Americans help us or not."

Frankie rubbed his hands. "Please have some more tea," he told Lieutenant Yang.

"From Yunnan, you say," the lieutenant said, almost to himself. "Still tastes fresh, but you must have brought it over years ago." He drank more tea.

"It was mailed over," Frankie said gently to his old comrade. "We have a friend who's in business there now."

The lieutenant looked over his hands. "We're old men now, aren't we?" he asked.

"We are."

"This is where they take care of the elderly, right?" Lieutenant Yang looked around, noticing for the first time today people nodding off in their seats, or walking with assistance.

"It's a daycare center," said Frankie. "You live with your son's family."

"How old is he?" the lieutenant asked.

"He's forty-five," said Frankie. "You have two grandchildren. One boy, one girl."

"One boy, one girl," Lieutenant Yang said absently. He was beginning to slip again.

"Beautiful children," said Frankie. "Lieutenant, did you hear me? I said they're beautiful." The man didn't reply. Frankie stood. "I'm going to leave now."

"Will you be back?" the man suddenly asked. Frankie touched both of Lieutenant Yang's wrists.

"I come here every day," said Frankie.

DWAYNE WANDERED THROUGH THE center, admiring the art displays, and considered signing up for a few workshops that looked interesting. He was about to pass by a classroom when he noticed a group of seven men of Aborigine descent mostly in their 20s and 30s, big guys like him, sitting in folding chairs arranged into an oval. Most of the men were slightly hunched over, and their expressions ranged from ashamed to defiant. All seemed resigned to be there, however.

One older man in a white button-down shirt and khakis sitting in the circle noted Dwayne looking in.

"Please join us brother," he said with an outstretched hand to Dwayne. The only elders that Dwayne had the courage to defy were his parents, so he loped into the room and sat in a chair at one of the ends of the oval. He nodded at a few of the men but received no responses. "I haven't seen you before," said the elder. "My name is Paisol."

Dwayne nodded and said, "I'm . . ."

Paisol raised a hand as a stop signal.

"Wait," he said. "You don't have to give your name if you don't want to."

"I don't mind," said Dwayne.

Paisol shifted his jaw. "Well, in today's group, no one else is giving their names."

Dwayne pushed out his legs and crossed his feet. "I was going to give my English name." Dwayne turned to the most reticent-looking of the men. "Call me 'Dwayne.' I'm honored to be with you today, my brothers."

The man stared at Dwayne, straightened up, and thumped his heart like a baseball player showing love to his fans. "You call me 'Mike.' All of you can."

The six other men also came around, and gave English names. Paisol beamed at Dwayne. "Thank you for bringing in your positive energy, Dwayne. I'm quite grateful for that."

"It's good to be here with you," said Dwayne. Paisol put his hands together, between his knees.

"Today, we're going to talk about how we, as Aboriginal men, can show how much we have to offer the world while maintaining our culture." Paisol opened his arms to the group. "We're not looking for definitive answers. I just want to hear how you've been dealing with this issue, day to day." Dwayne raised his hand, and Paisol nodded.

"I might as well go first, since I'm new to this group. In my experience, I'd have to say that we're able to be our best when we're honest. When we're genuine. You guys know those little Aboriginal village tourist sites, where people pay to see us do our little dances and songs?"

A few of the men laughed bitterly in recognition. Encouraged, Dwayne continued.

"Those are rituals meant to be directed to our ancestors and to the gods. Not to tourists in return for their money. When we do that, we're literally selling our souls."

Mike cracked his knuckles. "I understand what you're saying, Dwayne, but there's also a lot of demand to see our culture. Why else do we have this 'Austronesian Cultural Festival' going on?" He planted his feet and leaned forward, elbows on his knees. "It is a voyeuristic demand, yeah, but that could mean jobs for our people, doing what's already in our culture, instead of putting on suits and ties, and being administrative assistants."

"Mike," said Dwayne, "I'm speaking from a place where I joined one of these 'Aboriginal villages,' and I felt like such a fake." Something in his throat caught and he could feel tears forming in his eyes. "Well, I got angry about it."

"It's all right to be angry," Paisol said. "Let's get all those bad feelings out. Don't hold them in."

"I get angry, too, Dwayne," said Mike. "I do. After *Cape No. 7* became a huge hit, everyone wanted to wear those necklaces of Paiwan glass beads."

"Everyone?" asked Dwayne. "You mean those hipster Han Chinese!" The group laughed again.

"I'm Paiwan, you know," said Mike, "and my kneejerk reaction was like, you people don't deserve to wear our stories around your neck!" Even Paisol was wiping tears of laughter from his eyes. It felt good to speak from anger while having a point. "On the other hand, our beads are so eye-catching, of course people want to wear them. Let's just charge them full retail, you know?" The men laughed even louder.

"That is a good point, Mike," Dwayne conceded. "As long as we stay true to ourselves, let's bring the money into our communities. I would also say this: we should make a point of giving money to the Hope Center. I'm really touched being here today. From now on, I'm going to donate two percent of my salary. It's not much, but together, you know, we're strong. I don't know what you guys do for a living, but I work at a stall in the night market. I make skewers and stews. They're pretty damned good, too, if you ask me."

Dwayne glanced at the other men and saw that he had their attention. Taiwanese society is one of subtlety, and a level of opaqueness is expected even between friends. It's frowned upon to speak directly or specifically about financial or personal matters. A person would never tell a stranger what one did for a living, much less how one chose to dispose of one's salary.

But Dwayne was being purposely confessional. He felt that he had met people he could immediately trust, and Dwayne hoped that at least Mike would feel some sense of closeness.

Mike did nod enthusiastically.

"I appreciate where you're coming from, Dwayne. You are a warrior for our people. When all my issues are cleared up, I'm going to do the same."

Dwayne nodded. Mike didn't disclose what he did, but that was all right. None of the other guys seemed willing to step up at the moment, but that was okay, too. Paisol seemed uncomfortable, and shifted in his seat while looking at nothing on the wall. Dwayne felt a little responsible. Maybe stating the exact percentage that he would donate was a bit too forward. It could have put all the men in an uneasy position.

Some might have families to support, and they didn't have money to spare, not even for a community center. Or maybe Dwayne's donation wasn't enough to please Paisol. Shit, he should've gone up to 3 percent!

Well, Dwayne couldn't control what other people thought, and his openness inspired Mike to give money at the end of the session, so that was a good thing. Mike had more to say.

"I've been making jewelry—we all have. Not the glass beads, because we can't get ahold of a butane torch." Mike looked over at the others, who nodded. "We can do a lot with what we've got, and we're getting better and better."

"In fact, Dwayne," said Paisol, "the shop downstairs sells the jewelry that the guys make." Mike shook his head and waved his hands, trying to make a show of discouraging the promotion of his work.

"I'll definitely buy some of your stuff," Dwayne said. "Please, don't be so modest, Mike. You should be proud of your work. All of you. Seriously." He'd at least look over the jewelry, he thought to himself. Dwayne rubbed his hands, hoping that he hadn't come off as having excessive disposable cash when he spoke about having money to donate.

Paisol checked his phone.

"Well, we are at the end of our time here, gentlemen. I'm sure you have someplace to be, and I'm sure that Dwayne does, too. We'll see you here again in a month. Dwayne, you're welcome back, as well. Third Thursday of the month, here at eleven o'clock."

"I will definitely consider it," said Dwayne. "I'm sorry I came in at the end. I hope I didn't sidetrack you guys."

Mike said, "We were glad you came in, Dwayne." Both men stood up and shook hands. Dwayne ended up shaking hands with all the men as they filed out of the room.

Paisol pressed an envelope into Dwayne's hands.

"What's this?" Dwayne asked.

"I don't know if you saw the posters downstairs or not, but there's an Australian circus performing in Taipei, the Flying Wonders, and they've been offering the Hope Center some half-off discounts. I thought you might want to go, since our brothers here won't be attending."

"They're pretty serious about their art, huh?"

Paisol stepped in line behind the men. "They are dedicated to their craft," he said. Ah, Mike and the rest of the guys might be in one of those artist communes in Taipei.

Dwayne waited in the empty room a few minutes to give the men some privacy on their way out. He himself was a bit of an artist, as well. Preparing and cooking food required some deft skills. It was easy, actually, to make food that tastes great, or looks great. Only masters could cook dishes that would garner both thousands of likes on Instagram, and five-star ratings on Tripadvisor and Yelp.

Dwayne wiped his face and snorted. Damn that Jing-nan. He has me thinking about how people see Unknown Pleasures on social media. The Han Chinese are savvy at marketing, and now that's rubbed off onto me.

He opened the envelope and read over the ticket offer for the circus. It was half off, all right, but it required the purchase of a minimum of five tickets to the Flying Wonders. Could Dwayne even find five people able to go on the same night?

Why would he need to go to the circus? The night market is enough of a circus. Famous people popped in all the time. Dwayne and Frankie shot a selfie with Jay Chou, but Jing-nan stayed out of the shot, making some bullshit excuse that there were too many people in the picture. The truth was Jing-nan hated Jay's music, and would have been mortified to be in a selfie with him. At the same time, that picture brought people to the stand.

Dwayne folded up the discount coupons, and stuck them in a back pocket. He walked out of the meeting room and shut off the lights. Might as well have a look at the jewelry the craftsmen had made. They all seemed to have the introverted, artistic temperament needed to create something decent.

Dwayne walked over to the gift shop, which was adjacent to the café he had sat in earlier in the morning. There were quite a few artisans' works, reasonably priced. He examined the knitted scarves, and some musical instruments including nose flutes and bamboo drums. But there didn't seem to be any jewelry out.

"Excuse me," Dwayne said to the saleswoman. She was sitting in a chair, resting her head on folded arms. She might have been tired or severely dehydrated. "Do you sell jewelry here?"

"Oh," she said, lifting herself up. The saleswoman walked to a storage unit at the end of the counter closest to the cash register. "The only jewelry we sell is made by inmates at Taipei Prison." She unlocked the case and opened the door.

"It's made by prisoners?" asked Dwayne.

"Yes," said the woman, as she placed a tray of necklaces before Dwayne. "I just had them steam-cleaned, and I forgot to put them back out. The artists just brought them over this morning. In fact, you just missed them."

Dwayne caressed the side of the tray and admired the craftsmanship involved in making the layered necklaces. So all of those guys were in jail. He wondered what Mike had done to end up there.

"What kind of stone is this?" he asked.

"Lapis lazuli," said the woman. "These products are quality stuff. The prisoners will have real livelihoods when they're released."

Dwayne raised one necklace with multicolored stones that rattled like a rainbow snake as he lifted it to his face.

"I want this one," he said.

DWAYNE STOOD AT A full-length mirror next to a garbage can in the lobby. He adjusted the necklace until most of the blue stones were near the bottom. This makes me look like a pharaoh, Dwayne thought.

Then he shifted it until the polished pink shell pieces were at the bottom. This seemed to highlight his white teeth more.

"You're beautiful and you know it!" called out a familiar voice. Dwayne turned around.

"Frankie, what are you doing here?"

Frankie gave one of his big smiles. "I was here to see if the center had any programs or interest groups for veterans of Aboriginal descent," he said. "I found that while there's a support group for incarcerated artists, there's nothing for the veterans. That sends the wrong message, doesn't it? Why is there rehabilitation for people convicted of breaking the law, but nothing for those who served their country?"

Dwayne thought back to his empty and angry years before he met Frankie. He cringed slightly out of shame for his prideful acts, which had only caused pain for all parties concerned.

"People can make mistakes," Dwayne said. "The great thing about our country is that we can help people out once they've paid their debt to society." He wrapped the bottom of the necklace around his right fist. "Look, Frankie, now you've got me defending Taiwan, which has been marginalizing the people the Hope Center is trying to help. Nearly everything here is volunteer-run, as you know. And by the

way, I ran into Linh this morning." He related the café incident to Frankie, who nodded his approval.

"I do love the Hope Center," Frankie said. "I love everything it stands for."

"Why don't you visit Linh since you're here?"

"Where do you think I just came from?"

"Hey, Frankie, I have a great idea. Why don't you start
up a group to help Aboriginal vets? I mean, you're a veteran
and you were held in that . . ." Dwayne's voice trailed off as
he recognized that he could possibly upset Frankie by talking
about his time in prison.

"I don't think I'm qualified," said Frankie. "I don't even
have what it takes to help one old friend of mine."

"Frankie!" said Dwayne suddenly. "Did you hear about
Captain Huang?"

"Yes," said Frankie.

"What do you think?"

"It's not good."

The two men walked out of the center and to the MRT station. Neither said, "We should head into work now," but that's
what they were doing. Most people would probably balk at
the suggestion that their culture viewed commitment to work
as a virtue. But everyone was dedicated in their own way to
their occupation, and for many, this meant starting early or on
time, and staying at least an hour or two late each night.

Dwayne and Frankie didn't talk on the MRT. Frankie
seemingly stared at nothing, but in reality he was eyeing the
faces of all the passengers. None seemed familiar, but Frankie
continued to subtly scrutinize them, not looking for anything
in particular. He had a sixth sense about people who were up
to no good.

Dwayne skimmed the news feed on his phone while his
thoughts were still focused on the men he had stumbled upon.

He should have asked for Mike's email address. Did inmates have access to email? It probably depended upon their crime.

Years ago, before Jing-nan's father hired him at Unknown Pleasures, Dwayne was drinking heavily, and moving from one meaningless job to another. Getting into fistfights at nightclubs wasn't even the low point. That came after one brawl, when Dwayne, the last man standing, was offered a job selling drugs to club-goers.

Dwayne had pretended to be wasted, staggered to the bathroom, and then left the club through an emergency door that he knew wasn't alarmed.

What would have happened if he had opened that other door? Less than a week after Dwayne left the nightclub scene for good, there was a major raid of the clubs and karaoke joints. The cops bagged up ketamine tablets and low-level dealers. Sentences handed down were longer than the gaps between Ang Lee films.

Dwayne could be sitting in jail with Mike right now, making jewelry instead of buying it.

When he thought Frankie was looking away, Dwayne bowed his head, closed his hands over his phone, and said a quick prayer to Jesus to help Mike.

"How about lunch, Frankie?" asked Dwayne.

"Sure."

They could have deliberated about where to go to eat. Even before the night market opened, the neighborhood had choice and cheap places to eat. Instead they continued on to open up Unknown Pleasures. After all, who else could cook to their satisfaction better than themselves?

CHAPTER 16

Jing-nan read every story he could about Captain Huang's murder. It was a bigger shock to his system than the torture session less than 24 hours ago. This story said that Boxer and the captain had been killed by the same person, but another said it couldn't have been. Was Captain Huang decapitated or was he strangled?

They were still seated in a busy campus dining hall, although Siu-lien had gotten up twice to get more coffee and a candy bar.

"Jing-nan," said Nancy after nearly 15 minutes of silence. "I don't think it's good for you to keep reading those stories."

"I just want to know every detail of what happened," said Jing-nan.

"These journalists," said Siu-lien, "they don't know anything. Either they make it up, or they take the word of some cop. They write anything to get you to click on their stories and save their jobs."

"I know something no one else knows," said Jing-nan. "Well, one other person knows now. Nancy, I told you that Captain Huang brought me down to the station for questioning, but I didn't tell you that he tortured me to try to get a confession." Her hands gripped the edge of the table, while Siu-lien stroked an earring. "It wasn't that bad, although it was headed in that direction. He handcuffed me to the chair and brought in a guy to twist my arm. Just when they thought they had me, I punched myself in the face, to show evidence I was being beaten. I had a bloody nose, too."

"Why the hell didn't you tell me this?" asked Nancy.

"It wasn't something I wanted to say on the phone or a text," said Jing-nan. "You know, if you had stopped by Unknown Pleasures when you came to the temple . . ."

"That was smart, Jing-nan," said Siu-lien. "I'll bet seeing blood all over the place made them stop."

"The guy torturing me ran out of the room!"

Siu-lien touched his wrist and looked over his nose. "You turned the tables; good for you. Still, I'm sorry I got you involved in all this, Jing-nan." Her hand crept back to her nearly empty coffee cup. "I thought he would be so shocked by seeing you, he'd hand over the rest of the money. I had no idea he'd spend it so quickly. Well, everything's more expensive these days."

"I'm sorry we didn't stop by that night, Jing-nan," said Nancy. "It was a really stressful situation. Captain Huang harassed us that night, too. I went to the bar after we talked on the phone, and he surprised me by showing up there. He was saying all this stuff about Boxer right in front of Arlen Chen."

Jing-nan slapped the table. "Arlen Chen! He was in one of the news reports I saw. I'll bet he gossiped to all his friends."

Jing-nan's phone buzzed. He and Nancy both saw the caller. "I think my day just got a little worse," said Jing-nan. He picked up the phone and said, "Hi, Peggy, how are you doing?"

"How am *I* doing?" asked Peggy. "*What* the fuck are *you*

doing? From what I hear, you're involved with both murders, Jing-nan!" Peggy was an old high school classmate from one of the richest mainlander families in the country. Peggy was friendly at times, uncaring at others, and sometimes both, like right now. Was she calling to check in on his welfare, or was she mostly mocking him?

"I'm not involved at all, Peggy. Yes, I recently saw Boxer and Captain Huang, but I had nothing to do with their deaths. That's it."

"That's it, huh?" The mouthpiece of her telephone scraped against something. "Hey, would you mind if we switch to a video call? I can't tell when you're being sarcastic by your voice alone."

"Not right now," Jing-nan said to a dead line. A notification popped up that Peggy's video call was waiting for him to pick up. He mouthed, but didn't say, "Fuck."

"Who is this person?" asked Siu-lien, who was adept at reading lips.

"An old friend," said Jing-nan. He placed the phone on the table and tapped the screen. "Hi, again, Peggy. Slow day at the office?"

She was standing. Her phone camera was close to her face, making her nose seem bigger than it really was. Her ink-black hair was cropped short and combed back. Her eyes were so bright and dark, they seemed to float above the screen. Edges of the frame seemed to show track lighting above and walls on the sides.

"Having a small break from intense negotiations," said Peggy. "This big American bank is pulling out of Taiwan, and we're looking to buy up the assets. You know, bleed 'em for everything. Anyway, I heard that you were beaten up in Captain Huang's office. Is that true?"

"You have no idea what's going on."

"I actually do know. My family's your landlord at the night market, and we hire some of the precinct's cops for security there. One guy told me he saw you staggering out of the captain's office with your face a mess." She brought the camera closer to her face. "I will admit, though, that you don't seem to be injured."

Nancy leaned in. "I don't mean to be rude, Peggy, but now is a bad time to be talking."

"Ah, sweet Nancy. I was worried about Jing-nan, so I called him. Isn't that what friends do?" Siu-lien moved over to get a better look at the owner of the blithe voice. "Oh, is that . . . are you Nancy's mom?"

"Yes, I am."

"I am so sorry for your loss. Really. It's terrible what the news people are saying about Boxer. It was really tasteless of that one reporter to go count the number of brothels on the same block. At the same time, doesn't twenty-five seem like an exaggeration? I mean, I never go there so I wouldn't know. Would you?"

Nancy could feel her mother grinding her teeth.

"Peggy," said Jing-nan, "can you tell me anything else the cop told you about me?"

"Hmmm. He saw an informant leave Captain Huang's office, and then you came out and washed up in the bathroom. Then the captain left the room and hid in an interrogation room while his office was cleaned. Also, that you have a legitimate motive to kill him."

"I didn't touch the guy!"

"Well, they're going through the surveillance-camera footage to check your movements." She paused. "I know that in all likelihood, you probably didn't do it, Jing-nan. You can count me as a supporter, you know, if you have to make bail or something."

Jing-nan held his right hand outside the camera's view and gave Peggy the finger. "Thank you so much for that," he said.

"Oh, one more thing. The cop said some of the boys were thinking of visiting you at Unknown Pleasures tonight."

JING-NAN PACED IN FRONT of Unknown Pleasures. Sure, he was worried about the police who might be visiting. But primarily he was itching to get more business. It was 9 P.M., a time when people realized they had forgotten to eat, or they were hungry again. There should be more customers by now! The success of his food stall, particularly in recent months, made Jing-nan feel less secure on nights when the line of customers seemed thin.

Shit, maybe people are staying away because stories about the two murders mention Unknown Pleasures! Wait, that couldn't be true. Tourists don't read newspapers, and they can't understand the TV programs.

He commanded himself by the name of his night-market persona, the barker who corralled tourists to buy his food. C'mon, Johnny! You got this! He closed his eyes, cracked his neck, and then looked around, expecting to see that everything had changed. Nothing had, but his attitude was better.

"Dwayne and Frankie," he called. "I'm going fishing."

"Yeah," said Dwayne as he took a seat. Frankie slapped his arm.

"Hey, that doesn't mean take a break. Let's put some skewers on the grill, get some of that aroma in the air!"

Jing-nan walked away to check foot traffic at the intersections.

There had to be a big group of tourists, functionally illiterate in Taiwan, but dying to spend to feel something authentic. Jing-nan looked to the left and right, but he couldn't spy big groups of indecisive Americans—his favorite prey. They weren't victims, though. He was doing them a favor by roping them into eating the best food that Taipei offered, and not wasting their money on merely adequate fare.

C'mon, Johnny, he told himself again.

ON NANCY'S SUGGESTION, JING-NAN had begun to keep a running spreadsheet of his weekly and monthly revenue and profit. He crunched all his numbers himself for taxes, and this year was going to be a doozy. Nancy thought having something that only needed small updates every day would make running Unknown Pleasures less stressful for Jing-nan, but it had the opposite effect.

Jing-nan began to obsess over the daily take. If it was less than the previous day, he panicked. If it was more, he checked it against the same day the previous week. If the latest day was still better, he'd find another reason Unknown Pleasures had failed that day. Getting more serious about money was also causing a personality crisis. He had long ago accepted his fake persona, Johnny, as a part of doing business. Now when he was keying numbers into the calculator app and spreadsheet, Jing-nan heard his teenage voice mocking him for being a sellout businessman. When he was out at the day market searching for new ingredients for special, even artful, creations, the voice taunted him again. Why are you haggling for lower prices? Isn't it hard enough being a farmer in Taiwan? You're taking money out of the mouths of their kids. The good thing about this rupture was that he'd been able to leave it at work and not bring it home. So far.

DWAYNE WATCHED JING-NAN AS the night went on. That kid is off his game. Well, he's got good reason to be melancholic. Being tied to two murders would be enough to sidetrack anybody who wasn't Michael Corleone. Dwayne brushed off his sleeves. Jing-nan would beat this, anyway, with his luck. They got nothing on him.

Dwayne walked over to the large stew pot and lifted the lid. The smell was a little off. Dwayne knew the sense of smell was stronger than taste, and if it smelled too salty . . .

He ladled out a small circle of liquid and held it under the light. The color was good. He slurped. Yes, too salty. Dwayne went to the cutting board and diced a long turnip and tossed it into the pot. The mild-flavored vegetable would absorb the salt and balance out the soup. He replaced the lid and saw that Frankie the Cat was looking at him with one eyebrow raised.

"I thought you'd salted it too much," Frankie said. Dwayne shifted his feet and shrugged his right shoulder. You couldn't get anything by Frankie.

"Yeah, a little bit."

Frankie lowered his eyebrow and spoke gently. "Turn down the heat a little, too."

"I was just going to," said Dwayne as he obeyed. "Honest."

Frankie patted his shirt pocket and headed out for a smoke. Dwayne followed him.

"Say, Cat?"

Frankie turned, his cigarette already lit. He said nothing and Dwayne continued. "Have you noticed that Jing-nan seems a little down lately?"

Frankie removed his cigarette and thoughtfully blew out a trail of smoke. "Yes," he said.

"We should do something," said Dwayne.

Frankie spoke this time from the side of his mouth, cigarette back between his lips. "Why?"

"Don't you want to help out a guy who's down?"

Frankie let out smoke from the other side of his smile. "He's going through a life test."

Dwayne rubbed his temples. "We're making more money than ever. That should cheer him up," Dwayne said mostly to himself.

"If you think money alone makes you happy," said Frankie, smoke leaking from his lips, "you'll never have enough."

Dwayne shook his head. No way was he buying this. "I'd have a limit," said Dwayne. "Gimme ten million bucks and I'll be happy. Quit this job and fuck this place." Frankie crossed his arms. "Ah, nothing personal, you understand."

"Anyway," said Frankie, dropping his cigarette and squashing it with his foot. "Jing-nan's not so bad off. He has a girlfriend to talk to."

Dwayne held up a finger. "But we've known him longer."

"We don't sleep with him," said Frankie.

JING-NAN SURVEYED THE NEARLY empty walkways in the vicinity of Unknown Pleasures. It was like Moses had parted the Red Sea of customers and left nothing but a dry seabed. Boxer and Captain Huang seeped back into his thoughts. Was the whole thing a setup? Had Siu-lien somehow planned the double murder to sabotage her daughter's relationship with him, and his business, as well? Siu-lien couldn't be that crazy, could she?

Jing-nan straightened up and thought it through. Nothing made sense. The past two days were like a crime film with no imagination, budget, or second takes. He turned his head and saw two larger-than-average men in suits walking purposefully toward Unknown Pleasures. These had to be the boys Peggy had told him about. He decided to play it cool with them, and looked the other way.

He spied a group of five young tourists approaching cautiously. He smiled. Maybe they'd read about his notoriety. If they were Japanese, they'd probably buy a lot and not ask any questions. If they were Asian American, though, it'd be the opposite.

He was looking for clues in their clothing when a man's voice politely asked, "Are you Chen Jing-nan?" He turned to see that the two men were standing nearby, sizing him up.

"Yes, I am," he said lightly. The man who had been speaking was looking him directly in the eye, and seemed bemused by Jing-nan's simple answer. The other man stood back and viewed Jing-nan with openly hostile suspicion. So that was their game.

"You been here all night?" the suspicious cop asked. He seemed to be in his late 40s, and had a wide, frowning face and a nose like a hawk's beak.

"I got here before the night started," said Jing-nan. "I like to be prepared."

"I'm Detective Kao," said the polite cop. "That's Detective Wu. We're both with the Shilin precinct." Detective Kao was also in his late 40s, and had the smooth, light skin of a scholar. "By now you know that Captain Huang's been murdered."

Jing-nan lowered his head and nodded. "Yes, it's sad. You guys know I had nothing to do with that, of course."

"Why don't you cut the crap?" asked Detective Wu. "We know you were one of the last people to see him."

Detective Kao feigned embarrassment. "We know you probably had nothing to do with the murder. But there is the fact that his appointment with you was his last order of business for the day. We wanted to know if you could tell us anything that might help the investigation. If Captain Huang was acting a little odd, or if he mentioned anything that seemed unusual."

Jing-nan stopped himself cold from saying something snarky. The guy was dead, after all. He should respect the man's spirit, even if he didn't respect the man.

"Captain Huang brought me down and accused me of killing Boxer, which isn't true at all," said Jing-nan.

"We know you're innocent of that, as well," said Detective Wu. "The timing of your visit and his death don't work out. He was probably just probing you, to see what you knew."

"You didn't give him much, according to his notes," said Detective Kao. Wait, he was supposed to be the good cop, thought Jing-nan.

"Maybe I should add that he had some guy in there twist my arm, someone named Li."

"What, do you want to file a complaint against a dead detective, Jing-nan?" asked Detective Kao, while his dour expression suggested that that would be a very bad move.

Jing-nan looked around for Dwayne and Frankie for backup. Hey, where'd they go? "Guys?" he called out. "Where are you?"

"Yeah?" called out Dwayne as he reappeared from the back. Frankie followed.

"These two detectives are asking for information about Captain Huang," said Jing-nan. "Since he stopped by the stand before he encouraged me to come down to the precinct, I was wondering if you two noticed something amiss with the captain."

Dwayne crossed his arms and looked from Jing-nan to the two detectives, to some anxious-looking tourists.

"He seemed his normal self," said Dwayne. Frankie leaned against a side counter and eyed the two cops.

"Say," said Detective Wu, "where were you just now, Dwayne and Frankie?" Dwayne raised an eyebrow. They must've found our names online, he thought.

"Me and Frankie, officer? Well, we were in the immediate vicinity of this esteemed food joint, right around the corner. We didn't sneak off and attack anybody."

Detective Wu pointed his index and middle fingers at the arches of Dwayne's eyebrows. "You looking to fight someone, tough guy?"

"Mr. Officer," Dwayne said slowly, "we've been here all night. If you don't believe us, check all the camera footage around here." He waved his right arm in a circle.

"Don't tell us how to do our jobs," Detective Kao told Dwayne. "We know you had nothing to do with Captain Huang's murder. The evidence exonerates you all, actually. We've gone through enough footage. The guy we're looking for is shorter than you, Dwayne."

"He's in better shape, too," Detective Wu added, pausing to rub his beak. "You ought to hit the gym, son." Dwayne brought his hands together and cracked all ten knuckles, imagining that each was a vertebra in the detective's back. Couldn't everybody lose some weight? That gave him an idea for a comeback.

"You're not so skinny yourself, pal," Dwayne said to Detective Wu.

Frankie quickly stepped between the two men and asked Detective Kao, "Can you please tell us exactly what happened to Captain Huang? The media is giving mixed messages." The polite-again detective met eyes briefly with his partner before speaking.

"Around midnight, Captain Huang was leaving a bar near Chiang Kai-shek Memorial Hall. Actually, that was the second bar he'd been to that night. The first was BaBa Bar, where he had a verbal confrontation with Nancy's mother, Siu-lien, and other unruly patrons.

"Judging from the way he was walking on the camera footage, before he was attacked, Captain Huang was quite drunk. The captain turned to go down a small alley that seemed to be a shortcut to the MRT station. Then a dark male form dropped on top of him. Captain Huang was taken by surprise and had no chance to defend himself. After suffering blows to his head, the captain fell to the ground, and was choked to death. The attacker ran away."

"It looked like he kinda *danced* away," said Detective Wu. "There seemed to be a bit of glee in his step, like how a super-villain might move."

Frankie looked up and lazily stretched his arms. "You didn't get a good look at the attacker's face, did you?" he asked the night sky.

"No," said Detective Kao.

"What makes you say that?" Detective Wu asked Frankie.

"Well, you guys are here," Frankie said languidly. "I think you wanted to size us all up, considering that Jing-nan was one of the last people to see the captain alive. I also think that nobody at the bar gave you anything useful.

"Lastly, it's quite embarrassing for the department that a high-level cop drank himself into a stupor, and once the foot-age hits the news, as it inevitably will, everyone in the Taipei City Police Department will lose face."

With all eyes on him, Frankie paused to stretch all four limbs, one at a time.

"Oh, I should add that this was no random attack," Frankie continued. "It had to be someone Captain Huang had offended deeply at some point in his colored career. Maybe someone he had arrested, or someone else who otherwise felt aggrieved by his actions . . . or inaction. You guys are here now because it's probably impossible to narrow that number below 1,000. Anyway, if you look carefully through his files, you'll probably find a lot of people who shouldn't have been pinched to begin with. If prosecutors get wind of that, there could be a string of lawsuits and firings."

No one said anything. The detectives looked at the ground.

Jing-nan remained focused on sending telepathic messages to curious bystanders within earshot to buy food. Dwayne was thinking about how he would definitely make it to the gym tomorrow.

"Well, gentlemen," Frankie said to the detectives, "I think that this particular branch of the investigation has ended, as well."

Detective Wu walked away.

"Good night," said Detective Kao before leaving. After the detectives left, five young tourists approached Jing-nan.

"Those guys were cops, right?" one woman asked in stiff Mandarin, indicating it was learned in college.

"I think I'm allowed to say that they were," said Jing-nan, as he gave her a conspiratorial look.

"What happened?"

"I'm not supposed to say." Jing-nan let his words hang for a beat. "You're not Americans, are you?" he asked in English. The woman was taken aback by how articulate Jing-nan's English was.

"No, we're Canadian," she said.

"Oh, I love Canadians!" said Jing-nan. "You're so much cooler than people from the States!"

Man, Jing-nan would do anything to make a sale, Dwayne thought, and not for the first time. Unknown Pleasures was doing well because Jing-nan was so good at his job. Look at the fish he was reeling in right now. They were buying so much, they'd have to sit down to eat. Dwayne rolled his shoulders and prepared to cook some more skewers. He was the only one who knew how to do it right. That was his job, after all.

Frankie stood by the sink, lifting another batch of meats out from their marinade. Dwayne adjusted the flame on the main broiler unit and explored his feelings of repulsion at what Jing-nan did, glad-handing strangers with chumminess squeezed from a bottle. Dwayne wouldn't do that for any amount of money. He'd rather help Frankie peel apart animal tissue. It was a slimy task, but at least he didn't have to pretend to be friendly.

Dwayne lifted the skewers on the grill and turned them over—never rolling them—in a gentle and caring motion that belied his size and demeanor. He watched the flames lick hungrily between the sizzling meat chunks, and he thought about death, Captain Huang's in particular. Dwayne had never liked the captain much, but he certainly didn't want the guy dead. Who did he want dead? Dwayne rubbed his nose with the back of his right wrist. He searched his memory and heart, and came to the conclusion that while there certainly was a longish list of people he disliked, Dwayne didn't want any of them to die. He was surprised to find that he felt this way, and a little abashed. Dwayne glanced back to see if Frankie had noticed his lapse in manhood.

Frankie worked his fingers into a marinated beef shank and felt the sinews dissolve and yield like warm butter. He encountered no strings or knots, which meant that the lime juice had done its job over the past two days. Frankie separated the beef into thinner strips. Without moving his head he registered that Dwayne had shot him a guilty look. Frankie didn't give it a second thought. He had learned long ago that as much as he'd like to, he couldn't control the way people felt. Sure, Frankie would do what he could to comfort the afflicted, especially if they were acting in a way that was publicly mortifying, but for the most part he preferred to let people feel what they felt. It was a gift, after all, to be honest with oneself, and nothing was more truthful than emotions.

Frankie thought about Captain Huang's passing. He hadn't liked the man very much, but the veteran also had a measure of empathy for the cop. Frankie saw in him the damaged bravado from a lack of job advancement. That frustration was expressed in the way Captain Huang had bossed around Jingnan and other stall operators at the night market.

Many Taiwanese say they aren't religious, but that only means they don't adhere to any one dogma and instead have fluid ideas about divinity and what lies in the Great Beyond. Frankie removed his gloves and made sure to scrub away any residue of meat or blood on his arms above the wrists before doing what most Taiwanese did when someone they marginally knew passed away. He bowed his head slightly and quietly mouthed a Buddhist prayer for all beings to have happiness, and to be free from sorrow. The wind shifted and a small column of smoke from the main grill snaked by his face and twisted up into the night sky.

CHAPTER 17

Nancy woke with a start and immediately began rubbing her sore neck. She had dreamed about lifting her head to watch something floating in the sky, and the strain must have carried over in real life.

She was scared that something up there was going to fall, but she couldn't remember anything else.

If Jing-nan were with her, he would be massaging her neck. But she had wanted to spend another night at her mom's. It was the right thing to do, but tonight, she'd go back to Jing-nan's place. If her neck still hurt later, she'd ask him to put a Salonpas patch on it.

She did miss Jing-nan. Had he been in her dream? He must've been. He always was, even though Nancy wasn't always happy about it. She'd had to save him a number of times, and he never seemed grateful. Even though it was just a dream, it did reflect what she was feeling in real life, right?

She sat up on the couch and realized that she had worked her body up until her head was on a cushioned armrest. So that was the source of pain. Standing up made it worse, but Nancy had to get up. Her stomach was growling.

She peeked into the bedroom. Her mother continued to sleep on her side of the bed. Was Siu-lien living a lonely life? Her mother certainly seemed to have a lot of fun when she was younger, chasing her dream. Standing in the doorway, Nancy felt that old dread again, wondering if her mother was going to be mad or not when she woke up. It was the sort of fear that a kid felt when she thought something bad was her doing, her fault.

Nancy knocked lightly on the doorframe. "Mom, I'm going to make us some breakfast now," she declared. "It's almost nine o'clock." Her mother stirred.

"Thank you," Siu-lien managed to moan.

Nancy went to the kitchen. The refrigerator was empty apart from jars of sauces that were stuck in place on the shelves. She found a packet of instant breakfast grains in one of the cabinets. The hot-water dispenser on the counter hadn't been kept filled, so Nancy put a small pot of water on the stove and waited. There had to be something else to eat. Her mother could eat stale boiled grains, but Nancy needed something more substantial. She turned off the heat and yelled, "Mom, I'm going out to grab something!"

JING-NAN FELT HIS COMPETITIVE streak kick in as he strolled through the day market. Other night-market proprietors were on the prowl for fresh ingredients, too. They would circle back and sort through the same vegetables that Jing-nan had selected from.

The people who operated stands at the day market were just as savvy as their nocturnal counterparts. Some regularly chopped up samples of their herbs to keep the fresh scents in the air, in hopes of luring in buyers. As Jing-nan walked on, he took inventory of the day's offerings based on what he was smelling. Cilantro, chives, something like a leek, spring onions, and was that cinnamon?

He stopped at a stand where a man in his 60s wearing a farmer's hat to shade his eyes was grating cinnamon bark into jars.

"That smells incredible," said Jing-nan.

The man glanced at him, then lowered his head until the brim of his hat hid his face. "This is probably the first time you've smelled real cinnamon," he said coolly. "This isn't that cassia crap from China. I only sell the real deal from Sri Lanka."

So the bargaining had already begun. Sri Lanka was pretty far away, and there would have to be a handling premium. Jing-nan cursed himself for showing interest too early.

In the end, he paid only a little more than what he thought was fair. The man had given him tips on using the cinnamon in tea, but he winced when Jing-nan said he planned to use it to dust some chicken skewers. Well, don't knock it until you try it, Jing-nan thought.

What else went with cinnamon? Something sweet, something spicy, something full of carbs, too. Jing-nan picked up two jars of honey from a woman who said she played classical music to the bees to make them happy, and a bag of dried hot chilies from a man who tried to push a spicy sauce, as well.

Jing-nan also loaded up on the usual suspects—chives, onions, and garlic. He recalled eating at a Buddhist temple for some ceremony when he was young. Jing-nan knew that the food would be vegetarian, but he was surprised by how bland it tasted. He still remembered asking one of the monks for some garlic sauce and the big man let out a jolly laugh.

"If there was any of that here, there could be trouble," was all he could say. Jing-nan later read online that Buddhists believed that strong herbs aroused sexual desire. Eating onion rings and garlic noodles in the temple would drive the devout to forget their celibacy vows in a frenzy of sexual abandon. You'd think bad breath would be a turnoff.

The place would really go wild if someone brought in coffee and donuts.

Ah, donuts! That could be the carb! Grilled donut pieces on a skewer would absorb the cinnamon taste and help offset the mouthfeel of the chicken. He'd have to watch it, though. If the chicken was dry, the donut would only make the situation worse. Well, Dwayne never ruined chicken, or anything else.

He walked into a Mister Donut near the east exit of the day market and found Nancy staring at a swatch of mochi donuts, paralyzed by hunger.

"Hey, how are you?" he asked her.

"Oh, Jing-nan, you're doing your morning shopping," she said.

"I came here to get ingredients for a creation." He looked around the donut store, and decided to remain cagey in public. You never knew who was listening. "I'm going to try a little something."

"I'm here to pick up breakfast," said Nancy. "My mother doesn't have anything in her kitchen."

"She lives around here?"

"Yes, just a few blocks away."

"Nancy, don't eat this crap. I'm going to get a decent loaf of bread from a bakery, we'll pick up some eggs at the 7-Eleven, and I'll make you guys French toast."

"Really?" Nancy exclaimed.

"Yeah, I've even got some great cinnamon for it."

On the way out, Jing-nan noticed the cashier's sour look. "Oh, I didn't mean to call your donuts 'crap.' I just meant that your coffee is so good that everything else pales in comparison."

The man wasn't buying it. Jing-nan decided to pick up donuts later, from another location.

NANCY WALKED INTO SIU-LIEN'S apartment and held the door for Jing-nan.

"I'm back, Mom," Nancy called out.

"You were right," said her mother. "That stale cereal is inedible . . ." Siu-lien stopped speaking when she beheld Jing-nan, who was awkwardly looking for room on the floor for his shopping bags while stepping out of his shoes.

He regarded Siu-lien in her threadbare robe that bore images of Betty Boop and he bowed slightly.

"You have a lot of nerve to let him in here," she said to Nancy while glaring at Jing-nan. "This man could be a murderer."

"He's not and you know it," said Nancy. "Anyway, he's here to make us breakfast, if you'll let him use the kitchen."

"Fine! Go use the kitchen! I'll be in the bedroom!" Siu-lien's robe swished like a startled fish's fins as she left. They heard a door slam.

"Uh," said Jing-nan. "Did I miss something here?"

Nancy shook her head. "An old cop friend came by BaBa Bar last night, and he was saying not-so-nice things about you."

"Um, this wouldn't be a Detective Kao or Wu, would it?"

"How did you know? Detective Wu was the guy. He's helped out my mom in the past, and she trusts him." Nancy began to unpack Jing-nan's bags. "Well, she trusts him more than you because they have a long history. Also, I think Boxer's death is really hitting her now."

Detective Wu, eh? Jing-nan hadn't forgotten the irate-looking, beak-nosed detective. There's a saying that a man shouldn't fall in love with a woman who has a nose like a bird's beak, because she'll henpeck him all the time. There should be a saying about men with hawk beaks who talk shit about you.

Jing-nan gestured to the closed bedroom door. "Now I'll have to cook without an audience," he said.

"I'll watch you," Nancy offered. Jing-nan felt inspired.

"You won't just watch. We're going to cook together for a change. Crack those eggs into a bowl and whisk them."

"I don't think they had a whisk."

"What do you mean 'they'?"

Had he forgotten already? "My mom and Boxer. They lived here together." Jing-nan shrunk slightly.

"Oh, right," he said.

"I'll use a fork instead on the eggs."

Jing-nan raised his eyes to the ceiling. "A fork? You're completely ruining my French toast already!"

Nancy slapped his arm. "You're joking around too much. You can be funny when you're with your boys, but this is my mother's house."

Jing-nan nodded silently. The bedroom door flew open. Siu-lien was carrying some pieces of cloth.

"Here," she said to Nancy. "Put on these burlap armbands. Use these safety pins. Detective Wu reminded me that we're a household in mourning."

"Where did you get these from, Mom?"

"The last funeral I went to. One of Boxer's friends." She glanced at Jing-nan and the ingredients he had laid out. "We shouldn't even be eating French toast. We should be on a vegetarian diet, not cracking eggs and ending more lives!"

"They weren't going to hatch, anyway," said Jing-nan.

"How can we eat vegetarian if you don't have any vegetables, Mom?" Siu-lien stomped her foot.

"Just making excuses! You two do whatever you want!"
She flew back to the bedroom.

"Should I go?" Jing-nan asked Nancy.

"Just make breakfast, Jing-nan. I'll look in on her." They
embraced and comforted each other for the first time in what
felt like forever.

SIU-LIEN WAS LYING FACEDOWN on the mattress, her
legs hanging stiffly over the edge. Nancy entered and closed
the door behind her.

"Mom, you seem especially upset. It's not fair to be mad at
Jing-nan because of something Detective Wu said."

"I saw Boxer," Siu-lien said into the sheets. "He came to
visit me in my dream." Nancy stood by her mother, not sure
if she should touch her.

"Oh," said Nancy. What else could she say? "What happened in your dream?" Siu-lien rolled over, and without
lifting her head regarded Nancy from the corners of her eyes.

"He told me that he was sorry for all the pain he ever
caused me, including stealing the lottery ticket. Also, seeing
Jing-nan might have been too big a shock. Boxer said that he
felt it when we prayed to Guanyin and Dizang last night. He
wants us to do more mourning for him to ease his suffering."

"Do you want to go to a temple today, Mom?"

Siu-lien sighed. "I don't have time because I have to pay
the goddamned rent." She propped herself up. "I have to
work to make money."

"But that's not until later."

"Well, I want to at least sleep some more first." She eased
back down onto the mattress and threw her right forearm
over her eyes. Nancy moved to leave, and Siu-lien called out
to her. "Boxer told me who killed him."

"Who was it?"

"He said it was his picture, the one we found in his stuff."

"His childhood picture?"

"Yes."

"A childhood friend killed him?"

"I don't know what he meant." Siu-lien said. "He never spoke clearly."

Someone knocked on the bedroom door.

"Hey," Jing-nan said from the other side. "Sorry to bother you, but we have guests." Nancy opened the door. Her boyfriend looked worried. "It's the police, yet again," he whispered. "They have some questions."

BY THE TIME SIU-LIEN washed up, put on some makeup, threw on another robe—a thick, white cotton one—and emerged from the bedroom, she found Jing-nan, Nancy, and two police officers eating breakfast at the dining table.

"Siu-lien," said Jing-nan as he stood up, "we saved some French toast for you."

"I don't want any," she snapped. The officers looked away from her. Siu-lien recognized them. They sometimes passed through the bar, scanning the crowd and never ordering drinks. The woman in her 40s would come up to the bar and say hello once in a while. The other one, a man in his 30s with a pockmarked face, was like a ghost, suddenly vanishing into the crowd and reappearing seconds later several feet away.

They weren't detectives, only beat cops, and each regarded Siu-lien with a cautious smile. The woman officer spoke.

"We were just telling Jing-nan that it was so coincidental that the three of you are connected with two recent murders in the city." She paused to wipe her mouth with a napkin. "Not that you're suspects, but we, Officer Li and I, wanted to talk to you because there's a chance that the murder suspect is known to the three of you."

"We now think that it's one suspect for both cases," said Officer Li. A scrap of French toast was stuck in the front teeth of his lower jaw. "Officer Song and I see some similarities."

"What similarities?" Siu-lien snapped.

"We haven't disclosed to the public," said Officer Li.

"We can tell you one thing," said Officer Song. "The murderer is an incredibly strong man who seems to know the streets well. Siu-lien, are there people that the three of you know who might fit that description?"

"My friends are not their friends!" Siu-lien said.

"I was thinking," noted Jing-nan, "that Captain Huang was a fairly well-known character. Boxer, as well, in his own way. Way more people than just us three knew both of them."

Officer Li put his hands together in a praying gesture, still holding a syrupy fork, and faced Nancy's mother.

"Oh, we'd be remiss if we didn't say that you had our sympathies, Siu-lien," he said. "Down at the police station, we always thought that Boxer was a charming person."

Siu-lien crossed her arms. "You people used to beat him up!" she spat.

Officer Song shook her head. "Boxer would fall down all the time and hurt himself," said the female officer. "He was usually drunk."

"He hasn't touched alcohol in years!" Siu-lien declared. The cops exchanged glances with raised eyebrows. "Okay, that's it," Siu-lien barked. "Time for you two pigs to go, now that you've sat around and eaten."

The two cops stood.

"I know Detective Wu!" Siu-lien warned them.

"He's a fine man," said Officer Song.

"I'm going to tell him you harassed me in my home!"

Officer Li said, "It was Detective Wu's idea for us to come

by and see you and Nancy together. We're glad Jing-nan was here, too, because that saved us a trip."

"Thank you very much for your hospitality," said Officer Song.

"I should charge you for eating my food," said Siu-lien.

"Actually, it was my food," ventured Jing-nan.

"Well, you cooked it in my house with my gas and my pans, and used my utensils and my plates, so all this is my food!"

Jing-nan was about to counter her statement when a sharp look from Nancy stopped him cold. He coughed loudly instead.

The officers moved to the door and slipped on their shoes. Siu-lien watched them with so much hate that her glowing eyes could guide ships at sea. Officers Li and Song gave brief nods and left.

"Some investigation!" declared Siu-lien. "They only wanted to solve the Case of the Free Breakfast!"

Jing-nan stood up, sure that he had overstayed his welcome as well. Siu-lien slid into a chair at the dining table and tilted her chin up at him.

"And you, Jing-nan," said Siu-lien. "I'm sure you have some business to attend to."

"I do, I do," he said. Jing-nan scrambled to the kitchen and removed his vegetables from the refrigerator. He looked longingly at the carton of eggs. He had some idea that he was going to do something with the other half, but not now. Siu-lien needed them more than he did.

"Don't touch anything that doesn't belong to you," said Siu-lien as he gathered his things. Jing-nan understood that she was referring to Nancy in addition to her meager offerings. He couldn't restrain himself from making a sarcastic remark.

"Siu-lien, I wouldn't dream of taking your expired ketchup," he said.

"I'd squeeze it into the toilet before I let you take it," countered Siu-lien as she withdrew once more to the bedroom.

Jing-nan decided not to point out that he was only kidding.

"She had a dream," Nancy told him. "Boxer told her it was his childhood picture that killed him."

"A picture of Boxer as a kid? What did he look like?"

"Kinda tan and happy." Then she added, "Innocent."

"Maybe a picture can give you a paper cut, but . . . well, it's just a dream," said Jing-nan with a shrug. He had dreams, too. Dead people often had messages for him but he always forgot what they said right after he opened his eyes. But Jing-nan usually remembered the tastes of the dream meals that he shared with them. His parents, and his grandfather and grandmother, too. The five of them would sit at a big round table and eat out of a hot pot in the center. Jing-nan had dreamed about such meals on a regular basis, but the odd thing was that this scenario had never happened in real life. When they were all together, Jing-nan's family members were working and never ate at the same time, much less even faced each other. There was always more work to be done. The young Jing-nan had discovered solace in being busy, and no one had the time or need for family conversation as long as everyone had a job to focus on.

Maybe that's why he never wanted to listen to Nancy's suggestion that he cut back on his hours at Unknown Pleasures. It would be hard for Jing-nan to find another worker who was good and who would fit in to pick up the slack. It would be even more difficult for him to spend "quality time" with Nancy, as she put it. His relationship with her was really his first as an adult that wasn't tied in with work. When he was with Nancy, he felt the urge to tend to his social media platforms. That behavior wasn't good for them. He could see that now.

"Jing-nan, are you all right? Don't let what my mother said upset you."

"I'm not upset. Anyway, she's right, I do need to get ready for work." He pointed to Nancy's burlap armband. "Are you keeping that on? People will avoid you in the street if they see you're in mourning." She fingered the armband.

"I'm keeping it on because we're going to a temple today, to pray for Boxer. I think my mother would be really glad if you came, too." She exhaled. "I know she can be so hard to deal with, but it would really make things better between you and her."

"I just can't today, Nancy." Jing-nan looked into her eyes and knew that their relationship had matured. The carefree, fun times were no longer separated from the difficult parts of their individual lives.

He and Nancy had been together for almost a year now. Jing-nan had been wondering if he should do something to mark the anniversary; once so marked, the relationship's egg timer would be set. It was a countdown to either getting married or breaking up for good. He hoped it wasn't the latter, and as he took her hands in his, he knew she hoped the same.

He did love Nancy, and he believed they should be together for the rest of their lives. That didn't seem to be a long-term proposition at times, considering the things they'd gone through. Speaking of proposition, one day, he would have to get down on his knees and bow his head, and ask Nancy to marry him. And when you marry someone, you marry their parents, too.

"Nancy," said Jing-nan, "I will go to the temple with you and your mom. I can make the time. I just need to bring these groceries home." He glanced down at his Swervedriver T-shirt. "I'll have to change, too, of course."

Nancy looked relieved. "Can you be back here in an hour?" she asked. "We can get on a bus together."

"Yes. Are you sure I'm not going to make things worse if I come?"

"I'm sure she wants you to be with us. More people will make the prayers more powerful."

Conscious of Nancy's mother seething in the next room, they had an arms-length hug, and Jing-nan left.

Nancy was glad that Jing-nan would be going to the temple, even if he was just doing it for her sake. There seemed to be something formal in his manner, and she sensed that he was at least thinking of proposing. After all, their anniversary was approaching.

The bedroom door flew open.

"Is he gone?" asked Siu-lien.

"Yes," said Nancy. The news was met with a grunt of approval. "But he'll be back to go to the temple with us." Siu-lien nodded, and made her way to the dining table.

"His French toast, is it good?"

"It's the best. Wait, don't eat it cold, Mom. Let me heat it up for you." Nancy tried to grab the plate from her mother's hands, but Siu-lien turned and stuck out her elbows, putting up a defense that not even the People's Liberation Army could penetrate.

"This is fine," Siu-lien said. "It's already getting too warm to eat hot food."

CHAPTER 18

Jing-nan sat behind Siu-lien and Nancy. He had expected a charter bus. Nothing fancy, but something big. At least bigger than this. Instead they were crammed into a glorified van that seated about 20 in five paired rows of double bench seats. He had many childhood memories of riding in vehicles like this, going up mountain roads to Buddhist temples to say prayers for dead people he had met once or twice, in many cases only as an infant.

The entire van was filled with people silenced by their personal pain. No one visits a Buddhist temple when there's nothing wrong. It's said that people ask Daoist gods for less-than-altruistic favors, but they visit Buddhist temples after a calamity, and only seek comfort and a way forward. Older people in the van had lost their siblings and friends. Younger people had lost their parents.

There was no air-conditioning, and wind from the open windows didn't clear the air of the odor of nutritional-supplement breath.

Jing-nan's seatmate was a woman who may have been in her 70s or 80s. Her head was bent forward. Her left hand was pressed to her forehead. The other covered her right ear. She wore a burlap vest over her white blouse, clear signs she was serious about her mourning. The burlap spoke for itself, and white is the color of choice for the bereaved.

This is so depressing, thought Jing-nan. Everyone on this trip is praying for loved ones who either have died or are pretty much about to. When you've lost all hope, you find yourself riding to the top of a mountain to beseech the gods to somehow make it a little better.

Boxer's killer would probably never be found. The trashy magazines had already moved on from their obligatory consideration of Jing-nan as a suspect to pronounce that the killer was some random lowlife in the area. He actually agreed with that assessment. Boxer's hideout was not in a safe area, especially for someone buying and using drugs. Still, Siu-lien was going through the worst kind of hurt, and she was the type of person to lash out at those closest to her. He didn't take personally the abuse she had heaped on him at her apartment.

Jing-nan didn't believe in the spiritual realm, but he wasn't strident about it anymore. His mission for this trip was simple: pretend to pray for the sake of Boxer's spirit in order to make Siu-lien like him more and put Nancy at ease. Jing-nan wouldn't go through the motions of mourning for Captain Huang, though. Let other people bow down and spend money on that guy.

He felt something drop into his lap. It was a 25 NT coin. Another one followed. Then a 50 NT coin rolled in.

The beaded pocketbook slung over his seatmate's shoulder had a hole in it. Coins were rolling out. Jing-nan didn't want to wake her up. He could just hand them to her when the ride was over.

Then a foreign coin encased in a plastic holder bounced against his crotch. The coin seemed too heavy for its size. He realized the coin was made of gold, and he stared stupidly at the horned animal on the obverse. *Krugerrand*, he read. What country was that? His nervous fingers turned the coin over and nearly dropped it. South Africa. Mystery solved.

For three seconds, he thought about keeping the coin. Then he looked at the woman. She had probably been holding on to this coin for years, and maybe it represented her life savings.

The van angled upward as it started on a mountain path, and another Krugerrand tumbled out. How many did she have? How many had she already lost? Light dappled on the gold coins as Jing-nan held them in his palm. He closed his fingers over them, and leaned over to his seatmate.

"Excuse me," Jing-nan whispered to her. "I'm so sorry to bother you." The woman turned her head. She hadn't been sleeping. "I think you've dropped these." He held up the coins in his open palm. The bags under her eyes quivered. She looked at the coins, then brushed them aside and back into Jing-nan's lap. The woman grabbed Jing-nan's empty palm with two hands, and her open mouth formed a crooked trapezoid as she studied the lines.

Jing-nan was surprised but too polite to pull his hand back. The reading even hurt a little, as the woman flexed his fingers. She then dropped his hand and frowned at him.

"You need to see my priest," she told him with a seriousness usually reserved for the worst medical news.

"I do?" asked Jing-nan.

"Yes. You do."

"Do you see something wrong?"

She leaned over and he could see the remnants of breakfast in the corners of her mouth. "People around you are dying, aren't they?"

"People are dying all the time."

"They die after they see you!" she said in a chiding whisper. "Your bad luck rubs off on everybody but doesn't stick to you. I can tell by your smooth hands." Jing-nan pointedly collected the coins in his lap. He now considered keeping them as compensation for this undeserved pronouncement.

"If your reading is true, aren't you doomed?" he asked the woman. She gasped, then looked around the van. Not a seat was empty. She sniffed and managed to compose herself.

"That's all right," she said. "I have protections in place."

Jing-nan sighed. "In that case, please take your coins back. Maybe you should fix your purse, too. Anyway, I'm not going to curse you, I promise." He poured the coins into her hands. She weighed them in her palm.

"You know these are gold coins from South Africa," she said.

"I know that now."

"Why didn't you take them?"

Jing-nan had to smile. "Because they belong to you."

"Would you take the coins if I gave them to you?"

Jing-nan shrugged. "Well, I wouldn't leave them on the seat if you refused to take them."

"These coins didn't simply fall out of my purse. It was a test."

Jing-nan glanced at the roof of the van. Was he on some new hidden-camera television show?

"Please, just keep your coins," said Jing-nan. He turned away and took out his phone. Of all the seatmates, why . . .

"I wasn't joking about your palm, you know," said the woman.

"I'm sure you weren't."

"I've seen you on TV."

"I'll bet you have."

She pointed at his nose. "Nothing but trouble."

The conversation ended. A few minutes later, the road evened out, and the van pulled into the parking lot of a temple complex. The driver stopped the vehicle and cranked open the door. Indifferent from years of steeling himself to the pain borne by his passengers, the driver sprung up from his seat, bounced out of the vehicle, and stood a good distance away from those disembarking. By the time Jing-nan came out to the fresh air, it was already being polluted by the driver, who was near the end of his second cigarette.

Most of the passengers headed single file to the entrance of the complex.

"This way," said Siu-lien. She led Nancy and Jing-nan away to a side entrance. A monk wearing jeans under his robes was leaning on a door, propping it open. Siu-lien put her hands together and bowed, and he returned the gesture. She turned to Jing-nan and said, "Give him a tip."

Jing-nan fished out a NT$100 bill and handed it to the monk, who perfunctorily slipped the note into his right back pocket. Jing-nan and Nancy followed Siu-lien into the building. The monk remained outside and let the door swing back, but he shoved a folded map of the temple complex in front of the strike plate to block the latch from catching.

"Why did we come in this way?" Nancy asked Siu-lien.

"We want to avoid the line, and all the propaganda and donation boxes." Her raised eyebrow suggested that Nancy should be appreciative of the maneuver.

"It seems wrong to sneak into a Buddhist temple," said Jing-nan.

"Well, we didn't sneak in by ourselves, did we? A monk went out of his way to personally open the door for us. That makes it even more holy." Siu-lien waved a hand to indicate that she wouldn't entertain any more questions of this nature. "Let's go."

Nancy and Jing-nan tried to keep up. Siu-lien opened the door to what seemed to be a classroom, and class was in session. A woman was reading a book to a dozen seated children.

"Oh, pardon us," said Siu-lien as she backed up but left the door open. Nancy lowered her head and followed her mother down the hall. Jing-nan tried to slink away, too, but doubled back and courteously shut the classroom door.

Siu-lien opened another door, this time to an empty classroom, and walked to a back corner. She pushed aside a large cardboard box filled with foam cushions. A door that had been behind the box could now fully swing open.

"I don't think we should . . ." Nancy said.

"It's fine," said Siu-lien. She twisted the knob and pulled. The door made a sound like cracking wood as it opened. "See?" Nancy shielded her face as she followed Siu-lien through, in case people were watching to see who was coming through the door. Jing-nan made a feeble attempt to pull the box back into place before following the two women.

Jing-nan found himself standing in a large hall. He could hear voices echoing from the line of visitors standing between the velvet ropes that guided people to a Guanyin bodhisattva statue that stood probably a good 30 feet tall. Siu-lien and Nancy were already fast-walking toward the figure, ready to cut in near the front of the line. They had to walk against a path that was an exit for people who had already appealed to the bodhisattva.

Jing-nan followed his girlfriend and her mother. He noticed that they had the same nervous gait, an alternating stutter step. The crowd's grumbling rose in volume as the three tactlessly zoomed ahead, sometimes dodging people merely trying to get out.

As Siu-lien advanced, she saw open hostility in the eyes

of those more patient. It made her screw up her face. She already faced the worst society had to offer at the bar. Did a bunch of mourners think they had any edge on her?

Siu-lien hunched her shoulders and put out her elbows to make herself look more menacing. Hadn't she spent more time in this temple than nearly anyone who wasn't a monk? Hadn't she already come here more than any person should in a single incarnation? Hadn't she already suffered more than one lifetime on this earth could bear?

Siu-lien singled out a man who looked particularly soft, timid enough to leave enough space in front of him for her to step in. "Please excuse us," she said to his shoes. Siu-lien puffed out her chest and stretched out her arms to make more room until Nancy and Jing-nan entered the line.

"Thank you, Siu-lien," Jing-nan whispered. She nodded.

He wasn't so bad, after all, this boy. Jing-nan had come along on this trip to offer prayers to the spirit of someone he didn't really know. Of course, he was just doing it for Nancy, but this deed boded well for their relationship. Siu-lien felt an ache in her side. How well had she known Boxer? She knew that he battled his demons, and was usually able to keep himself together. He'd never really been able to shake off the alcohol, although he assured her that he was long finished with the drugs and the other women. Boxer had sometimes gone off and come back blotto, but she'd never found evidence of a serious slipup. She knew he wasn't smart or careful enough to make himself presentable if he'd spent time testing some other girl's mattress.

Well, Boxer's lack of money until very recently was probably more of a deterrent to going astray than his moral values ever were. Look what happened on his last night. Drink. Drugs. At least one girl. In Siu-lien's dream, Boxer told her the picture had killed him, but did he apologize for taking her money, and for dying in a way that embarrassed her? No. He continued to disappoint from the afterlife!

Apart from in dreams, though, Boxer wouldn't be annoying her or anybody else ever again. Not if she prayed for his spirit. Siu-lien relaxed her arms. She felt hollow in the region of her heart where she used to hold hard feelings for him. The poignancy of his absence worked its way through her circulatory system.

Soon it was their turn to stand before the bodhisattva and bow. The three of them lit incense and dipped three times. As they planted the joss sticks in a censer, the man that Siu-lien had rudely cut in front of entered their space before they had fully stepped away. Siu-lien, Nancy, and Jing-nan's intrusion had detained the man by 30 seconds at most, but maybe Mr. Timid was learning to be more assertive. And the misdeed mattered enough for a large monk to appear from nowhere to confront Siu-lien, Nancy, and Jing-nan at the exit ropes.

"Hello brother and sisters," he said in a pleasant growl. "I would be honored to have you three as guests in my office." Nancy noticed that although he was smiling, his two angry eyebrows seemed to point directly at Siu-lien. The monk's arms, outspread in feigned generosity, blocked any deviation from where he wanted them to go. The sleeves of his robe hung loosely, leaving plenty of room for what assuredly were large triceps and biceps.

THERE WAS NO FURNITURE in Hsing Sun's office. The four of them sat on a rug and faced each other. Light from the window shone behind the monk's head, and Siu-lien, Nancy, and Jing-nan had to squint when they looked at Hsing Sun's face, which was surrounded by a blinding halo.

"You've taken a lot of shortcuts today, haven't you?" the monk asked a small space on the rug between Siu-lien and

Jing-nan. Satisfied with the lack of a reply, Hsing Sun closed his eyes and continued. "You entered our space through a side door, disrupted a classroom filled with young children, broke through a sealed door in another classroom, and then cut in line ahead of devout followers in order to bow before a bodhisattva that you supposedly believe in." The words hung in the air and the room was heavy with spoken truths.

"Our case is rather urgent," said Siu-lien. "We needed to get in and out as quickly as possible. Jing-nan here operates a famous night-market stand and he's on a schedule."

Hsing Sun opened his eyes slightly. Jing-nan dipped his head at the monk and if the latter noticed, he made no sign of it.

"What good is it," said the monk, "to do things as quickly as possible? The less effort we put into an act, the less meaning it has." He was seated in lotus position and rubbed his knees. "I know there are many material annoyances involved with visiting our temple. The lines can be long. You may feel the wait is unbearable when you're already in a distressed state. And yet, if you try to avoid suffering, are you truly paying tribute to the person you love or are you simply going through the motions of mourning while avoiding real pain?"

Nancy tensed up. She didn't need to hear condescending shit from men, including her university professors, cops, or even monks.

"Did you know that her partner was murdered?" Nancy asked pointedly. Hsing Sun shook his face hard and his features changed. He looked a decade younger, and all his features were now marked with complete surprise and wonder.

"You were married to the drug guy?" he asked. "I know the cop wasn't married."

Siu-lien bristled. "I wasn't married to him, and he wasn't a 'drug guy,'" she said. "Boxer was a man. He wasn't a perfect man, and sometimes he was a terrible man, but not everyone can be a monk, can they?"

"Yes, that's true," said Hsing Sun, who had now reverted to his humble days as a disciple. The suggestion that he had been egotistical had cowed him. "A tragedy, indeed, a national tragedy, but existence is suffering."

"The circumstances of his death are out on display for everyone to see," said Siu-lien. "Many people have their theories of how he died, but I prefer to remember how he lived. Parts of it, anyway."

"Yes, yes," said the monk.

"We could even say that money was his downfall." Siu-lien raised her hand, as if about to take an oath before testifying in court. "You know the winning lottery ticket belonged to me? After Boxer cashed it, he saw that it was too much money to let go of, even if it didn't belong to him."

"Yes, yes," said the monk.

"Yes, yes," said Jing-nan softly into his armpit. Nancy elbowed him for mocking Hsing Sun. Siu-lien rose to her feet and straightened her back.

"Now that we're done paying tribute to Boxer, we'd like to leave so that Jing-nan can get back to his business, Unknown Pleasures."

The monk smiled broadly. "Of course I know that business," he said as he turned to Jing-nan. "You're the young man who used a big pot to block bullets from a gun."

"That's me," said Jing-nan, his voice inflected with false modesty. He had heard the story told so many times by others, he no longer corrected details that were wrong. He expected the monk to mention him in connection with Boxer's death, and was relieved when none came.

Jing-nan and Nancy stood. "We're sorry we caused so much trouble here," he said.

"Yes, yes," said Hsing Sun, who remained sitting. "Of course, there is the matter of doing penance for your trespasses. You've all caused much distress today for others and for your own karma." He turned to look at Siu-lien directly before continuing. "It would be difficult for me to see how one could act this way and remain a true follower in our faith." Siu-lien bowed her head slightly.

"What do you want, money? How much?"

The monk held up his hand. "No money. I need you to represent us. President Tsai has asked a number of faiths to follow the government's guidelines to make amends to Taiwan's Aborigines. This includes volunteering at the relevant agencies." Hsing Sun looked over the three of them, contemplating what they'd be good at.

"I get it," said Siu-lien. "It's an election year, so we have to pitch in for Tsai's 'third period of critical advances' for Aboriginal rights. What sort of goodies has she promised you to help her get reelected?" A vague smile appeared on the monk's face, but he said nothing.

Nancy quickly asked the monk, "What can we do, Hsing Sun?" The big monk stood up in three distinct stages, and opened a cabinet.

"I think the three of you should consider this." He handed them a sheet of paper with an address and a telephone number. "This is an assisted-living facility focused on serving Aboriginal people. They need volunteers to do things." Jingnan looked over Nancy's shoulder and shuddered slightly. The facility was named Brighter Days. The address was in Datong District, many parts of which were a bit run-down. He sure didn't want to go to Datong.

"What would we be expected to do?" asked Jing-nan. "Are we talking about sweeping floors and emptying bedpans?"

"Oh, it's not manual labor," said Hsing Sun. "You'll be

keeping people company. Talking to them, listening to their stories. I know you're very personable, so you'll be a natural at this."

Jing-nan was about to make excuses, but he saw there was no need. They should just say thank you, leave, and ditch this assignment like extra math homework.

"Thank you so much, Hsing Sun," he said. "For your generosity and wisdom."

"Thank you, Hsing Sun," said Nancy. The monk nodded at the two of them.

"Do we have to make a proper exit from the temple, or would you mind if we took a shortcut?" asked Siu-lien. "I know you think it's bad to take shortcuts in life, but, seriously, we're just looking to leave."

Hsing Sun raised his chin and pointed it at the door. "Listen for the music coming from the gift shop," he said. "That's the fastest way out."

CHAPTER 19

As Frankie and Dwayne approached Unknown Pleasures, Jing-nan greeted them. "You needed a bodyguard today, Dwayne?" Frankie smiled and said nothing, but Dwayne spoke up.

"We were hanging out at the Hope Center," he said defiantly. "You know the place, all the nonprofits struggling against the Han Chinese Man."

"Actually, Jing-nan," said Frankie, "it's a little odd seeing you here this early."

"This certainly is a change," said Dwayne. "Did you come early to tell us that we've been replaced? Frankie, can you believe this guy? He didn't even have the decency to call us at home to tell us not to come in."

Jing-nan kept his face neutral. "I went to a Buddhist temple today," he said. That killed Dwayne's jokey demeanor right away. Such a journey, generally to an out-of-the-way location, meant that there was something serious to deal with, such as the death of a loved one, or a loved one near death.

Both Dwayne and Frankie waited for Jing-nan to continue, wary of asking the wrong question.

"Well, it was for Boxer," said Jing-nan. "We went to say prayers for his soul." Relieved that there wasn't any new bad news, both Dwayne and Frankie nodded solemnly. "Dwayne, I want to ask you something, ah, related to Aborigines."

Dwayne crossed his arms. In his experience, this couldn't be good. "What?"

Jing-nan put his hands in his pockets and tilted his head. "Do you know anything about assisted-living centers for the Indigenous?"

Frankie raised an eyebrow but said nothing.

"I know they exist," said Dwayne. "Why?"

"Well, I'm going to be volunteering at one," said Jing-nan. He had planned on tossing the address of the Brighter Days facility, but he couldn't do it. It was a miracle. Or maybe just deep-seated guilt that he'd never volunteered for anything that wasn't self-serving.

"Dwayne," continued Jing-nan, "I wanted to know what sort of dress is acceptable. You know, if short-sleeved shirts are disrespectful, or if hats are frowned upon. Things like that."

"You know what's disrespectful?" Dwayne asked in a challenging tone. "You Han Chinese stealing our land, digging up the graves of our ancestors, and destroying our language and culture! That's disrespectful. All of you people should be giving up money and time to help Aboriginal people. You majorly owe us!"

Jing-nan shrugged. "As a small-business owner, I employ a workforce that is half Aboriginal. Who else can say that?"

Dwayne let out a guttural laugh because he couldn't think of a good answer.

"Where are you going, Jing-nan?" asked Frankie.

"There's this Aborigine-focused facility called Brighter Days," said Jing-nan. He showed Frankie an emailed receipt for his volunteering reservation with the address.

Low-key as ever, Frankie casually said, "I happen to know that place."

"Get outta here!" said Dwayne.

Frankie lit up a cigarette. He blew out some smoke before adding, "I've been looking into facilities. For a friend."

"Wow, Frankie, you get around, don't you?" said Jing-nan.

Frankie walked to his station. "I get around because he can't get around," he said. "An old buddy from the orphan brigade." He turned on the hose to wash out organs and other cuts of meat. "It's a decent place," Frankie said to Jing-nan. "They do a good job."

Jing-nan nodded. "I'm going there tomorrow with Nancy."

"It's good that you young people are doing something like this," said Frankie. "Well, I'm going to do some reconnaissance." He left to survey the competition as they were setting up.

"This is an overdue start for you, Jing-nan, that's for sure," said Dwayne. "Did a monk say you had a shitload of bad karma, or something?"

"No way. We're going in because we were so moved by what we felt at the temple." As he said it, Jing-nan couldn't help but squirm.

Dwayne's eyes narrowed. Jing-nan had never voiced interest in volunteering for any cause, although he had spoken kindly of some groups and gifted some percentages of sales to charity. Notably, Jing-nan had donated every fall to Taipei Pride. That was mostly for the publicity, Dwayne thought, but what was in it for Jing-nan to personally do volunteer work?

"This is for some tie-in with the Austronesian Cultural Festival, right?" asked Dwayne.

"Honestly, I'd forgotten it was even happening," said Jing-nan.

"What are you going to be doing? Like, giving sponge baths? Clipping toenails?"

Jing-nan rubbed his hands. "No, I'm actually going to be more like a companion. I'll be conversing and listening. Science has shown that loneliness kills at rates comparable with some terminal illnesses."

Dwayne thought about his life outside of work. Unlike Jing-nan and Frankie, he didn't have a partner. He wasn't in love with anybody. Maybe he had never been. Dwayne's last relationship ended when he was 22, about a decade ago. He dreamed sometimes about holding babies, cradling their heads with one hand and wrapping a muscled arm around their little bodies. Sometimes, upon waking up, he had the feeling that he was holding himself.

Imagine me being a daddy, he thought. The idea of fatherhood jolted Dwayne back to the task at hand, stoking a fire for the main grill. Dwayne left Jing-nan, wiped his hands on his shirt, and laughed uncomfortably at his thoughts. He lifted the cooking grates and dumped in wood charcoal bricks from a sack, stopping twice to toss in fruitwood twigs and sugarcane that had already been squeezed dry. Then he drizzled in about a pint of grease trapped from yesterday's cooking. He struck a match and paused a ceremonial two seconds before dropping it to start the fire.

Dwayne stood back and felt the warmth from the flames billow out. His face went slightly damp with perspiration, and he wiped his upper lip with the back of his right thumb. Dwayne poked the coals with a pair of long tongs, which he then used to close the cooking grates. He thought about the inmates he had met and sat with. They were locked up behind bars as the years burned away from their lives.

"Dwayne, have you never seen a fire before?"

Dwayne stepped back and looked at a bemused Jing-nan. "I'll light a fire under your ass," said Dwayne. He suddenly thought that a threat like that could land him in court and then jail. Especially in the wake of two murders. "Ah, just kidding! I would never hurt you for real." He smiled painfully.

Jing-nan was more unnerved by Dwayne's apology than the insult. Something must be up. Well, it was wrong for one man to ask another's personal business, so Jing-nan put his concerns aside.

In any case, there was a business to run, and everyone knew what had to be done. Even Frankie over there. Whoa, when did he get back? Jing-nan shook his head and did his part by getting into his salesman persona. He strutted out to the middle of the front path and looked both ways.

A few stalls down, toward the temple, he saw a family of four Americans. They had to be Americans. The father was wearing a fanny pack, and he kept a hand on it as if everyone in Taiwan was a pickpocket. This should be easy.

"Hey," Jing-nan yelled at him. "I've got some really awesome skewers here for you to try!" The man was relieved to hear English and familiar words. He shepherded his family and brought them to Unknown Pleasures.

"I can totally get into skewers," said the father. "What kind do you have?" He and his wife were in their late 40s, and the boy and girl were almost teens. This was probably their first time in Asia, Jing-nan surmised. They had probably just landed, and hadn't eaten or bought anything yet, judging by their empty hands and jetlagged, lethargic demeanors. If you had made it through the five alleys of the Shilin Night Market to get to Unknown Pleasures without buying anything, you were cautious but also curious.

Better not confuse them with too many choices.

"I've got chicken and beef," said Jing-nan as he swept his hands to the mirror that displayed his wares. "Of course, vegetable skewers, too. But if you're feeling really adventurous"—at this point he dropped his voice to a stage whisper—"I also have spicy cinnamon donut skewers."

"These two are vegans," the mother said of her children, shaking her head with a mix of helplessness and admiration.

"The grilled tofu skewer is one of our specialties," Jing-nan declared.

"We'll take two of them," said the father. Jing-nan jumped back behind the counter. "You mentioned the donut skewer. I'll have that."

"Me, too," said the wife.

"You've got it!" Jing-nan moved to the smaller grill and squirted a shot of oil into it. Flames shot up and the kids gasped. He had them.

AT NINE THE NEXT morning, Jing-nan and Nancy boarded a public bus. "This will be something new for us," he said.

"I never thought we'd be doing something like this together," said Nancy.

"Best of all, it's in Datong." He rolled his eyes.

"Don't make fun of the district! What if you lived there?"

"Let's not even consider that!"

Nancy smiled. "My mother was so happy you came with us yesterday. She said more prayers were needed because the police will probably never solve Boxer's murder, and definitely not before Captain Huang's."

"I think she's right. The captain's murder will definitely be the priority case. But I'm glad I was there for your mom, and I completely understand that she doesn't feel like coming today. I believe in comforting the living, as you know."

"Well, we were a pain in the ass, too. Let's not forget why we're here! We were in the principal monk's office."

"First time for me," said Jing-nan. "You know, I was a really good student when I was a kid."

"No way."

About 45 minutes later they arrived at Brighter Days. Like any commercial building in Taipei dating from the 1980s, it didn't resemble any of the surrounding structures, and yet it was also nondescript.

It was drizzling and the poured concrete of the exterior had taken on the same gray color of the sky.

Jing-nan yanked open the building's front door, which required more effort than he had expected.

"This place must be underfunded," he said as Nancy walked in first.

"I'll bet the volunteers do everything," she said.

A woman was seated at a lobby desk that may have been cast off from a high school administrator's office. She herself looked like a principal at one of the hooligan-reform schools. *One wrong step*, her watchful eyes seemed to say, *and you'll taste my belt.*

She stood up and came out from behind the desk as Jing-nan and Nancy approached. The woman was tall, about five foot five, and carried herself like she was being graded on posture. Maybe she was in her late 30s.

"I'm Captain Tang," she said, folding her arms across her chest. "Air Force. Retired." Nancy made a small wave with her right hand.

"I'm Nancy."

"I know," said the captain. "I read the registrations of all the volunteers."

"That must be a lot of work," said Jing-nan.

"I wish it were," said Captain Tang, her eyes crinkling. She allowed herself an unguarded smile. "You're Jing-nan. I've enjoyed what I've read about you, fighting off a gang with a metal pot."

"That's not quite what happened," said Jing-nan.

"It is a better story, though," said Nancy.

"And about the back-to-back murders . . ."

"I had nothing to do with that," said Jing-nan quickly.

"I know you didn't," said Captain Tang. "The real story doesn't come out for a year, if ever." Jing-nan nodded. "You, Nancy," said the captain. "I've read some of the studies that you did at Taida, and I wish I had your mind because I couldn't understand any of it."

Nancy lowered her head in modesty. "It's very simple stuff," she said.

"She knows more about robobiotics than her advisor," said Jing-nan. "Or is it biorobotics?"

Nancy smiled even though she never liked Jing-nan to talk about her studies. He never seemed to be able to describe what she did. Heck, he couldn't even remember the right name. Yet he listened to all her complaints about the department's politics and awful advisors, and always voiced support for her. One time he cracked her up by putting on a fake *Godfather* voice and saying, "Your enemies have become my enemies, and they will fear you."

The captain returned to her seat behind the desk. "I'm sure you've read a little about our home, but we're maintained by the Council of Indigenous Peoples and the armed forces. You'd think it was good thing, having more than one group supporting you. Sometimes, though, the two of them play off each other and blame the other agency for not living up to their obligations." She gave Jing-nan a meaningful look. "So quite often we are underfunded."

He cleared his throat and looked down, embarrassed that the captain had heard his remarks as they entered. Nancy cut in.

"You'll have to forgive Jing-nan's remarks. He has the mentality of a night-market barker. He says what's on his mind without really thinking." She clasped her hands. "He really is the kindest person I know, though."

The captain nodded absently. "Most of our residents have eaten breakfast already, so I think they're amenable to having visitors and some conversation. Nancy, I'm going to ask you to speak with two residents on the fifth floor. Jing-nan, I'd like you to speak with two lovely men on the third floor."

The printer on the desk whined and spun out two pages. The captain handed one to Nancy and the other to Jing-nan.

"These are the names and room numbers of your new friends," said the captain. "Even if offered, please don't smoke or drink alcohol with the residents. Please don't discuss politics, it could lead to something really unpleasant. And, listen, if you ever feel uncomfortable, or if you feel like you need to leave, please come down here, immediately."

Jing-nan wove his fingers together. "Have there been any unfortunate incidents?" he asked. Captain Tang exhaled slowly through her nostrils.

"We have had issues," she said. "For one thing, one volunteer claimed he saw a ghost." Jing-nan felt a chill run through his body. Nancy touched his hand, knowing that despite all his talk about being a rational person, he could still be spooked. They had once binge-watched spooky things uploaded from Taipei's network of security cameras, and he screamed more often and louder than she did.

For her, nothing topped that vacation video from the 1990s, the one that showed a mysterious little girl in red following a group of hikers. One of the hikers died days later, and supposedly his doomed face appears obscured in the video, but everything was a little blurry because the footage was shot long ago on Super 8 film.

"But there's no such thing as ghosts," said Nancy, more to Jing-nan than the captain.

"Of course," said Captain Tang.

"Yes," said Jing-nan.

THE FIRST PERSON JING-NAN visited was Private Tung, an 80-year-old man who seemed to be in tip-top shape. His hair was still mostly black and though it was on the thin side, there wasn't a bald spot anywhere.

Tung's face looked like a relatively smooth walnut with two sparkly eyes.

"So, I'm three times older than you," said Tung, as he came back from his small kitchenette with a can of Taiwan Beer for Jing-nan.

"It's a little early for me to drink," Jing-nan said warily. "And I was warned not to drink alcohol while visiting."

Private Tung waved an arm in disgust. "If you don't have a beer with me, then how the hell are you going to be able to sit through a visit? Hell, you'll be lucky enough if I don't die on you, ha ha!" The can of beer remained in front of Jing-nan's face, shaking slightly in the old man's grip.

"Thank you," said Jing-nan, taking the beer.

"Attaboy," said Private Tung. There were metallic wrenching sounds as the two men tore open their cans.

"So, how are you doing, Private Tung?" asked Jing-nan.

"How am I doing? I'm old, how the hell do you think I'm doing?" He laughed emphatically as Jing-nan chuckled. "Hey, what did you think about the election?"

Jing-nan froze. "I was also warned not to talk about politics."

"Because you have no opinion about anything? I'm tired of these neutered visits where I can't even have a real discussion! Now, tell me, are you DPP or KMT? Don't bullshit an old man!"

The DPP, the Democratic Progressive Party, is the

conventionally liberal party that leans toward an independent Taiwan. The KMT, the Kuomintang, is relatively conservative, and holds that Taiwan is a province of China. Beyond and between these two main political parties are a number of smaller groups with their own agendas.

"I'm a businessman," said Jing-nan. "I'm not an activist."

"So then you're KMT, aren't you? Don't you know how much better Taiwan's economy would be if we were formally a part of China?"

"Would you trust the Chinese government after what it did to Hong Kong?"

"Ah, listen," said Private Tung as he leaned forward with his elbows on his knees. "You know what, I trust the Chinese government more than the KMT or DPP. After all, the KMT and DPP have let us down so many times with broken promises over our land, our tribal rights, and our representation, we can't believe anything they say. They're the two ends of the same snake. I'm not sure which is what end, you know?"

Jing-nan nodded noncommittally. This first visit was a mix of amusement and restraint. Surely it wasn't time for Jing-nan to explore his own muddled thoughts about politics. He decided to hijack the conversation.

"Private Tung, do you like rock music by any chance?" he asked.

The private rubbed his chin thoughtfully. "I do like the Beatles. Do they count?"

NANCY CHECKED TO MAKE sure that the woman was still breathing. She was. Nancy carefully removed the digestive cookie from the plate still clutched in her hands.

The woman, the singularly named Lu, had fallen asleep midsentence, her head rolling forward and shoulders slumping, nearly sending her cookie sliding to the floor.

She looks so small, Nancy thought. Lu could pass for a student napping in middle school. Upon opening her door, Lu had apologized for taking too long to answer Nancy's knocks. Her medication made her sleepy and hungry, she said, a bad combination.

Nancy placed the cookie on the bare counter, which looked clean enough. Then she took a pillow from the bed and put it behind Lu's head. She tried to take away the plate but the woman wouldn't release it, even in her sleep.

Maybe Lu was dreaming she was holding on to a steering wheel. Nancy returned to her hard plastic seat opposite Lu's cushioned recliner.

Should she try to wake her up? If the medicine made her sleepy, then maybe she should sleep. Nancy hugged herself in indecision.

She looked around Lu's room. It was small, but adequate for Lu. A television was on the left nightstand, and Nancy could imagine her dozing off every night to some talk show. She didn't seem to have many belongings. A woven cloth lay across the edge of her kitchen sink. It seemed too festive to serve as a dish towel. There were two windows in Lu's room, and even though they were less than ten feet apart, they offered two different views of a Taipei morning. One window was bright and sunny while the other framed a cloud that looked like a dirty cauliflower.

Nancy turned to her phone and began to read a paper in a chemistry journal that she liked.

JING-NAN FOUND HIMSELF WALKING down the hallway for his next visit. He didn't know how to evaluate the first appointment. Jing-nan blamed the beer, and drinking on an empty stomach.

The room doors began to look a little shabbier as he continued down the hall. Maybe the cheaper rooms were farther away from the elevator. He began to hear faint sounds of music from the end of the hall. He hurried down.

Yes, it was definitely "The Drawback," an early song by Jing-nan's favorite band, Joy Division. The song lurched with the nervous energy of young punks, but the themes that Joy Division would explore later were also present: sonic and lyric claustrophobia, and paranoia.

Oddly, the room that the music was coming from didn't have a number. It had a sign that read THE END in English. Jing-nan checked the room that he had been assigned. Yup. It was "the end," all right.

He knocked on the door and waited. When it didn't open, Jing-nan knocked again, more insistently.

"Hi, I'm here to visit," he said as he checked the slip of paper again for a name, but there was none. "I'm here," he called again.

There were sounds of rustling inside before the door opened. Jing-nan stared into the face of a man who looked familiar. But how was that possible? How could he know someone more than twice his age?

The man gave Jing-nan a knowing smile and waved him in. Was he mute? He wasn't deaf, because he was listening to music. The apartment was the same size and layout as Private Tung's but it was crammed with CDs, records, posters, and other music-related detritus. Numerous nonmatching speakers blaring Joy Division were stashed randomly in whatever free spaces there were: a subwoofer on one of the nightstands, a woofer under the bed, and a tweeter cracking open a kitchen-cabinet door.

The music was loud but not unpleasantly so. Well, Jing-nan was biased. He loved the band. If his eardrums were bleeding from the volume, he'd still be casually nodding his head in time with the music.

Jing-nan fixed his eyes on the man, who had thinning white hair and patches of dry skin on his face. The man's hands shook as he opened the nightstand drawer and slowly pulled something out. It seemed to be a framed picture. He handed it to Jing-nan.

Jing-nan took the frame gingerly, thinking it would be an old photo of the man from his active service days. Instead, it was an upside-down picture of a young couple. Jing-nan righted the picture and stared into his own face. He was standing next to Nancy, and they both had vacant expressions on their faces, as if they weren't aware of each other. Two people standing next to each other on a crowded subway train.

Slowly, the two figures drifted apart until neither was in the frame. Jing-nan was spooked. The photo seemed too thin to be a tablet. He examined the back of the frame and didn't find any ports, or anything else that indicated it was an electronic device.

Jing-nan gave the picture back to the old man and shook his head. The old man's lips stretched into a tight grimace.

Then Jing-nan knew that he was the old man. This is who he would become without Nancy.

Jing-nan took a step back.

The old man grabbed his shoulder and said, "Are you all right?"

Jing-nan woke up to find Private Tung shaking his shoulder.

"I wasn't going to disturb your rest," he said, "but then you were whimpering like a scared puppy."

"How long have I been out?" asked Jing-nan.

The man rubbed his hands. "About half an hour! Boy, you young people are supposed to be the energetic ones!"

NANCY TOUCHED LU'S HANDS—STILL clutching a plate—in one last, unobtrusive attempt to gently awaken her, but it didn't work. She didn't like the idea of leaving without saying goodbye, and yet she had to. Nancy was already a few minutes late for her next visit.

Nancy closed Lu's door behind her, but it remained unlocked.

She hoped the next visit would be more meaningful. Nancy wanted to feel useful, like volunteering here was bringing some positivity into the world after the two murders.

She had certainly involved herself in unpleasant activities in the past. After all, she had decided to become a tech company executive's mistress in exchange for an apartment and a car, two things her mother couldn't afford herself, let alone provide for her daughter. Nancy wouldn't be where she was now had she not had those comforts, although she sold the car as the MRT expanded its route.

Nancy was well aware that she had benefitted, overall, from society's conventions while others had been forgotten. For all of Dwayne's posturing, he had a point: Aboriginal groups were only paid lip service before elections, and almost never got what was promised. Siu-lien didn't feel the same way, but she was still struggling, Nancy knew. At times she worried that her mother would fall through the cracks of her piecemeal employment and land on Nancy's couch, or worse, in government-subsidized housing. It might be inevitable. Siu-lien couldn't keep working forever, and she couldn't have much in the way of savings, which made this whole stupid thing even worse, what with Boxer stealing her mom's best chance to move up from serving drinks to drunks.

Yet this whole chain of events had led to her and Jing-nan volunteering at Better Days, a deed Nancy could never have imagined. It was undeniably good that they were here. As a couple, they had never "given back" together.

Nancy took the stairs down to her next appointment, and noted that the stairwells were clean, well-lit, and competently maintained. The stairs weren't the cluttered fire hazard that many apartment stairwells were.

She reached the landing and opened the door to the hallway, which smelled freshly vacuumed. As far as assisted-living facilities went, this place was pretty good, but whether it represented the norm or the high-end, Nancy didn't know.

She walked by a TV lounge and took note of a group of women laughing and chatting just like kids in college.

As Nancy continued down the hall, a door opened and a spritely woman emerged.

"You must be Nancy," the woman said as she rubbed Nancy's right arm.

"Yes, how did you know?" Nancy returned the gesture.

"They know I like to greet people before they knock on my door." She reached up and hooked her arm through Nancy's. "Please come in."

"I'm so sorry," said Nancy as she removed her shoes. The woman had already laid down a pair of slippers for her. "I don't know how to pronounce your name. Could you please tell me?"

"You can call me 'Bannie.'" They entered her room, which apart from a row of framed photographs was as sparse as Lu's room.

Bannie dispensed two cups of hot water from a counter brewer and drew her hand across two clear-plastic containers filled with different teabags.

"Please, Nancy, choose one."

"I would love to," said Nancy, "but before I do, may I use your restroom?"

"Yes, right over there," said Bannie, adding, "please don't look in the shower!"

"I won't!"

Nancy stepped into the bathroom and shut the door. As she sat down, she saw a photo that shocked her so badly, it put a temporary hold on her ability to pee.

When Nancy was done and had composed herself, she opened the door and casually reentered the room.

"I think the mint is the best one," said Bannie, "but of course, you're free to choose. We live in a democracy, after all." She was already seated at the kitchen table, and drinking mint tea, based on the fragrance in the room.

Nancy walked over, picked up a random teabag, and dropped it carelessly into her cup. She glided over to the kitchen table, sat with Bannie, and asked, "Do you by any chance know someone named Boxer?"

Bannie opened her mouth into a hard O and breathed mint breath all over Nancy. "I know him, yes, I do. I guess you know him, too, Nancy?"

"You see, Boxer was my mother's boyfriend. You might have seen the story about him."

Bannie stacked her hands flat on the table, and her body went rigid. "Boxer was my son-in-law."

"I didn't know he was married," said Nancy.

"You know, I . . ." Bannie began to cry.

"I'm so terribly sorry," said Nancy. Bannie already had a tissue in her hands.

"I hadn't thought about him in years, decades, until I heard about his end."

"Yes."

"Shocking."

"Yes."

"Nancy."

"Yes."

"Listen to me. Boxer was not a good man, not when I knew him. I did not hold affection for him. My daughter wanted to marry him when she was only 16. I couldn't stop her. She was smart. She was headed for college." Bannie held up one hand and curled her fingers, pulling back the years. "He ruined her."

"I'm sorry to hear that," said Nancy. She took a sip of the tea. It had a weak chrysanthemum flavor. Nancy really should have gone with the mint, which smelled so much better. She wanted to hear more about Boxer, and she didn't have to wait long.

"I knew he was a loser the first time I saw him," said Bannie. "He would sit out in late-night restaurants, always at a table close to the sidewalk so he could keep an eye out." The open-air format was still popular today. "What business does a 30-year-old man have whistling at schoolgirls? I'm sure you had no dealings with older men when you were a teenager, Nancy."

Nancy blinked and tried to keep an even expression. "I actually think some older men can't help themselves."

"You're darned right, they can't!"

"You know, Bannie, girls who grow up with a single mother may be trying to find a father figure."

"Do you think I was a single mother?" Bannie snapped. "Why would you bring up a negative stereotype about Aboriginal people?"

"I'm talking about me," protested Nancy. "*I* grew up with a single mother!"

"You did, huh?" said Bannie. "Well, I *was* a single mother, so maybe I am at fault."

"You didn't do anything wrong," said Nancy. "Society just shapes these expectations, and young people are susceptible to having these values impressed upon them. You're made to feel like there's something missing in your family and your life if you grow up with one parent."

Bannie crossed her arms defiantly. "That's an idea the Han Chinese have pushed. Where I come from, you respected all your elders as if each of them were one of your parents." Bannie paused to wipe her bottom lip. "Unfortunately, that wasn't the case for Juna, my daughter. She was in daycare when I was at work, and they just kept the TV on all the time. I blame the shows, with all the women trying to find older men. Every single one."

Nancy nodded. Bannie tilted her head and asked, "Can you see how someone would want to kill Boxer? For years, I think I could have. He cheated on my daughter, and she ran away. Juna was too ashamed to come back to me. I wish she weren't."

"Where is she now?"

Bannie wiped her nose roughly. "I don't know."

"If you hate Boxer so much," Nancy ventured, "then why do you have his picture on your bathroom door?"

Bannie's eyes grew wide. "What?"

"Boxer's picture. Well, when he was a kid."

"That's not Boxer's picture," said Bannie. "That's Boxer and Juna's son. My grandson. Well, I was more of a mother to him, after both his parents abandoned him."

Nancy ran to the bathroom and ripped the photo from the door, even though such an action was absolutely too forward for a guest in someone's home.

"This is your grandson?" asked Nancy as she held the photo up to Bannie.

"That's him. Christian. Just Chris. He lives in Australia, but he was just here," said Bannie.

"You mean, he was here in this room?"

"A few times," Bannie laughed. "He's performing with that circus, you know, the Flying Wonders."

"So he must have heard that Boxer was killed," said Nancy. "I mean, he knew Boxer was his father, right?"

"Yes, he did," said Bannie. "Chris knew exactly how I felt about Boxer, too."

Nancy slapped the photo down on the table.

"Did Chris kill Boxer?"

"He certainly would've been capable of doing so." Bannie sipped more tea. "And I don't care if he did. Boxer got what he deserved, and, as for the captain, well, I hate cops."

"He killed Captain Huang, too?"

Bannie traced the lip of her mug with her right index finger. "Oh, did I say that?"

Nancy gasped. By her appearance, no observer would think that the kindly looking, tea-drinking elderly woman was capable of advocating cold-blooded murder.

Bannie sipped more tea and said, "Now, tell me more about yourself, Nancy. Have you ever traveled to Japan?"

"No, I haven't," said Nancy. "I'd like to." She was speaking idly because she was focused on what her next step should be. Maybe Bannie wasn't all there. Still, the picture had been in her bathroom, and now it was clasped in Bannie's right hand. Oh, that would wrinkle it. Nancy decided to call Siulien. Her mother would know what to do.

"When you go to Japan," Bannie said with marked sincerity, "you have to bring warm clothes. It's quite cold there. Here, we never think about the cold too much, being so close to the equator."

"Oh, my, I forgot something!" said Nancy as she stood up suddenly. "My boyfriend is being discharged from the hospital today. I have to go see him."

Bannie leaned back and slipped the photo into her blouse.

Nancy cursed herself for not taking a picture of it. "What was wrong with your boyfriend?"

"He had a kidney thing," said Nancy. She clasped Bannie's hands. "It was so nice meeting you. I'm sorry that I have to go."

Bannie rose to her feet and nodded to Nancy. "Well, you're welcome to come back anytime."

I might be coming back sooner than you think, thought Nancy.

CHAPTER 20

Nancy ran into Jing-nan in the lobby.

"What are you doing here?" she asked him. Jing-nan shrugged and gave her a small, embarrassed smile.

"Oh, I'm just answering some questions on our Facebook page," he said. "Some foreigners don't know how a night-market stall works, and they actually want to make reservations."

"You're here to spend time with people, Jing-nan!"

He glanced at Captain Tang, who seemed engrossed in her phone. Under his breath, Jing-nan said, "I fell asleep at the first visit, and when I woke up, I was already late to see the second person, so I figured I'd just come down to the lobby and wait for you."

Nancy shook her head. "That's a little irresponsible, Jing-nan."

He narrowed his eyes. "Nancy, how come you're not doing your visits?"

She clenched her hands into fists. "Oh, I came down here because I saw something!"

"What did you see?"

Nancy moved in close to Jing-nan. "I think I know who killed Boxer and Captain Huang!" she scream-whispered. His mouth fell open. "I'll tell you, but I need to call my mother first!" Nancy called Siu-lien and explained what had happened, and Jing-nan got the gist from half the conversation. Siu-lien told Nancy to stay put.

After about 20 minutes, Siu-lien strolled into the lobby of the center. Captain Tang, who had previously been quietly focused on her phone, leapt up and came out from around her desk to block the path to the elevator.

"Hello, are you a visitor? We don't allow anyone in until they register online." Captain Tang nodded her head at Nancy and Jing-nan. "These two are the only ones registered for today."

"I had planned on volunteering today, as well," said Siu-lien, "but I was feeling a bit under the weather last night."

"Captain, this is my mother," said Nancy. "Bannie said she wanted to meet her."

"Are you sure?" asked the captain. "Bannie's not the most social person."

"We got along great, though," said Nancy.

"I've always treasured the contributions of our Indigenous peoples," said Siu-lien in a sugary voice that reeked of insincerity to both Nancy and Jing-nan. But Captain Tang smiled.

"Oh, well, seeing as you're an ally, I can't say no. Um, you're not with the police, are you?"

Siu-lien gave a lusty laugh. "Hell no, I'm not a cop!"

The captain stepped aside and gestured to the elevators. "Please come in. You'll be really glad to meet Bannie. She's one of my favorite people."

Siu-lien smiled and winked at Nancy. "Great, great," she said as she grabbed Nancy and Jing-nan and sandwiched herself between them. The three of them walked to the elevator.

"I can't wait to meet Bannie," Siu-lien called out to Captain Tang. She viciously jabbed the down button with her right hand.

"That's the wrong button," said Jing-nan. Siu-lien bumped her shoulder into him. "Ouch!"

"Quiet, Jing-nan!"

"Mom, I'm glad you're here," said Nancy.

"I should've brought a knife," said Siu-lien under her breath. "Then I could get the real story out of this stupid old woman."

The elevator seemed to stop at every floor on the way down.

Jing-nan whispered, "I think, actually, um, Nancy and Siu-lien, maybe this is a police matter. We really shouldn't be meddling on our own."

"You don't know anything," growled Siu-lien.

The elevator bell rang and finally the door opened. They entered and Siu-lien pressed the button for the basement.

"That's the wrong button again!" Jing-nan said a little too loud.

"Ah, I'm so clumsy," she declared, in case Captain Tang had heard. The doors closed. Siu-lien jabbed Jing-nan with her right elbow. "Stop talking!"

"Mom," said Nancy, "is everything all right?"

"Everything is not all right, but I've enlisted an old friend to help out."

They exited after the doors opened. Siu-lien led the way to the back of the basement, away from the boilers. She seemed to be looking for something, and then spotted the emergency exit door at the top of a wooden stepladder.

Siu-lien ascended and examined the door's alarmed release bar. She smirked. The bolt was unlocked, so no alarm would go off. This was typical, as security guards often needed shortcuts for cigarette breaks.

She pushed the door open, and Detective Wu entered.

"It's disgusting here in this alley," he said as he stepped down. "People drink and smoke here, and piss right on the wall."

"You've seen worse," said Siu-lien.

"Right," said Detective Wu. He looked over at Nancy and then let his eyes linger on Jing-nan. "You, again," he said.

"Hello," said Jing-nan as he stared down the stern beak-nosed officer.

"So based on what I'm hearing," said the detective, "it looks like you may not even be a person of interest in these murders after all, Jing-nan."

"Wow, you should be up for promotion," said Jing-nan.

"You never know when to keep your mouth shut," said Siu-lien. "He's here to help us on his own time, and you only have annoying things to say!" Jing-nan decided to stay quiet to remain in the good graces of Nancy's mother.

The elevator ride up was silent. Nancy led the way out and knocked on Bannie's door.

"Yes?" Bannie asked from behind the door. She sounded like she was calling out from the bathroom. "Are you back already, Nancy?"

"Yes, it's me again."

"I thought your boyfriend had an emergency," Bannie called out.

"I was confused," said Nancy. "I had the days mixed up."

"Just a minute," said Bannie. The sound of a toilet flushing followed. We've really caught her off guard, Jing-nan thought.

Footsteps approached and the door opened. Bannie smiled. "Oh my, Nancy, you've brought some friends, I see," she said.

"I'm her mother," said Siu-lien. "The one whose boyfriend was Boxer."

"Yes, I remember Nancy saying," said Bannie. "That good-for-nothing bastard." She hadn't altered her light and cheery tone at all, which made her words chilling.

"Hi, Bannie, I'm Detective Wu. I'd like to ask you a few questions, if you don't mind."

"I knew you were a cop just by the way you looked at me," said Bannie as she walked to the dining table and took a seat.

"And how did I look at you?" asked Detective Wu.

"Like you were better than me," she said. "Like you were going to get one over on me." Bannie stretched her legs out and scratched her kneecaps. "I'm afraid I won't be offering you anything to eat or drink because I truly despise your kind and anyone who associates with you." Detective Wu wiped his mouth with his left thumb and chuckled.

"I'm glad you're honest about it," he said. Nancy looked over the bare dining table, and then went directly into the bathroom and stomped back.

"Where is it?" she asked Bannie.

"Where is what, my dearest darling?"

"The picture of your grandson," said Nancy.

"Why, I have no idea what you're talking about, little girl. You did say that you were a little confused about calendar dates, right? Well, that's not all you have mixed up." Jing-nan detected the slightest smile on Bannie's face.

"You had a picture of Boxer's kid in your bathroom," said Jing-nan. "You said his name is Chris, and you also said he was in the Flying Wonders. But the only Taiwanese Aborigine in the troupe is named Umaq." He couldn't help his accusatory tone. Detective Wu stepped in.

"Is Umaq your grandson, and did he kill Boxer and Captain Huang?"

"Why, these questions are preposterous," said an unruffled Bannie.

"Did you just flush Chris's picture down the toilet?" asked Nancy.

Bannie's small smile became slightly bigger.

"I didn't reach this age without learning a thing or two," she said sweetly. "Nancy, dear, I knew you were making an excuse. I knew you'd come back with the cops."

"One cop," said Detective Wu.

"You're just the symbol of an ineffectual and immoral force," said Bannie.

"Just a minute, here," said Detective Wu. "I have a witness who recorded what you said about your grandson killing Boxer and Captain Huang. That'll stand up in court."

"I'm afraid that it won't." Bannie stood, pushed her chair in, and rested her hands on the dining table. "You see, even if little Nancy really did record me, which I doubt, I've already been diagnosed with dementia. I'm afraid that anything that I say likely won't be admissible." She nodded her head at Nancy. "That includes anything you thought I said regarding some murders, my dear. I might have been repeating something I saw in a movie a long, long time ago."

"You don't have dementia," Nancy spat.

Bannie dropped her sweet old lady act. "Oh, yeah, missy? How about I pick up a kitchen knife and slash your face? Not a single jury would convict me!" She stomped her foot. "Now, all of you get out of my home!"

DETECTIVE WU AND SIU-LIEN went their own way, saying they would think about what to do. Jing-nan and Nancy also considered next steps as they rode the MRT to the Shilin Night Market. They stood and swayed as the train moved on. Jing-nan remembered the picture that he had seen in his dream and purposely moved closer to Nancy.

"Bannie can't win like this, can she?" asked Jing-nan.

Nancy shook her head. "We're talking about murder here," she said. "The murder of someone dear to my mom, and the murder of a police captain. We have to do something, Jing-nan, even if you don't like the police!"

"Why do you think I have a problem with the police?"

"Don't you?"

"Nancy, I've been abused by a number of members of law enforcement. Even Captain Huang himself." Jing-nan wiped his chin against his right shoulder. "But he didn't deserve to die like that. Maybe he should have had his performance reviewed and been fired, though."

"We have to figure out how to get to Chris or Umaq," said Nancy.

"You heard what Detective Wu said, right? There's nothing to make a case out of this. And that Bannie? I could totally see her following through on her threat to put on a dementia act for the court."

"Jing-nan," said Nancy, "I *saw* that picture."

"I know you did," he said. "But what's a jury going to think?"

Nancy sighed. "Dwayne and Frankie might be able to help us. They're going to be at Unknown Pleasures, right?"

"Of course. They're more reliable than me." He checked his phone. "Whoa, it's only noon. Naw, they're probably not there yet. In a few hours."

"You owe them your life. Literally."

Jing-nan nodded his head solemnly. "That's absolutely true. Well, I think the three of us are all interdependent." The train slowed for a stop, and he reached into his coat pocket.

"You're going to put in your earbuds and not talk to me?" asked Nancy.

"I'm trying to think, and I think best when I'm listening

to music." Nancy's stoic face was unnerving to Jing-nan. "Music helps me step outside of my usual boundaries."

"I don't think you're stepping outside your boundaries at all," said Nancy. The train began moving again, and Jing-nan had to hastily reach for a grabhold. He nearly fell over.

"Nancy, are we all right?" Jing-nan asked. He was annoyed but tried to keep that feeling in check.

"It's just that our anniversary is coming up, Jing-nan." She looked at the floor. "What are our plans for the future?"

Was she talking about marriage? Children? Was he getting fat?

"I take things day by day, Nancy," said Jing-nan. "I'm trying to keep my business on track, and it sure hasn't been easy for me these last few days."

"I mean about us, Jing-nan. What kind of future are we going to have?"

"We're going to have a great future," said Jing-nan.

"What if Unknown Pleasures has to shut down? Then where would you be?"

"I wouldn't let it shut down. But even if the place burned down, I'd start something else. Right now, we're doing better than ever. Do you know how many followers I have?" He realized immediately how weak that sounded. "And you're my favorite follower. Thank you for hearting almost every post." God, that was even worse.

"What if the stand doesn't do so well in the future?"

Jing-nan felt self-conscious speaking of failure in a public place. Just talking about it felt like he was tempting fate. "I'll make sure it does."

"Jing-nan, I've thought about it a lot but I've never told you. I think you need to get a college degree."

"You . . . you have told me before."

"I have?" Nancy was genuinely surprised.

"A few times," said Jing-nan. The train lurched and he

found himself staring at an ad featuring a college student in a library, ecstatic that he had discovered how to open the lid of his Acer notebook.

"Maybe I don't remember because you never say one way or another what you want to do," said Nancy.

"I've never said because I don't know."

"You're smart, Jing-nan."

"I'm a smart businessman."

"It would be better for your business if you had a degree."

What the hell was going on? thought Jing-nan. We're mixed up in murder investigations, but now I have to make a decision on college? But he knew that Nancy was saying that it would be better for their relationship if he had a college degree. She was thinking about the long term, the big game. Nancy was a beautiful young woman attending the nation's most prestigious school. She certainly wouldn't lack prospects, if she were looking. She'd be set for life with some asshole from business school.

A gloomy feeling overcame Jing-nan. Indeed, he was bright enough to get into a good American college. But he had to leave UCLA in his sophomore year because his father was sick with cancer. Soon after he returned to Taiwan, both his parents died. Now he was stuck doing what he had vowed not to: running the family night-market stall. Of course, the only family he had now were Dwayne and Frankie. And in the future, maybe Nancy, too.

She was going to be a prominent figure in biotechnology. No doubt. Nancy was already co-authoring important research papers. Meanwhile, Jing-nan was prancing around the festive environs of the night market, a role that didn't even call for an education, only audacity. Well, at least he had that. The average Taiwanese guy couldn't even talk to a stranger without feeling a little shy.

Nancy wasn't going to come out and say it, but maybe she was a little embarrassed that Jing-nan didn't have a degree. Certainly her colleagues looked down on him. Still with that guy who makes late-night snacks for tourists, huh?

That was nothing new to him, the world looking down on him—and vice versa! Jing-nan had grown up listening to Western punk and post-punk, and his English was good enough that there were no subtleties lost on him. Jing-nan remembered the first time he heard Joy Division's "Atrocity Exhibition," in which singer Ian Curtis played carnival barker to entice listeners to embark on a tour of human misery. Later, when Jing-nan heard the bootlegs of live Joy Division concerts, he was shocked at how vehement Ian's vocals were on the song, menacing the crowd with adlibbed lines: "You want to see some more? Step inside!"

He knew that Ian was daring the audience to explore the ugliness of their own minds, their prejudices, their hate for their fellow human beings.

Jing-nan didn't care what the world thought of him, how he lived his life, how he made a living.

But he cared what Nancy thought, and he knew she was right in this matter. Sometimes, when dreaming big about the future of Unknown Pleasures, he wondered what the larger picture was. Surely, not just a stall twice as big as the one he had now. Not even an outpost in every night market in Taipei.

Jing-nan looked at Nancy and tried to glimpse the years ahead. He was scared to want what he'd never had. A stable family life, one that wasn't under the constant stress of striving at the night market. What was that word the Japanese anti-hoarding woman used? Ah, joy! A life of joy. That's what scared and tantalized him.

Nancy had an expectant look on her face, and Jing-nan realized that he hadn't said anything for quite a while.

"You're right, Nancy," he said. "I should finish school. I can take a class or two during the day. I have no excuse not to." Her eyes opened and she couldn't help but smile.

"What are you going to study?" she asked him.

He said something he never thought he'd utter, as the punk spirit in him writhed in pain. "Business and marketing."

CHAPTER 21

Jing-nan and Nancy spent the afternoon making love and napping at his Shilin apartment. Hours later, they went to Unknown Pleasures. Frankie and Dwayne were already trimming meats for the evening's stews and skewers. As a matter of courtesy, because a lady was present, Frankie put out his cigarette, and Dwayne wiped the blood from his arms.

"Is it a special night?" Dwayne asked Nancy. "You don't usually come here this early. Are you here as a second set of eyes to check up on us?"

"I'm here because Jing-nan and I had the strangest experience at the nursing home," said Nancy.

"What happened?" asked Dwayne. Nancy relayed the details. Dwayne nodded and let out occasional exclamations while Frankie listened so stoically he didn't seem to blink or breathe.

When Nancy was done, Dwayne declared, "Frankie, it's that circus again, the one with posters all over the Hope Center!"

Frankie smiled and nodded. "The Flying Wonders," he said.

"We should go check it out," said Dwayne.

"Well," said Frankie, "we could let Siu-lien's police friends handle this . . ." He left his words hanging to show how futile a hope that was.

"Detective Wu said he probably couldn't do much," said Nancy. "After all, there's no evidence to go on, and my word that I saw the picture means almost nothing."

"If we go to the circus," asked Jing-nan, "do we try to tackle Umaq? Also, doesn't it cost like two thousand bucks to go?"

"I happen to have a coupon for half off," said Dwayne.

"How about we go tomorrow, then?" said Jing-nan.

"I thought you said there was no point in going?" said Nancy.

He tapped his forehead. "My business and marketing instinct is telling me that the risk-reward proposition is better with those coupons. More importantly, I can tell Frankie's already thinking of a plan for us to get the guy."

All heads turned to Frankie, who said nothing but gave the slightest wink.

"Yeah, the Cat can do it," said Dwayne.

"Won't you have to close Unknown Pleasures if we're all going to go?" Nancy asked.

"That part sucks, but it's just one night," said Jing-nan. "It's not going to kill anybody." He realized what he had said, gave an embarrassed grunt, and washed his hands. "I mean, it might create more demand by announcing a one-night closure."

"Dwayne," asked Nancy, "do you have enough coupons for my mom and Detective Wu?"

"Sure," said Dwayne before adding, "can you make sure I don't have to sit with the cop?"

Jing-nan and Nancy had never been to Taipei Arena before, mainly because they didn't like any musical acts that were commercial enough to fill it. Dwayne had been to the arena in the past to see Jeremy Lin play against the Indiana Pacers. Funny thing was, he couldn't remember what team Jeremy was with, as he had worn so many different jerseys.

It was Frankie's first time in the venue, but he was familiar with it because he had studied the floor plans online. Frankie had been to this part of the city before, though, having seen a number of games at the old Taipei Municipal Baseball Stadium, which was knocked down in 2000 to build the arena.

Siu-lien had seen A-Mei, probably Taiwan's biggest contemporary singer, at the arena. Siu-lien still yearned to sing, an undiminished longing from her younger days. She had never sung anywhere nearly as big as Taipei Arena, but her voice could probably shake its rafters after some rehearsing.

Siu-lien had belted her heart out in those clubs for drinks, short conversations, and tips. It never went any farther than that, not for Siu-lien. She had heard from other singers that if you went to a three-hour hotel room down the block with one of the grandpas in the audience, they'd always be unable to perform out of shyness or other failings. Then you'd have to endure the stories about their broken families and estranged children, but there would be a folded NT$500 note for you at the end.

The grandpas died off, as they tend to do, and the red-envelope clubs folded for good one by one. Now Siu-lien's place was behind the bar. The closest she came to music these days was when she handed out songbooks and wireless mics for karaoke nights.

She remembered her dream about Boxer, and how he told her the photograph had killed him. How strange it would be if that boy, now a man, really was the murderer.

Detective Wu brought food from one of the arena's restaurants. "I have a burger and yam fries," he said to Siu-lien, "but if that's too much like bar food, I also have a chicken salad."

"What's wrong with bar food?" she asked with feigned indignation.

He laughed awkwardly. "Nothing," he said.

Siu-lien grabbed the burger and fries as Detective Wu looked at the chicken salad with a grim smile. This wasn't supposed to happen. He hated salads. They reminded him of a childhood spent eating vegetable trimmings back at his parents' languishing restaurant. They were still at it, too. He opened the lid and poured half of the French dressing into one corner of the plastic container.

He had been to the arena in the past, chaperoning his niece to the Ice Land skating rink. Seeing her face light up during her triumphs and comforting her after bad stumbles, the cop had the passing thought that maybe it would be fun to have a kid. But he knew that he was only seeing the best of the parenting experience, and that there was all kinds of shit—literally—that he hadn't had to deal with.

Besides, even the cutest kids can grow up to be killers.

Detective Wu breathed in deeply and looked around carefully for suspicious behavior. He caught Dwayne's eye and nodded. Instead of returning the gesture, Dwayne acted as if he hadn't seen him and turned away.

Detective Wu forked some salad into his mouth and chewed thoughtfully. Some people just don't like cops. He didn't take it personally. A few cops really did suck, and unfortunately that was enough to tarnish the reputation of the entire force in a society teeming with anti-authoritarian sentiment. A few decades of martial law will do that.

Still, he'd rather endure unspoken hostility than stand next to a hot grill and hand over skewers to tourists all night. How much money did Dwayne make at the night market, anyway? It couldn't be more than him, could it? Then the detective thought about his stocks and how they only seemed to go down. After that, it hit him how expensive the arena food was. On top of all that, he was stuck eating the fucking salad he had gotten for Siu-lien!

The PA speakers announced that the show was going to start in a few minutes and then began to list government organizations of Australia and Taiwan that had helped to bring the show to the arena. Carefree voices addressed the audience in Mandarin, Taiwanese, Hakka, and English.

As he listened to the announcements, Dwayne's annoyance grew. He understood parts of all the languages—English, less so—but if the show was supposed to bring out the Taiwanese Aborigines and celebrate their culture—ahead of the Austronesian Cultural Festival, no less—why weren't their languages represented? There hadn't even been a token "Naruwan!" Not that the greeting in Amis alone should suffice to address all the different Indigenous groups, but it might have shown the bare minimum of giving props.

Was it already fated that the Indigenous languages would die out? He looked around the arena and crossed his arms. Maybe we should just make English the national language, Dwayne thought. At least it'll make it harder for China to take over.

Nancy stared hard at the headshot of the acrobat named Umaq, who was supposedly Bannie's grandson and Boxer's son. She wasn't sure he was the same person in Bannie's photo. Jing-nan was also scrutinizing the headshot.

"Doesn't seem to look like Boxer," he said. "Is this our guy?"

"I can't be sure," said Nancy. "I couldn't testify in court

that it is." She sat back in her seat. "Even if this man turns out to be Boxer's son, that doesn't prove he's a murderer."

"The cops could take his fingerprints and try to match them to samples in Boxer's apartment."

"There aren't any legal grounds for them to do so," said Nancy. "Hopefully, Frankie's plan is going to work out, and make him slip up in front of Detective Wu."

The announcements ended and the arena went dark. A spotlight scraped across the ceiling and stopped to focus on a man high in the air hanging upside down. It looked like his feet were tied to a rope. Then, as he began to move, swinging his legs down, it became apparent that he wasn't tied to the rope at all. His grip alone was preventing him from falling. The man made his way down, with bug-like meticulousness, holding the rope in his hands or between his thighs.

Jing-nan's heart was in his throat. He hadn't seen any safety nets. Phones in the audience lit up like fireflies. When the man was about 50 feet off the ground, he seemed to do a split in the air and began to swing like a pendulum.

There was a thunderous crashing sound and the audience gasped. It was only the beginning of a musical piece. Several of the arena's screens lit up with video footage of Taiwan from the air. The man seemed to fly above the Taipei 101 tower, leap over Mount Ali, zoom through Taroko Gorge, and then dive into Sun Moon Lake. A giant wave of water splashed through all the screens and when the lights came on, the man was nowhere to be seen.

"Amazing!" a voice boomed in Mandarin from the speakers. "Let's give a big hand for Umaq, a young man who is a native Taiwanese!" The crowd broke out into applause as stagehands wheeled out a multilevel platform. "And now, ladies and gentlemen, let's give a big Taipei welcome to the Flying Wonders!" The crowd responded, but after no performers emerged, the cheers ebbed into a confused murmur.

Jing-nan worried that maybe Umaq was already on the run after being tipped off by his grandmother. Nancy thought the same. Then she noticed that a part of the platform seemed to be coming loose. Not only was the troupe a no-show, their equipment was falling apart!

Then a platform beam kicked out two legs and soon, the entire structure crumbled. The crowd watched in disbelief as the platform dismantled itself and became a group of human figures clothed in black and silver. They formed an outward-facing circle and tore off their masks with excessive flourish to show their faces and measured smiles.

Nancy scanned the faces for Umaq, and wasn't sure he was there.

Eight performers bounded away to grab ropes that had slinked down from the ceiling. Four others remained in the center to set up a base structure. A doddering, long-haired stagehand whose job was to collect the masks was bumbling in his work, dropping as many as he managed to pick up. One of the acrobats took exception to his poor performance and began to berate the poor man with exaggerated hand gestures. The stagehand scurried about, dropping even more masks.

That was the last straw. The acrobat drew one foot back and kicked out where the stagehand would have been had he not done a backflip and landed on the shoulders of another acrobat. The stagehand tossed away his baseball cap and wig. It was Umaq.

The acrobats on ropes swung down and after several passes, no one was left on the ground. They climbed higher and played on the trapeze bars that hung down at various heights.

Dwayne watched the ropes sway, and his eyelids grew heavy. A dim memory from childhood surfaced. He remembered seeing a circus, an American act that included men and women doing tricks while standing on the back of a galloping horse. Dwayne slid down his seat until he nearly fell on the floor.

Frankie the Cat sat still, his hands on his knees, and took in everything. Despite the distracting video screens and booming music, he kept track of where Umaq was at all times, registering that the stunts the young man carried out with aplomb required years of training and strict discipline.

"I can't believe there's no safety net," said Jing-nan. Nancy nudged him.

"They all have harnesses and wires," she said. "They wouldn't be flying around without something holding them up." Nancy watched the acrobats crisscross each other as they leapt from bar to bar, defying gravity. Why aren't they getting tangled up? she wondered.

Siu-lien's eyes were glazing over. She never understood why people liked to watch shows like this. One trick wasn't that much different from another. One person switches with another one over there, and they both do a little spin. So what? Then a song by A-Mei kicked in and Siu-lien sat up straight. The moves were in time with the music, and she thrilled to hear A-Mei's plaintive voice. "Anger, envy, jealousy." Siu-lien silently mouthed the lyrics.

Detective Wu found himself swept along with the show. Everything was tinged with the unexpected, and he was tickled. The detective tapped his feet and allowed himself to smile. At one point, he became conscious that he was holding Siu-lien's hand. Had he reached for her? Had she grabbed him? He didn't know, but he maintained his relaxed hold. Siu-lien seemed oblivious to the physical contact. Jesus, was she singing now?

He rubbed his mouth with the knuckles of his free hand and gazed upward. Something could happen at any second.

CHAPTER 22

Jing-nan had expected an intermission, but instead, the monitors began to play a documentary about the hardships that the troupe had undergone to create the current show.

Each performer had at least one minor injury over the course of the eight-month process, and the film made sure to show each one.

At one point the performers all piled into SUVs and headed into the outback where they performed to and with Aboriginal communities. Umaq seemed to take a special interest in the people he met, saying there were similarities with the marginalized Indigenous peoples of Taiwan.

Dwayne watched closely. The Australian Aborigines had been uprooted and forced to renounce their sacred animals, trees, and landmarks. He knew his ancestors had that common experience, and he was galled to see that the history and culture of Australian Aborigines were also being used to promote tourism—as was this "documentary!" He crossed his arms and bit his bottom lip.

Nancy leaned against Jing-nan. She liked the shots of Sydney. A few months ago, a recruiter from a university there had tried to entice Nancy to move. She had dismissed the idea without really considering it. Everything there looked new and organized in a way that Taipei wasn't. Sydney had space, and Australia had big money. The economy was stronger than Taiwan's, and Australia's immigration policy was friendly to the highly skilled, the recruiter had reminded her, as if Nancy would move there permanently.

As the video moved on to the troupe's living quarters, which, frankly, could have been anywhere in the world, Nancy thought about the things she would miss about Taipei. Daytime deluges. Nights walking around on the wet pavement as bright as the streetlights. All the food, too. And, of course, Jing-nan.

The video came to a close, with a credit to Tourism Australia. Dwayne slapped his knee and thought, I knew it!

As the screens faded, Umaq flew out over the crowd as if shot from a cannon. After a few backflips in the air, he came to rest on an invisible perch.

Frankie appreciated the athleticism. Umaq made it look easy, but that could only come from years of constant self-denial. Reaching that level of performance required near-psychopathic tendencies. Frankie had seen crazy men do incredible feats in the military.

Umaq wouldn't be easy to trap. Frankie wouldn't have an advantage in a one-on-one confrontation. No one in their group would. That kid was a beast. Frankie would have to use the considerable resources of his mind, and Dwayne as a prop. He was sure there were stringent security measures in the arena, but every switch, button, and lock was still controlled by a human. Those were the weak points.

He turned to Dwayne and said, "You sure you're up for doing something stupid to get that guy? You might get hurt."

"My body doesn't feel pain," said Dwayne as he cracked

joints in his wrists and elbows. "You're still fine-tuning plans, right?"

"I'll tell you in the bathroom." Frankie stood up and nodded to Detective Wu. The cop, Frankie, and Dwayne left. Nancy glanced over but didn't say anything. She took her phone out of her bag and placed it in her lap, to make sure she wouldn't miss any texts.

Two minutes later, Siu-lien checked her phone, stood up, and left.

Five minutes later, Nancy received a text noting the location she and Jing-nan were supposed to find. He followed her up the aisle to the exit.

FRANKIE HAD WATCHED RECORDINGS of the show online. He knew there was a period of about 15 minutes when Umaq went backstage, underwent a major costume change, and was wheeled back onto the arena floor inside a box.

One thing Frankie wasn't sure about was how secure things were backstage. Were there only guards near the front, or along the length of the hall where Umaq's box was wheeled down?

Frankie wasn't afraid of being tactless in order to carry out a mission, so he ducked into a bathroom while Dwayne ran frantically down the escalators.

Despite all his talk, Dwayne still hadn't made it back to the gym, so he wasn't faking being out of breath when he arrived at the information desk.

"Help! My dad's legs gave out when he was on the toilet! Do you have a spare wheelchair so I can get him out?" Dwayne wiped the sweat from his forehead and tried to pant extra hard so he wouldn't be able to laugh out loud at the ridiculousness of the setup. The man at the desk looked like a boy-band backup dancer. His hair was styled into a swoop that spoke of ambition beyond customer service. His nametag said, *Ivan*, and Ivan was immediately freaked out.

"Oh, no, let me get . . . someone!" Ivan's hands shook as he picked up the phone receiver. It was clear that this was his first emergency. It might've even been the first time he'd picked up the receiver.

"It's the northwest men's room, on the third floor," said Dwayne, realizing that he was sounding suspiciously precise.

"Yes, someone will be there soon," said Ivan. A voice came on the line and Ivan stuttered the details. Dwayne jogged back to the escalators and rode up to see Frankie.

"I should take a picture of you looking helpless," Dwayne said to Frankie, who was lying on the bathroom floor, his shirt untucked and his hair disheveled.

"If you do," warned Frankie, "I'll kick out and break your fucking legs right now."

Three young men in orange vests entered the bathroom. "Is this the man who needs help?" asked the one in charge, pointing to Frankie on the floor.

Dwayne refrained from saying something sarcastic. "Yes, my dad is in distress." The other two men rolled in a large wheelchair, each of them holding a handle. Dwayne noticed they were both equipped with long flashlights that could be used as billy clubs, depending on the situation.

Dwayne helped lift Frankie into the wheelchair. As he hoisted Frankie's legs into place, Dwayne was amazed at how muscular his calves were underneath the pant legs. Like tree trunks still rooted in the ground.

"Should we call an ambulance?" asked the man in charge.

"I want to see the rest of the show!" cried Frankie. "I don't want to leave!"

"He'll be fine, his legs just give out sometimes," said

Dwayne. "Would you mind if we moved to a section that accommodates wheelchairs?"

"That's no problem." The man spoke to someone on his walkie-talkie and soon his coterie escorted Dwayne and Frankie to an empty third-floor balcony overlooking the show.

When the security guys had left, Frankie held up a ring of keys.

"You got that from the leader?" asked Dwayne.

"He was talking and not paying attention," said Frankie, running his fingers over the keys. "I can tell by the way they feel that there's a few elevator keys here, so we can jump to the shortcut plan."

Frankie texted Detective Wu, who had been posted elsewhere in case they needed to go the longer route. The detective in turn texted Nancy and Jing-nan.

Frankie waved his right arm in a circle, and Dwayne wheeled him out to the public concourse.

"Let's go to the end here," directed Frankie. "There, that looks like the service elevator!" They rolled up on a pair of doors. Frankie fiddled with the keys and got it right on the second try.

"I'm worried someone might be looking at us," said Dwayne. He glanced back at the few people walking around.

"Don't worry," said Frankie, as the elevator car moved to their floor. "Nobody pays attention to people in wheelchairs. They'll either ignore us or feel bad for looking."

The doors opened without a sound. Dwayne wheeled Frankie inside. When the doors shut, Dwayne used the key to put the elevator on hold. Frankie stood up and peeled off his shirt. Dwayne nearly gasped. Frankie had a six-pack. How was that possible for a man his age?

"If you keep staring at me, at least stick some money in my pants," said Frankie. Dwayne cleared his throat and

rummaged through his gym bag, handing over various arti-
cles of clothing: a blue shirt, red leggings, a bag with a heavily
embroidered strap, and a multicolored cloth headwrap.

"This is really fucking offensive," Dwayne muttered as
he watched Frankie dress. "Some Chinese guy trying to pass
himself off as Amis. I'm glad my people aren't watching."

"The ancestors are always watching through your eyes,"
said Frankie.

Dwayne wasn't sure what to say, so he grumbled, "What
do you know about it?"

"You know there's a hole in this shirt?" Frankie asked
as he buttoned a flap with a zigzag-shaped border. "If you
respect your culture, remember to take care of your clothes."

Dwayne scratched the back of his neck and tried to
think of someone he could blame for the state of his shirt.
It had been hanging untouched in the closet for years. He
should have put it away in a plastic box with something to
kill insects. But then, that would have made it smell funny.
All in all, he could live with a little hole. A little physical
defect can be easily hidden, but you can't really hide a bad
smell.

Frankie, who was now seated in the wheelchair, lightly
elbowed Dwayne's side to get his attention. "How do I look?"
he asked.

Dwayne walked over to the front of the wheelchair. Frankie
had made his mouth small, his eyes unfocused, and his face
slack. The transformation was remarkable.

"Man, Frankie, you look old!" said Dwayne.

"Do you think I can pass?" Frankie asked.

Dwayne thought about how at gatherings he never looked
too long or too closely at elders. The older generations had
been closer to the years of unbridled disenfranchisement.
They felt the loss of their lands and traditions more keenly.

It was all over their faces, and the pain and the shame were palpable.

"Yeah," said Dwayne. "You can do it." He texted the rest of the group to meet at the second-floor doors of the private elevator. Then he walked over to the control panel and turned the key.

As the elevator began to move, Frankie got up and stretched. "Who knows how long I'm going to be stuck in that thing?" he said. Dwayne jumped into the empty wheelchair. "What are you doing, now?"

"Well," said Dwayne, "who knows how long I'm going to be on my feet?"

SECURITY WAS FAIRLY LIGHT at the basement level where the dressing rooms were. After all, it wasn't accessible to the public.

The two security guards at the desk were alerted that the private elevator was arriving. More curious than concerned, the two women watched the monitor that connected with the elevator's camera. They saw a group of six people, including an elderly man in a wheelchair who seemed to be the center of attention.

"Who the hell's that?" asked Zhao. Her average height and willowy build belied her prowess at tae kwon do. For a while Zhao had the same coach as Tseng Li-cheng, who had won a bronze medal at the Olympics, but now the sport was only a hobby. She was in her mid-20s now, and graduate school was more important. Zhao idly adjusted the tint on the monitor.

"They look like a delegation or something," said Lian. Zhao regarded her partner with mild disdain, as always. After all, Zhao was worried about becoming her. Lian was unmarried, in her late 30s, and given to sighs and worry. "I hope there's no trouble," Lian added.

"Trouble," spat Zhao. They watched the group exit the elevator, and prepared for their stop at the security desk. Lian walked forward and crossed her arms. She liked to act so brave for the security cameras, thought Zhao.

Detective Wu led the group, followed by Dwayne pushing Frankie in the wheelchair. Siu-lien, Nancy, and Jing-nan followed, heads slightly bowed.

The detective flashed his shield and said, "I have an emergency visit for Umaq from Master Ayal." Lian took half a step back.

"You're a detective?" she asked.

"You might have seen me on the news," said Detective Wu. Jing-nan chuckled to himself. What an ego, he thought.

Nancy froze. She recognized Zhao from campus, although she didn't personally know her. Nancy decided to keep her movements as small as possible.

"I haven't," said Lian.

"Well, then, maybe you've seen Master Ayal," said Dwayne. "He's on Taiwan Indigenous TV all the time." Lian looked at Frankie's solemn face and then quickly looked away.

"I watch TITV," said Zhao. "I've never seen or heard of Master Ayal. Also, we weren't notified that any guests were arriving."

"I'm sorry that nobody dropped you a line," said Detective Wu. "Then again, this was something that came together at the last minute. Master Ayal decided less than an hour ago that this would be the correct time to meet with Umaq." He bowed his head slightly when he said "Master Ayal." The detective added, "It is only the master's awesome reputation that allows us to be in this private area of the Taipei Arena. Your superiors upstairs immediately gave us the private elevator keys upon hearing Master Ayal's request."

Lian rubbed her hands. Zhao felt her colleague wavering.

"Look here," said Zhao. "I don't care who he is, and in fact I don't care who any of you are. You're not on the guest list, and you can't come in."

Frankie raised his arms and cracked his knuckles. Oh no, thought Jing-nan, Frankie, please don't start any trouble with these women. Frankie held his arms to his sides and then brought them to his face. He began to sob loudly.

"Oh," said Zhao. She saw her own grandfather in the wheelchair. "Oh, I'm sorry, ah, Master Ayal. We just have our procedures, that's all."

Frankie milked it even more, lowering his head in a truly heartrending portrayal of a broken, elderly man. Jing-nan dug his nails into his palms to prevent himself from laughing.

Zhao wiped away her tears and said, "Let them through, Lian."

Her counterpart struck an indignant tone. "I *was* going to let them through," she said. She wanted to tell Zhao that she had been unnecessarily cruel to an old Aboriginal man whose fame obviously preceded him.

Dwayne pushed the wheelchair ahead, and Frankie kept his face covered with his hands. Dwayne eyed Zhao carefully. She could have some Aboriginal blood, he thought, and he was annoyed that she had fallen for Frankie's act.

Siu-lien walked by calmly, betraying nothing. She was skilled at such things.

Jing-nan got the sense that Nancy had wanted to walk ahead of him, rather than aside. He lagged behind and followed at an impersonal distance.

Nancy was keeping pace with Siu-lien when Zhao stepped in front, holding an imposing stance.

"You go to Taida, don't you?' asked the security guard.

"Yes, I do," said Nancy, conscious that her facial features

were being scanned and memorized by Zhao's unblinking eyes.

"Do you really follow Master Ayal? Is he for real?"

"I find him very inspiring, and his teachings are ageless," she declared. Zhao frowned, but only because she was disappointed that Nancy seemed to be telling the truth. Zhao stepped aside to let Nancy through.

"You!" Zhao said to Jing-nan. "I've seen you on television for sure!"

"My night-market stall is very famous," said Jing-nan.

"Yes, that's it," said Zhao, who was acting a little too thrilled for Lian's taste. Ask the guy for an autograph, she thought.

"I'm one of the celebrities who is in awe of Master Ayal," said Jing-nan as he reverently pressed his hands together. "So many are."

He caught up with Nancy.

"We're getting too well-known to sneak around," she said.

"We're not sneaking," said Jing-nan. "We have nothing to hide." The group walked to the end of the hall, all of them listening for some music cue that would tell them when Umaq would be alone backstage.

Siu-lien looked back at Lian and Zhao. "If we wait here instead of going in, the guards are going to get suspicious."

"I've got it," said Jing-nan. "Let's hold hands and bow our heads like we're having a prayer thing."

"Great idea," said Frankie. They made a semicircle around the wheelchair. Jing-nan made sure to grab Nancy's hand. They gave each other gentle grips just strong enough to be reassuring.

"I can't believe I am participating in the desecration of my people with this shtick," muttered Dwayne. "Passing some Chinese guy off as an Indigenous shaman is sick and insulting."

"Well, you wouldn't fit in this wheelchair, would you?" asked Frankie.

"Doing what we did got us this far, already," added Detective Wu.

"What if Umaq is innocent?" asked Siu-lien.

"There's no way he's innocent," said Jing-nan. "Did you listen to what your daughter said?"

"Do you ever really listen to my daughter, Jing-nan?" hissed Siu-lien.

"Mom and Jing-nan," said Nancy. "Please stop."

"Whether someone's innocent or not, that's never something I think about," said the detective. Everyone turned to him with raised eyebrows. "It's not my job to decide that. I'm responsible for bringing in likely suspects, and the court or the jury, if it comes down to that, finds them guilty or innocent. Even if we don't have a trial, then these dirtbags get a taste of what it's like getting arrested. Most of them need to be scared straight. Maybe no one can prove they committed a certain crime, but when I bring in someone, it's because I'm already sure they've got a foot or two on the wrong path."

"Cops shouldn't try to find dirt on everybody," said Jing-nan, who had been harassed by the police and other authority figures in recent years. "You're supposed to be enforcing the law."

"I know my duties, kid," said Detective Wu with a smirk. "That's why I'm here."

"You're not here in an official capacity, though," said Jing-nan. "You said there wasn't enough evidence for the Taipei City Police Department to get involved."

Detective Wu leaned across the handles of Frankie's wheelchair to get into Jing-nan's face. "Look here. Would you be surprised to know that I made my biggest drug bust while in an unofficial capacity?" The detective's eyes were unblinking and unfeeling. "I'm going with my gut here. When we grab Umaq and get a confession and other evidence, no one's going to be asking if I went about it the 'right' way. We'll just say I happened to be in attendance at the show, coincidentally ran into him, and then one thing led to another."

Jing-nan thought about what Detective Wu had said. When high-profile crimes were solved, there did seem to be a high number of coincidences.

A FISHING CREW WAS recently accused of exploiting undocumented Vietnamese men, keeping them at sea while depending on smaller motorboats for resupplies and hauling away the day's catch. Some police who happened to be partying on a yacht claimed they saw the men in chains. The cops stormed the ship and arrested the Taiwanese captain and his subordinate officers.

Then there was a syndicate of loan sharks that was busted when a moving van driven by a detective slammed into the driver's side of an SUV just as it was pulling out of a garage. The cop had said it was his day off and that he was getting some stuff out of storage. The cop claimed that the SUV driver had shot out into the road and that he had no chance to brake. Funny that the pictures of the accident seemed to show that the moving van had struck the SUV before the latter even rolled past the sidewalk.

There had been three men in the SUV, and all had long criminal records. The driver had been killed immediately, and the other two had concussions and couldn't remember what had happened. The evidence of a cache of pellet guns (a favorite underworld torture device), notes totaling NT$20 million, and receipts strewn across the back seats and road were all the public and courts needed to see.

The whole thing actually became a public-safety

promotion, with a picture of the strapped-in detective giving a thumbs-up. The caption read, *I was wearing my seatbelt, so I lived, and didn't get a concussion!*

IN THE ARENA, THE speakers began to play an instrumental knockoff of a Celine Dion song. Jing-nan snapped his fingers.

"Guys, this is 'My Heart Will Go On.' That's our cue to move."

Detective Wu pushed open the door to the private dressing rooms and sauntered in, followed by Frankie and Dwayne. Nancy was next and Jing-nan tried to follow her, but Siu-lien shoved herself between them.

CHAPTER 23

Umaq wrapped faux-leather straps around his calves and eyed his phone with disdain. Why was his grandmother calling him so many times when she knew he was in the middle of a show?

Maybe meeting up with her during this tour had been a big mistake. Well, this trip had already had deadly consequences. Umaq pulled his arms back and stretched. He hadn't had the time or mental space to process it all yet.

Focus. Be here now. He eyed himself warily in the mirror. This is how he had gotten where he was today. Umaq had trained hard, and abstinence became his daily practice. No fun foods. No fun dates. No fun.

He had managed to persevere by vowing that if the group ever made it to Taiwan, he would go see his father.

He pressed his fingers into the back of his neck. That meeting couldn't have gone worse. His memories of his father, apart from scant images from his childhood, now included Boxer's last minute or two on earth.

THE FUNNY THING WAS that Umaq had avoided the building's entrance because he didn't want to be seen entering a building with such a bad reputation in an already seedy neighborhood. If a CC camera had filmed him, and if the footage had been made public, it could have tainted the reputation of the Flying Wonders. It would have sounded even worse if he had said he was visiting his father there.

Instead, Umaq had entered a nearby Daoist temple, walked through some full-sized dioramas of hell, and gone to the roof level, which was empty, as most visitors were on the ground floor begging the goddesses and gods for help. There, he threw a compact grappling hook across the alley to the roof of the building where Boxer used to hole up. The buildings were so close together, Umaq was able to run across the rope and retract the grappling hook in 15 seconds.

He hoped Boxer would still be in the same room, but in better condition.

Umaq entered the stairwell and headed down. When he reached Boxer's floor, he heard voices in the hallway. One man was asking about money and the other said he didn't have any left. It seemed to be some kind of drug deal.

When the conversation seemed to be winding down, as the exchanges became shorter, Umaq silently walked up one flight and stood in the shadows. The visitor opened the stairwell door below, and Umaq listened to his footsteps. Based on their cadence, the man heading downstairs was probably in his 20s, seemed to be in a good mood, and had a sense of rhythm.

Umaq waited for the man to leave the building, went back down a flight, and headed to his father's apartment. Before he could lose his nerve, Umaq knocked quickly on Boxer's door. He heard sounds indicating someone getting off the bed and shuffling to the door.

Umaq had seen this visit in his mind's eye for years. The door would open, Umaq would say, "Father." Boxer would smile, and maybe cry a little, seeing his son's apparent strength and resolve and also reeling from his own embarrassment for wallowing in squalor and addiction for so many years. Boxer would also be mortified to realize how absent he had been as a father to Umaq, and proud of his son for managing his way to manhood so well on his own. Boxer might even fall to his knees and beg for forgiveness.

Well, something like that.

The door jerked open. Umaq was the one struck with shame. He hadn't known that his father would look prematurely older, and that his manner of dress would show so little self-regard. And the smell of Boxer's apartment. A mix of bodily fluids and solids, and alcohol and drugs.

Boxer's expression of annoyance was familiar to the child Umaq once was.

"Hey, what do you want?" asked Boxer.

"I'm your son," stammered Umaq. This visit wasn't a good idea. Maybe he should just run now.

"My son?" Boxer asked his hands.

"Yes," said Umaq. "Your son with Juna," he added. The guy could have other kids, as well. Who knew? Boxer left the door open and walked back to bed. Umaq was still considering leaving until Boxer asked, "Aren't you coming in?"

Umaq entered, and his face twitched from the stink. The humidity was making it even worse. Sydney had none of that mildew smell that lurked around every corner in Taipei, and Umaq kept his own quarters spotless and odorless. He reluctantly closed the door behind him, cutting off the only source of fresh air.

Boxer sat on the edge of the bed and regarded Umaq.

"You are my only child," said Boxer. "Umaq. I also knew you as Chris."

Umaq nearly choked up to hear his father say both his

names. "I wanted to see you," he said. "I'm part of a famous circus now. The Flying Wonders in Australia."

"Australia," marveled Boxer. "What do you do?"

"Trapeze, tightrope, you name it."

"Wow, wow," said Boxer without full comprehension. He wiped his face. "You know, when you knocked on the door, I thought you were someone else."

"Who?" Boxer crossed his arms.

"Aw, who cares?"

Umaq surveyed the room, and his eyes fell upon a bra draped over the back of the only chair.

"Are you here alone?" asked Umaq. Boxer took note of his son's gaze.

"Oh, ignore that, please."

"Dad, how long have you been living like his?"

Boxer chuckled uncontrollably. "I've only been here one night, Umaq!"

"You're still in the same room that Mom said you were in years ago."

"Yes, but I only came here yesterday because I hit it big in the lottery. That's the complete truth! I normally live with my girlfriend in an apartment."

Umaq pointed at the bra. "Is that hers?"

"No, no. That's some whore's. She took a lot of my money. Funny thing is, I ran out on my girlfriend because I didn't want to share the prize money with her. Turns out I spent it and gave it all away, anyway. Now, Umaq, I wasn't around while you were growing up, but let me tell you one thing. Women are nothing but problems, and they're always out to rip you off. Got that?"

Umaq felt his face heat up. "What are you saying, Boxer? You know Mom and I really struggled without any help from you."

"Hey, that's not respectful, using my name. A son should always say 'Father.'"

"A father who's wasted his life like this doesn't deserve respect from anyone!"

"Well, fuck you, and fuck your mother!"

"Shut up, Boxer!"

"Maybe I should teach you some manners, you little half-savage!" Boxer swung out and struck Umaq's chest. The blow was a solid hit, but there was no force behind it. Still, Boxer moved side to side, looking for another opportunity to strike again.

Most children of Taiwan had been conditioned to endure beatings from their parents without complaint, and certainly without returning blows.

The compact grappling hook was in Umaq's right hand, and he intended only to use it to defend against Boxer's next attack. Then Boxer reared up and spat in his face and Umaq lashed out, striking Boxer hard in the left temple.

Umaq had underestimated his own strength. He always had, being an uncoordinated and skinny boy for so much of his life. Now, though, Umaq was muscular, conditioned by years of physical training, and his reflexes were as quick as thoughts.

Maybe even faster.

Boxer hit the ground before Umaq realized he had struck his father with deadly force. He stood there and watched blood pool on the ground near Boxer's open mouth. Half of the skull was caved in, and there was no point in CPR now.

Umaq wasn't sure how long he lingered, but the next thing he was conscious of doing was taking in the rope when he was back on the roof of the temple. It was clean, no signs of blood. His hands were slippery with sweat as he coiled the rope quickly and gave the grappling hook itself a quick examination. It looked clean.

He went downstairs to the men's bathroom on the ground floor. Umaq saw no evidence that he was a murderer in the mirror but thoroughly washed his hands and arms, anyway. He looked directly at his own face and saw the cold expression of Boxer. Incapable of caring, of loving. Umaq had waited for most of his life to see his father again. But the man had little regard for women, and even now had no regrets for his neglect of his wife and son. He'd struck Umaq, after all this time. Boxer had deserved to die.

Umaq flew through the air of Taipei Arena that night. Nothing had compromised his performance, physically or mentally. He had cut off Boxer as completely from his mind as his father had done to him.

THE NEXT DAY, THOUGH, after the show, he read reports of Boxer's death, and saw pictures of Siu-lien, who had been described interchangeably as his girlfriend and his common-law wife. Boxer indeed hadn't been living this whole time in the squalor of that seedy apartment building. The way Umaq had found him there—and killed him—must have been fated.

But by taking Boxer's life, Umaq had hurt another woman, Siu-lien, and that was the last thing he ever wanted to do. He knew what bar she worked at, and planned to do something nice for her—leave a large tip or contribute to a fundraiser—hopefully without implicating himself in Boxer's murder.

He left the next show by himself, assuring security that he would take precautions, as a murderer was about, and made his way to the bar. He wasn't expecting Siu-lien herself to be behind the bar. Yet that spoke to how dire her financial condition was, he assumed. He felt worse than ever.

Umaq left her what he thought was a generous tip, and

either she didn't take notice or had learned not to show appreciation to male customers. He settled with two drinks at a small table near a wall, contemplating how else he could help. Umaq continued drinking, unaware that his alcohol tolerance had tumbled in the months that he had abstained due to training. His emotions veered from rage at Boxer to extreme pity for Siu-lien.

Then that Captain Huang came in and started to harass and embarrass Siu-lien.

A cop should be a source of comfort, empathy, and safety—not unlike a father—but they never were, according to Umaq's grandmother Bannie. Umaq had grown up under her roof for as many years as he had spent with his mother, who had explained to him that Boxer wasn't giving her any money and she no longer had the means to take care of a child.

Most of BaBa Bar's customers were clearly disgusted, and Umaq delighted as some of the patrons confronted Captain Huang. Yet the laughs at the cop's expense didn't lessen Umaq's growing anger at the man.

The final straw was when Siu-lien pushed her way out of the bar with her daughter. Umaq saw a tear roll down Siu-lien's face. She wiped it away quickly, but seeing how the captain had hurt her nearly made Umaq's head explode with delirious fury. How many times had he seen his mother in tears while he had been powerless to do anything about it?

Now he could.

Umaq decided that he had to kill the captain. It was the only thing that could bring comfort to Siu-lien, and besides, there was a certain symmetry in that his first killing had caused her grief. Umaq tried to take a final gulp of his gin and tonic, but the glass was already empty.

When Captain Huang left the bar not too long after, Umaq

had waited exactly 15 seconds before following him out. He figured that he could make his move in whatever parking garage the cop had chosen. But the detective had walked on and on. Did he live nearby, or was he trying to walk off a buzz?

Umaq hadn't planned on killing him right on the street, but it was probably doable as there weren't many people out in this part of town.

The detective took a turn down a desolate alley. It was narrow and dark. Anything could happen there.

Umaq strolled behind. Murder. Again. He laughed at the thought that he had planned the killings, but the whole thing was no joke—it was an unfolding reality. And he did feel like he was in a reality show, a deadly one. His judgment was severely impaired, but his motor skills remained intact.

He began to sweat, but it wasn't his nerves giving out. It was Taipei's humidity, and a long-sleeve cotton knit was the wrong thing to wear, even in the relative cool of night. Yet it was the only all-black article of clothing Umaq had. He thought it would make him look inconspicuous in the bar, but now it served well as a disguise.

I killed my father, he thought. I shouldn't have any problem killing a stranger, especially a cop.

Umaq had a vague idea to knock the detective out first and then snap his neck. It turned out that his first blow—delivered via a jumping kick—did both. Still, he choked him in order to finish him off faster.

He woke up the next day with the knowledge that he had killed two men. Umaq blocked out the details. He couldn't wait to get back to Australia and never come back to Taiwan, so he could pretend that the murders were all just a bad dream, and not two absurdly easy killings that would haunt him for the rest of his life.

Umaq placed his right leg on the counter in front of his dressing mirror. The straps were on too tight. He would have to unwrap the entire thing and try again. The costumes had no buckles because they could scrape someone badly, and they could fail at the worst times.

Luckily, he was an old hand at it. In a couple minutes, the straps felt right. He walked around and squatted a few times. Still good.

There was a knock on the dressing-room door. Why? Who could be knocking? The stagehands were accustomed to swinging the door open slowly while calling out, "Hello!"

Umaq waited. Surely, the crew would handle visitors, wanted or not. More knocks came.

"Yes?" he yelled out in annoyance and surprise.

"You have a prominent well-wisher here, Umaq!" He had heard stories of famous people coming to visit backstage, but usually the meetings took place after the performances. Maybe Taiwan was different. Who could it be? A-Mei, possibly? Or perhaps Gingle Wang, the actress who had starred in that horror film set in Taiwan's White Terror period.

"Uh, thanks!" he said. "The show isn't over yet, though. Maybe the crew can find a place for you to wait?"

"This can't wait," boomed Detective Wu as he swung the door open with a flourish.

"Hey, that's supposed to be locked!" said Umaq. He was taken aback as a number of visitors streamed into his dressing room. Even worse, there was only one cute girl, but she didn't seem to be excited to see him. In fact, she seemed to be a servant of the old man in the wheelchair. They all were.

"Master Ayal has arrived!" declared the detective. Umaq regarded the seated figure. The old man seemed to be asleep, with his head to one side.

"I'm sorry, Master, I've never heard of you," said Umaq.

He was accustomed to deferring to elders. Frankie opened one eye.

"Never heard of me, eh?" Frankie asked, his voice raspier than normal. "I've been in your head, young man, and I know what you did."

Umaq narrowed his eyes, but didn't fully lose his composure.

"Hey!" Umaq yelled out through the open door. "I need some assistance!" He heard only a slight echo in response.

"If you're looking for someone," said Detective Wu, "I think they went on break."

"There's no break during a show," Umaq spat.

"I run a business," said Jing-nan. "I can assure you, Umaq, that there is a mandated break time for all workers. Or are you more comfortable if I call ya 'Chris'?"

Umaq didn't like the vibe in the room, and the apparent MIA status of the crew. He stood on his chair, ready to leap over people to get out. The older woman removed her shades and pushed back the brim of her hat to expose her face.

Then he recognized her. Boxer's girlfriend, Siu-lien.

He flew over the weirdo in the wheelchair, heading for the door.

Frankie reached up and grabbed both of Umaq's ankles.

Umaq broke Frankie's grip by tucking his body and doing a flip.

"Shit!" yelled Frankie. Umaq landed in the doorway in a crouch and scuttled away to the right. He started a sprint for the exit door, but saw Dwayne in the way.

Unknown Pleasures' most intimidating staff member stood square. With a nasty sneer on his face, Dwayne looked like a soccer goalie who played dirty.

"Hi, Umaq," he said. "Big fan right here."

Umaq bolted in the opposite direction, to the arena's main stage. He'd be early, but the rest of the troupe could deal.

He reached the center in darkness. The spotlights were high overhead. He planned to grab a rope, shimmy up, and stay there as long as possible. It wasn't a good plan, but he was sure he could refine it as the situation developed.

As his eyes adjusted, Umaq grabbed the nearest rope. He put hand over hand on the rope and ascended as casually and easily as many people ride an escalator.

CHAPTER 24

Jing-nan, Dwayne, and Nancy ran down the hall and entered the darkened arena. Detective Wu's voice was waiting for them.

"He climbed up two of the ropes," said the detective. "I lost track of which ones because I can't see shit in here. My Samsung died."

Jing-nan turned on his phone light and advanced. Dwayne and Nancy did the same. They might as well have remained in the dark. The performance area was way bigger than it had seemed from the seats, and none of them had any idea where to go.

Floor-based spotlights suddenly snapped on and pointed at a high-wire bicycle act, while some rotating lights—pointed down from suspended rigging to dazzle the audience—blinded them.

Jing-nan cupped his eyes with his right hand.

"Is Umaq in the bicycle act?"

"No," said the detective. "And there's nowhere to hide near all the spotlights. He has to be up there, somewhere."

Four ropes dropped from above and began to wriggle.

"I think the performers are coming down now," said Nancy.

Dwayne clapped his hands. "Let's grab the ropes and shake the hell out of them. He'll drop like a rotten papaya!"

"That won't work, Dwayne," said Nancy. "He'll barely feel it no matter how hard you shake. And anyway, we don't know who's coming down."

Jing-nan spoke up. "I think Dwayne's idea is half-right. We should wait by the ropes and guard them. Umaq could be coming down in disguise, you never know." He paused to look at his girlfriend. "Nancy, you should leave. You shouldn't have to do this."

She crossed her arms. "Why?"

"This guy has killed before. It's not safe for you."

"It's not safe for you, either, Jing-nan!"

"You're right, Nancy," he said. "None of us are ready to go one-on-one against this guy."

"How about this," said Detective Wu. "We'll each grab a rope and the first one who sees something suspicious, start yelling. We'll all jump in and finally catch the guy. He was never supposed to make it out of the dressing room."

"Just remember," said Dwayne, "if you can't grab hold of an arm or a leg, punch or kick him where you can to slow him down."

Detective Wu sucked his teeth noisily and grabbed a rope.

"He can't escape into the stands, because not even he could jump those barriers," he said. "And he can't go back to where we came in because Frankie will be ready for him."

Dwayne took the next rope. "Stay alert, you guys," he said. Jing-nan and Nancy jogged to the final two ropes.

"Which one looks better to you?" asked Jing-nan.

"The one on the right," said Nancy.

"I'll go left," said Jing-nan. "Good luck, and stay safe." Their hands touched briefly as they parted.

JING-NAN SAW HIS DESIGNATED rope jiggle. A figure was sliding down.

He was about to yell out when he heard Nancy shouting that Umaq was coming down her rope. Jing-nan rushed over to her, followed by Detective Wu and Dwayne. Nancy held the rope in both hands, feet planted. She looked ready to haul in a whale.

"Is that really him?" said Dwayne as his eyes followed the rope upward.

Detective Wu shielded his face against the swinging spotlights. "I see two people," he said. "Neither of them look like him." The house lights went fully up. The four of them took a few steps away from Nancy's rope. A light-skinned man and woman were coming down, and as they got closer to the ground, their expressions of confusion were visible.

The man reached the ground first.

"The hell are you guys doing here?" he asked in an American accent, more surprised than annoyed. The man was short, lithe, and muscular but not bulky.

"It's hard to explain," Jing-nan said in English. "But we're trying to find Umaq. The police need to talk to him." Jing-nan turned to make sure that the man coming down his designated rope wasn't Umaq. It wasn't.

"Right in the middle of our bloody show?" asked the female acrobat. She was now standing next to her fellow performer. Her Australian accent was so heavy it seemed fake.

"It's about murder," said Jing-nan. "Two murders, actually."

Detective Wu jerked at hearing the word twice. "Person of interest," he said in English.

An Asian Australian man who had come down Jing-nan's rope ran over.

"What's going on here?" he asked. Nancy told him in English. Jing-nan and Dwayne scanned the ropes and other rigging without seeing anyone who looked like Umaq.

Detective Wu looked to the stage exits. Umaq couldn't have made it out there, he thought. And he doesn't seem to be up in the rigging, either. The detective eyed the rest of the company gathering around them. They were all accounted for but Umaq.

"Are any of you hiding Umaq?" he accused in English.

The Asian Australian man laughed. "Look, mate, he doesn't need any help from us. If he's hiding, you won't find him."

A loud buzz arose from audience members as they wondered what was happening. The announcer boomed, "And now presenting Umaq for the show's finale!"

Jing-nan knew that this would be the point in the show where Umaq would climb up a ladder to a small platform for some crazy stunts on a high wire. Where the hell was that guy? Was he going to show up?

FRANKIE WALKED OUT TO the hallway and knocked on a storage-room door before unlocking and opening it, revealing a crew of about a dozen people, a mix of Australians and Taiwanese.

"Hi," he said. "Guess what. Detective Wu lied when he said you were under suspicion for dealing drugs. We just had to get you out of the way." Siu-lien came up behind Frankie and repeated what Frankie said in English.

A white man whose muscles were straining against a dark tank top stepped forward to Siu-lien. "Is the show still going on?" he asked in English.

"Yes," said Siu-lien. When she heard the announcement for the show's finale, she knew they still hadn't caught Umaq.

"Oh, shit," said the crewmember. "We don't have the safety net set up yet!"

"But you don't use a safety net," said Siu-lien.

A dark-skinned woman also in a tight tank top tried to suppress a snort. "We say we don't, but Taipei Arena's insurance policy requires it for Umaq's last act."

UMAQ STOOD UP FROM his perch in the crow's nest, which looked too small from below to be a viable hiding spot. He basked in the lights hitting him from every angle. Applause and cheers rose from below. It wasn't the loudest appreciation he'd ever heard, but for his final performance ever it would have to do.

He could tell the safety net wasn't set up yet. Maybe the universe was showing him the way to a grand finale. The Bible says that suicide is wrong, and Bannie had tried so hard to instill Christianity into him. Yet she had many views that diverged from their Presbyterian minister. Hadn't she even told him once that it was better to kill yourself than to let the cops take you alive? Well, this one's for you, Granny.

It couldn't look like a mistake. There were people filming him with their phone cameras, focusing in on his face. He wanted them to see how calm he was throughout, how satisfied he was with everything, and how much he intended to do what had to be done. He opened his arms and stepped out on the wire.

JING-NAN, NANCY, DWAYNE, AND Detective Wu stood on the darkened floor with their arms crossed as they watched Umaq start his routine without a care in the world. The other members of the Flying Wonders looked on, as well.

"We can't do anything but watch him," said Dwayne. "But he has to come down eventually, one way or another."

"If he falls and dies without confessing to the murders," said Detective Wu, "we could be charged with negligent manslaughter. We chased him up there early and threw him off his game."

"No way is he going to fall," said Dwayne. "He's done this so many times before, it's like drinking water for him."

The Asian Australian man approached them.

"Pardon the intrusion," he said, "but we think something's quite off. The safety net's not up. We usually help set it up when we come down with the ground crew."

"After bragging you don't use one?" asked Jing-nan.

"We tear it down when the act is over so the audience is none the wiser. I mean Umaq's never needed one, but it's a requirement in Taipei Arena."

The stage doors burst open and the crew barged onto the floor. The Flying Wonders performers mingled with the ground crew to pull out spidery arms from a contraption that was being pushed to center stage.

"Let's get out of their way," Jing-nan said to Nancy, Dwayne, and Detective Wu. "This could be life and death."

UMAQ MOVED ALONG. NOTHING fancy, just slow steady steps, dipping at times to hold the audience's eyes. He noticed a light flashing from below. It was the ground crew indicating that they weren't ready yet. It almost made him laugh and nearly threw him off, which made it all the funnier.

Couldn't they see he was already out on the rope, out on a limb?

"I CAN'T BELIEVE THAT crazy bastard's gone ahead!" yelled the dark-skinned crewmember. "That's a union violation for sure!"

"Let's get this net up now," said the white man, who seemed to be the crew boss. "Let's not have a literal postmortem about this situation."

"HE'S A QUARTER OF the way through," said Nancy. She pushed her hands hard into her armpits. "He's not following the routine I saw."

"He's crouching down," said Jing-nan.

Umaq was practically sitting on the rope now, balanced with one leg pointing straight down. He did a scissor kick and switched legs. If the audience hadn't been so tense they might have applauded.

The troupe and the workers were struggling to finish setting up the net. Well, Umaq's act was almost over.

One of the Flying Wonders was already halfway up a ladder to a midlevel platform. That was the person who would swing the flying trapeze out to Umaq. He was then supposed to catch it near the middle of his tightrope and swing back to safety.

UMAQ DREW HIMSELF UP and continued walking to the midpoint of the rope. How exactly should this end? He should ignore the trapeze. Maybe he should wave it away. Then he should drop and hold the rope with two hands. Then one hand. Salute the audience and let go. Yes, that was probably best.

THE WHITE MAN ON the crew was yelling at someone.

"Never mind! I'm going to do it, because I know you'd fuck it up, anyway!"

He began jogging out to the far end of the net, which had expanded to an impressive size, nearly half the ring on the ground. The man had a thick rope in his hand that ended in a spring hook that gleamed in the relative darkness.

The man tripped on something and tumbled. The metal hook landed on Jing-nan's left foot.

The crowd gasped and Jing-nan looked up. Umaq had dismissed the flying trapeze as it left him, instead of grabbing it.

Jing-nan knew right then that Umaq was planning to jump to his death.

The crew boss was down for the count, holding his knee and writhing in pain. No other crewmembers were near. Jing-nan glanced at Nancy. They both knew he had to grab that rope and finish the job.

Jing-nan picked up the hook. It was heavy and almost a foot long. He took up the rope in his other hand and bent down.

"What do I hook this up to?" he asked the injured man.

"There's a big metal pad eye, you can't miss it! Hurry!" the crew boss screamed.

Jing-nan ran off, eyes on the edge of the safety net's frame as it scrolled by. Pad eye, he chanted to himself. Where's the goddamned pad eye? The rope was nylon and felt like a cold, scaly snake.

THE FLYING TRAPEZE SWUNG by Umaq twice more and he ignored it both times. The arena filled with sounds of confusion. He folded his body in half and grabbed the tightrope with his two hands. Soon he was dangling from it like a pendant on a chain, his feet together like a diver. Some audience members screamed. Umaq looked around and took it all in. He couldn't see their faces but he could feel the audience's fear. He hadn't meant to make them feel that way.

But this wasn't a time for regret. He had to forge ahead.

Umaq's right hand let go of the tightrope.

JING-NAN RAN LIKE A tsunami was behind him. No pad eye. All he saw were metal rings already strung through with thinner nylon ropes. The hook wouldn't even fit through them. He felt the slack in the rope begin to tighten. That was a good thing, because it meant the pad eye had to be near. He picked up the pace.

Umaq swiveled on his left wrist and held a salute to the arena with his right hand. There was scattered applause from those still hoping that this was a part of the act, some sort of high-stakes joke. He opened his left hand and dropped.

Jing-nan saw a solitary flap of fabric. That had to be it! He reached out with his left hand and lifted it. A big metal pad eye was fastened to the frame under it.

The arena shrieked as one. Jing-nan whipped his right hand in the air, and slammed the hook onto the ring.

He scrambled away from the safety net and heard a metallic crunching sound as the frame buckled.

The house lights came up. The hastily assembled safety net had buckled slightly but remained intact.

Umaq looked like a swatted mosquito. Each bent limb pointed in a different direction. He was also intact, although one leg lay across the frame of the safety net. His eyes were open, and he was alive but too stunned to move. Dwayne and Nancy were already running to Umaq. Jing-nan rushed over, as well.

Detective Wu was the first to the side of the net, which was at shoulder level. He reached over and slapped Umaq's injured leg. The young man howled in pain.

"Well, look at that, you aren't a ghost yet," said the detective.

As Jing-nan came closer to the net, Dwayne ambushed him from behind and lifted him off his feet.

"You ran just like Yutaka Fukumoto!" he yelled, comparing Jing-nan to the Japanese stolen-bases king.

"I'm more like Tsao Chin-hui," said Jing-nan as Dwayne set him down. Tsao was the pitcher who was busted for fixing games, but never stole bases.

"Jing-nan, that was really something!" said Nancy. She touched his back lightly. "You saved Umaq's life!"

A crewmember wearing a baseball cap was coiling up the nylon rope that Jing-nan had been handling.

"You!" said the crew boss, limping over. "You're the reason I'm hurt!" The crewmember shook his head in response. Indignant, the boss pulled off the crewmember's hat. "Wait, you're that guy who let us out of the storage closet!"

It was Frankie, and one of his trademark big smiles curled up beneath his cheeks.

"Jing-nan!" he said, "please tell this man that it wasn't necessary to connect this rope for the safety net." Frankie elbowed Jing-nan. "Anyway, that run was epic. I've never seen you move so fast."

Jing-nan cleared his throat and addressed the crew boss in English. "He says it wasn't necessary to hook up that rope."

"I know what he thinks," said the crew boss, "but he's wrong."

"I'm right," Frankie declared in English, coiling the rope around his left arm.

"Bloody . . ." the boss grunted with resignation as he turned away.

The PA system told the audience to get home safely, and made chipper announcements of upcoming events.

Detective Wu pounded the safety net's frame and called up to Umaq, "Get down here, you piece of shit!"

"I think my ankle's broken," Umaq replied.

"You tried to kill yourself." The detective mocked him.

"Now you want to complain about a little broken bone or two?"

"I want a doctor," said Umaq.

"I'm your doctor," said the detective. "I'm prescribing you a pair of handcuffs. Roll onto your stomach, boy."

"I can't believe you helped catch Boxer's killer, Jing-nan," said Nancy. "What a crazy night it's been."

Jing-nan shuffled his feet. "I didn't do much," he said. "You heard what Frankie said. That hook I set up had no effect."

"But you believed in it." Nancy faced Jing-nan directly and pride glowed in her eyes. "You put everything into that run, and it was to save someone else's life. That was so selfless of you."

Jing-nan touched Nancy's hand briefly. "I'm glad you saw that. It's probably my last race."

"Hey!" yelled Detective Wu. "Get on your stomach, Umaq. I'm not telling you again!" His voice was menacing enough to convey that the next step was physical violence. Jing-nan looked around. Wasn't anyone going to do anything?

"That's it!" Detective Wu declared. "We're going to do this the hard way."

Dwayne finally spoke up. "Maybe you can chill a little bit?" he asked.

"Ah, I get it," said the detective. "You want to stick up for your fellow Indigenous person here. Did you forget that this little mountain boy is a murderer?"

Before Dwayne could make a single sound of objection at the slur, Umaq whipped his good leg through the air and caught Detective Wu on the right temple. The detective crumbled.

Umaq flipped off the safety net and cartwheeled away on his two hands and one good leg.

"Get the fuck out of here! No way!" yelled Jing-nan.

Umaq looked back as he prepared to land on his hands. A

length of nylon rope tore through the air, and lassoed Umaq's bad leg at the knee.

He landed on his head with a crunch. He hauled himself up and elbow crawled another ten feet before Dwayne planted himself on Umaq's back, careful to keep his face and eyes out of the reach of Umaq's fingers.

"Brother," groaned Umaq, "please let me go. You and me, we come from the same place."

"We did," said Dwayne, his hands clasped in prayer and his voice heavy with disappointment, "but somehow we ended up on different paths."

"I gave myself the name 'Umaq.' You know what it means? It means 'home' and 'family.' You're my family."

Dwayne closed his eyes and asked God for the courage to forgive Umaq. But he was jerked out of this frame of mind when Detective Wu swiftly kicked Umaq twice in the head.

"Don't get up, Dwayne," said the detective. "Keep that bastard down." Umaq tried to cover up with his arms. Detective Wu stomped on an exposed hand. Umaq never cried out but his body convulsed slightly with each strike.

"C'mon, detective," said Dwayne. "Enough is enough."

Detective Wu bent down, looking for an especially vulnerable spot.

"Think you can assault an officer and live?" the detective yelled.

Nancy touched his elbow. "I think you'd better stop," she said. "That's an Australian citizen."

"Hey, Umaq, is that true? You've turned your back on the Republic of China?"

"The ROC turned its back against us first," Umaq said.

Dwayne twisted his mouth but didn't say anything.

"So that's the play, huh?" asked Detective Wu. He stepped away and waited for more cops to come.

CHAPTER 25

The protests to set Umaq free started with a few hundred Taiwanese Aborigines and college students occupying Ketagalan Boulevard, a main thoroughfare that led directly to the Presidential Office Building.

The demonstration was lifted by a rising tide as more performers arrived for the launch of the Austronesian Cultural Festival. Troupes from Australia, the Philippines, Madagascar, New Zealand, the Solomon Islands, Hawaii, and elsewhere joined the protests, which grew bigger and louder, and the fierce fashions of the costumes alone merited major media commentary.

Groups in Taiwan shared video clips of Umaq falling from the tightrope, claiming that his act had been sabotaged, leading to his fall.

A leaked audio clip of Umaq's bedside confession, taken by detectives at the Taipei Hospital of the Ministry of Health and Welfare, made the rounds online. He clearly and plainly stated that he killed Boxer and Captain Huang, and the police said Umaq's groans and hesitations were due to the pain from his broken ankle. Protestors said they were indications that the young man had been tortured into making a false confession. In addition, Umaq had been forced to say that the first murder victim was his biological father. So this guy single-handedly killed his father, and then later murdered a captain of the Taipei City Police? Ridiculous!

The performers who had traveled to Taiwan to take part in the festival almost immediately took up the cause for Umaq. Apart from their common Pacific Rim heritage, they also shared two other things: dark skin and poor treatment by law enforcement.

Media teams that had traveled with the performers had expected to record shows, but they quickly began providing freelance coverage of the protests in English.

Ketagalan Boulevard was a popular site in Taipei for protests, not only because of its proximity to the president's office, but also because it was named to honor an Aboriginal people that the Taiwanese government ironically regarded as extinct, despite continued efforts by the descendants of the Ketagalan tribe for official recognition.

Demonstrations on the boulevard were usually shut down and cleared out by the police without much fuss. But the unrest reached a critical mass rather quickly. Also, it was an election year. No politician wanted to risk international ire for shutting down the expression of free speech by people that included Americans.

The venues for the Austronesian festivities were closed, and the organizers moved the performances to the sides of Ketagalan Boulevard. The merch tables probably had the most diverse offerings ever at a demonstration.

One popular, locally made T-shirt encouraged, *Find the Real Killers.*

On the advice of his lawyers, Umaq recanted his confession, saying it was made under "duress," without commenting on alleged police brutality. Linda Wyatt, Australia's minister for culture and the arts, who had come to Taipei originally to help launch the festival, declared that the investigation was either a "sham" or a "shame." Her accent blurred the line, but either worked. Wyatt, who was the first Aboriginal to hold the ministry post, declared that Umaq would fly home to Australia as soon as he could travel.

This was more than any old double-murder case. It lay directly and heavily upon old, unhealed wounds of the abuse of Indigenous peoples all around the Pacific Rim, and decades of broken promises.

Umaq's supporters saw yet another police setup. His grandmother Bannie said as much, at least for the first few days. Then she had a heart attack and landed in the same hospital as her grandson. Minister Wyatt invited Umaq's grandmother to Australia, as well, but she declined, saying that she had to stay in Taiwan and fight on.

After Bannie's hospitalization, Minister Wyatt also offered to change Umaq's Distinguished Talent visa into full Australian citizenship. The kicker was that Australia had no extradition treaty with Taiwan. If Umaq were allowed to leave the country, he would probably never be tried for the murders of Boxer and Captain Huang.

IT LOOKED LIKE YET another situation where Taiwan was going to be forced to bend to the will of a more powerful country. Taiwan and Australia had about the same population, 24 million, but Taiwan was much smaller in size, and had fewer friends. Most countries in the world didn't officially recognize the island, as most governments wanted to have good relations and trade with China.

If Australia wanted Umaq set free, it would probably happen.

Then something odd happened. Taiwan's Ministry of Health and Welfare announced that Umaq's DNA test showed that he wasn't Boxer's son. His lawyers called a press conference to respond to the finding. They noted that the claim was the most outlandish component of Umaq's forced confession to begin with, and that it didn't matter because their client hadn't killed the man, anyway.

But Umaq sat at the press conference, detached from the proceedings. He didn't answer any questions and kept his handcuffs hidden in the folds of his hospital gown. As he picked up his cane, a hot mic captured him remarking to one of his lawyers, "I don't know who I killed, then." It went out live around the world. In English.

Two days later, Minister Wyatt said she had to return to Australia. She expressed her appreciation of her time in Taiwan, and said that she was confident that Umaq would receive justice. The minister said it was a "personal matter of some urgency" that she had to attend to, but all Australian nationals who had come for the festival—including Umaq's fellow performers in the Flying Wonders—left on the same flight.

The Hawaiians left next, supposedly at the behest of the US government, an order relayed by the American Institute in Taiwan, which functioned as an unofficial embassy. The morale of Umaq's supporters took a hit when his comment played over and over on TV shows. Now that the largest entourages had left, the size of the protest was cut by more than half.

As the end date of the original festival arrived, all visitors who didn't want to pay the change fee for a later flight—in other words, everyone—boarded their planes and left, after posting videos expressing words of support for Umaq from the check-in lines.

Shortly after, on a day of heavy rains, the Taipei City Police set up barricades on Ketagalan Boulevard, pushed back the remaining 50 or so demonstrators, and reopened the road for traffic. What was left—street cleaners, dumpsters filled with signs and banners—was not covered by the media.

That morning, the lead headline was that Madonna had announced a return date to play the Taipei Arena. The last time she performed on the island, she had managed to irk the two main political parties, so the day was filled with pundits weighing in on what might happen with her next show. The future of Taiwan could hang in the balance over what the Material Girl did next.

AFTER UMAQ'S ARREST, THROUGH the surge and ebb of the protest, everyone in Nancy and Jing-nan's world had tried to go back to their lives.

Dwayne felt like he was being torn apart. He was sure that Umaq had murdered Boxer and Captain Huang. On the other hand, Dwayne was well aware of the Aborigine struggle in Taiwan. He also knew that Taiwan's conviction rate of more than 90 percent meant that if Umaq's case went to trial, he'd probably end up on death row. There was sure to be a trial, too, because there was no way Umaq could get a plea deal when the murder of a police captain was in question. What was that kid thinking? If he had only stopped at the murder of Boxer, he would've been in the clear. The cops were busy with other things, and not even the good ones would have stuck with investigating the death of a guy living on the margins. There were always financial scams that were more pressing for law enforcement. Online sexual extortion was still a big headline grabber, as well. Boxer's murder alone would have disappeared from the media in days.

Dwayne did what all Taipei residents did when they felt

helpless and frustrated. He prayed, and then threw himself into work.

JING-NAN WORKED EXTRA HOURS to accommodate the larger crowds at Unknown Pleasures. Frankie and Dwayne also put in more time. Online, Jing-nan downplayed the roles that the three of them had in the apprehension of Umaq, but the projected modesty was calculated to generate more publicity. Jing-nan was worried that Umaq's supporters would hold protests at his stand, but they tended to stay on Ketagalan Boulevard.

Nancy was annoyed with Jing-nan's longer hours, but he promised that he would start taking college classes in the spring semester. She had never imagined herself as the disciplinarian type, but she remained on Jing-nan's case to find and apply to programs.

Jing-nan felt trapped. Business at the night market was brisker than ever, and when he got home there was Nancy trying to pin him down to enroll in classes that would put even more on his plate.

Was there even going to be a convenient time for classes? Unknown Pleasures occupied nearly all his waking hours. Buying ingredients at the day market in the morning, taking pictures for social media in the afternoon, and then herding tourists.

During a brief lull at the night market, Jing-nan went to his stall's bathroom—an amenity that most night-market businesses lacked—and splashed cold water on his face. He looked at himself in the mirror, and watched the water drip from his eyes like tears.

It's true that he had never been able to capitalize on his academic smarts. He had been one of the top students at one of Taipei's top high schools. Hell, he had made it to fucking UCLA! If only he had been able to finish his studies there.

The only options now open to him on a part-time basis were schools no one had ever heard of. Community colleges, even. What a comedown.

Jing-nan shivered and toweled his face.

No sense in looking back at all the pain, missed opportunities, and bad luck. People who were gone were gone for good: Jing-nan's old girlfriend, the woman he had planned to marry; his parents and grandparents; and some old classmates, as well. There was only today, and hopefully tomorrow. He had to cherish the people around him now, especially the woman he now planned to marry someday. Nancy was on his case because she was trying to make him a better man.

Jing-nan left the bathroom and observed Frankie and Dwayne preparing and marinating skewers for the next night. He was lucky to be working with these guys, and Jing-nan realized that he really owed them something.

Getting a college degree was something way bigger than just him and Nancy, and even Unknown Pleasures itself. If he did better, he could pay Frankie and Dwayne more. One day, they could have people working under them.

The night markets were more popular than ever, but they still had a reputation for low-quality food, no matter how good their online ratings were. Certainly, they were expected to be bargain-priced. A small-business owner would have to be crazy to stay here.

Frankie cut vegetables into skewer-sized chunks while Dwayne poured sauce over completed skewers laid out in shallow trays.

Frankie looked at Dwayne and nodded his head at Jing-nan. Dwayne caught the gesture and set aside the pot of marinade.

"I've been lookin' for you, Jing-nan," said Dwayne as he

came walking over. He held up a crooked, brown seedpod. "These tamarinds. Where did you get them?"

Jing-nan shrugged. "From the day market, of course. Is there a problem?"

"Not at all, these are really good. The sweet and sour components are both strong, but they complement each other instead of fighting. Try to get them from the same seller." Dwayne rarely praised Jing-nan for anything, and when he did, it was in a grudging manner. Jing-nan took the tamarind in his hands and felt its surface carefully and examined the color. He was certain he could find the same product again.

"Dwayne?" asked Jing-nan.

"Yeah?"

"How would you feel if Unknown Pleasures became a bigger business?"

Dwayne narrowed his eyes. He had been dreading this moment.

"What do you mean, Jing-nan?" he asked. "Are you telling me that the stand is becoming more modern and that older workers like me and Frankie have to go because we don't fit the new concept?"

Was Dwayne joking? He couldn't possibly be serious, could he?

"You bastard!" Dwayne continued. "I knew you've been plotting something! Hey Cat, our young friend here is stabbing us in our backs!"

Frankie looked over warily at Dwayne and then Jing-nan before wiping his hands on his apron and producing a cigarette in the return motion. He lit it and crossed his arms without taking a drag. Jing-nan recognized that Frankie was waiting for him to speak.

"Listen, you guys!" said Jing-nan. "I would never get rid

of you! I will absolutely never fire you no matter what!" He was dizzy trying to think of more ways to assure them. "Do you want more money?"

"Yes!" blurted out Dwayne.

"No!" said Frankie, overruling both Dwayne and Jing-nan. "We can't afford it!" Dwayne signed with resignation and Jing-nan sighed with relief. "Jing-nan, how did this whole thing start?"

"I was just thinking of expanding the stall," said Jing-nan. "I mean, if I get my college degree, I'll be able to grow the business some more." Frankie finally took a drag on his cigarette and exhaled.

"And Nancy will be happy you'll be going back to school," said Frankie.

"Yes," admitted Jing-nan.

Frankie nodded. "Well, it would be a good thing. You can thank Nancy for looking out for you, because it means she's looking out for us, too."

LATE THAT NIGHT, FRANKIE and his wife sipped tea made with rainwater and dried flowers. They watched the first half of a Vietnamese gangster/romance film based on the life of Dung Ha, who had affairs with men and women.

"Are gangsters really like that?" Linh asked as she zapped the TV off.

"Nobody is really like that," said Frankie as he stood and picked up their empty magnetized mugs. "That's just the movies."

Linh stretched her arms and rolled her head to crack the bones in her neck. "But isn't the criminal underground exciting?"

"It's actually not," said Frankie. "It's like any other job. It's mostly mundane, but once in a while, it's someone's birthday and you get a slice of cake."

"You don't think your job is boring, do you?"

Frankie closed his mouth and ran his tongue over his teeth. "It's not. Well, especially since Jing-nan has been finding trouble. Or maybe the other way around. Is it boring being at Taiwan Is Our Home?"

Linh laughed bitterly. "No, it's the fight of my life!"

NANCY WAS ON HER couch, writing on a laptop with the TV on mute. Well, trying to write. Siu-lien had been texting almost every minute, even though Nancy had indicated that she was busy.

Siu-lien was excited. Happy, even. She said that the notoriety she had received from being a part of the group that captured Umaq increased business at the bar. People were asking for selfies with her, on top of giving big tips.

THESE PEOPLE, YOUR FANS, THEY HATE ABORIGINES, DON'T THEY? Nancy wrote.

THEY HATE CRIME, AND THEY HATE PROTESTS, TOO. MADE ALL OF TAIWAN LOOK BAD, Siu-lien wrote back. DON'T FORGET, UMAQ IS A KILLER. THAT IS ONE HUNDRED PERCENT TRUE. MY FRIENDS WHO ARE PROUD ABORIGINALS HAVE TOLD ME THAT UMAQ SHOULD BE IN JAIL.

Nancy shook her head, startled by the speed at which her mother could type, and by her use of the old "some of my best friends are those people" excuse.

MOM, YOU AND I HAVE TO AGREE TO DISAGREE ON THIS.

WHAT'S THAT SUPPOSED TO MEAN? Siu-lien fired back.

WE CAN HAVE DIFFERENT OPINIONS ON WHAT SORT OF PEOPLE COME TO YOUR BAR. It pained Nancy to type the next sentence. NEITHER OF US IS MORE RIGHT THAN THE OTHER.

THE PROBLEM IS THAT YOU DON'T KNOW PEOPLE WHO WORK, Siu-lien wrote. REAL PEOPLE DRIVE TRUCKS, WORK IN CONSTRUCTION AND FACTORIES.

I KNOW A LOT OF PEOPLE WHO WORK. JUST DIFFERENT JOBS.

YOU KNOW HOW TO FIX AN AIR CONDITIONER WHEN IT BREAKS? WHO AMONG YOUR FRIENDS CAN FIX A CRACKED WALL AFTER AN EARTHQUAKE?

I DON'T HAVE TO WORRY ABOUT EITHER SITUATION BECAUSE I'LL CALL YOU AND MAYBE HIRE ONE OF YOUR FRIENDS.

MY OWN DAUGHTER WRITES TO HER MOTHER SO RUDELY. MAYBE IT WAS MY MISTAKE TO LET YOU GO TO COLLEGE AND FORGET ABOUT MANNERS.

Nancy growled at her phone, and typed out, GOING TO COLLEGE WAS *MY* MISTAKE! YOU HAD NO PART IN IT!

UMAQ SAT IN HIS cell and looked up at the camera. The cops were probably tired of looking at him by now. Well, as soon as his ankle felt 100 percent, he could entertain them with flips. One of the cops could leak the footage to a TV station and make a few bucks. Though a video clip of Umaq was worth significantly less since the protests died down.

A high-profile law firm had been working on Umaq's case for no fee. One of the paralegals had told Umaq that the firm had been accused of being biased against Aborigines, so the case was key for their image. After the hot-mic incident, however, an intern visited Umaq to say his lawyers had quit.

The city government was now in the process of finding a public defender for Umaq, as the public prosecutor was moving forward with bringing charges against him. That night he had a dream that Bannie visited him and said nothing, but touched his face. The next day the guard who served him meals told him his grandmother had died at the hospital.

Two days later an older man in a white button-down shirt and khakis came to see him.

"Are you my new lawyer?" Umaq asked him through the handset at the visitor window, noting that the man wasn't wearing a tie, much less a suit. He had heard the public defenders were impoverished.

"No, I'm not a lawyer," said the man with a smile. "My name is Paisol. I'm someone who helps our people. I'm Aboriginal, too. We have a great history and culture that continues to endure, and can lift us up when we are at our lowest. God loves us." Umaq fiddled with the handset cord.

"You're a preacher?"

"I'm a minister," said Paisol. "But I'm not trying to convert you. I facilitate a group of incarcerated Aborigines and we explore our identity and how that can be an asset." Paisol tapped on the window separating him from Umaq. "You haven't been convicted of anything, so right now you're technically not allowed to join our group, but I'm working on that. I assume you'd be interested?"

"Yes, I would be."

"Good." Paisol hesitated and dropped his voice an octave before continuing. "I was encouraged by the state to ask if you had any interest in writing a confession to the two murders. But don't do it. If anyone asks you to write something, don't goddamned do it, okay?"

Umaq nodded woodenly. He couldn't believe he was hearing such language from a minister. This guy must really be for real.

"Good." Paisol nodded and resumed his normal speaking voice. "Now, I don't know how long it's going to take to get you in. It depends on your case, of course." He paused again. "I really loved your show. You were really something up there, Umaq."

"Thank you," said Umaq. Paisol nodded, replaced the handset, and walked away. Umaq was escorted back to his cell. He lay down on his mattress, which was filled with springs so dead they didn't even squeak. In a few minutes he was flying through the air and not looking down to see his little life far below.